BOUNTY

Bounty

ERIC
KRUGER

Space Monkey Press

The Benjamin Drake Adventure Series

Hauler

Bounty

Trapped

Alone

| one |

Sitting in the dark, Benjamin Drake nervously thumbed the crack in the steering wheel. Time had slowed, yet looking at the numbers on his Human Interface Console, it didn't. The screen, embedded in his arm, showed the seconds tick over like they had since the beginning of time itself. *Tik, tik, tik.* The numbers were moving, but not the world around him.

Night was falling, and down the street across the bridge, lamps flickered to life, illuminating the area. It didn't look like daylight, but it was bright enough to deter anyone from doing anything they would rather not have seen. Anything less than legitimate. Over there, just a few hundred meters away, things got done by the book.

He turned his head as the sound of feet hitting the pavement reached his ears. He was sitting in the dark, as there were no lights here. Here was a place that things happened in the shadows. Things that weren't altogether legitimate. The footsteps grew louder, and Drake started the ageing hydrocar. A vibration shuddered through the old rust bucket, followed by a low hum. Unfortunately, the hum didn't stay low for very long as it built up, getting louder and louder, higher and higher.

As it reached its whining crescendo, the passenger door of the hydrocar creaked open, and Jimmy Something jumped in.

"Let's go, partner!" he yelled, holding a small, brown box triumphantly in the air.

Time was of the essence, and the sooner they got back over the bridge, the better their chances would be. Drake slammed the hydrocar into drive and floored the accelerator. The whining became a screech, and a violent shudder went through the car, but nothing moved.

"C'mon, you bastard!" Drake yelled, and almost as if it was waiting for the instruction, the hydrocar bolted forward. Fortunately, there was nothing in front of them, and Drake quickly got control back of the bucking hydro.

Racing over the bridge, they entered the safety provided by the lights, and Drake eased off the accelerator a bit and kept it on the speed limit. The Data Display Unit finally finished booting up, and it superimposed a green line on the windshield, showing them the direction to drive in.

Looking at the rearview monitor, Drake said, "We are cutting it close, Jimmy. Too damn close."

"I guess, but we got the parcel, ya know?" Jimmy retorted, grinning from ear to ear, shaking the box at Drake.

Drake shot him a look that made him put the box down.

"Let's hope the drop off goes smoother than the pickup and that we actually make something out of this," Drake said.

Although light flooded everything, and cameras littered every wall and post, it was far from the safest part of New Franco. Drake didn't engage the Autodrive, but kept control of the hydrocar in case he had to make any snap decisions. He knew he was being overcautious and slightly paranoid, but they could not afford to screw up tonight.

"Look out!" Jimmy yelled, covering his face with his arms.

Drake saw the red hydrocar approaching the crossing just in time and applied the brakes. One of the first things he did when he'd bought this piece of junk was to root the DDU and get rid of all the AI safety protocols when in manual mode. The operator of the red hydrocar must have been in manual mode too, but unlike Drake's hydro, their AI realized they had a red light, and instead of speeding past them, was now also slowing down, increasing the chance of a crash instead of avoiding it. Drake made a reflex decision. He released the brakes and floored the accelerator.

"Hang on!" he yelled to Jimmy, who was already bracing himself. *Thanks for the confidence, buddy.*

The old hydrocar shook and whined, and for a second, Drake questioned his decision. The red hydro was now only meters away, sliding uncontrollably, smoke billowing from its screeching tires. Drake had no space to maneuver in, as buildings flanked him on both sides.

He knew what he had to do.

As the cars entered the intersection, it seemed inevitable that they were about to crash. Even at the increased speed of Drake's hydro, the red car would still hit its rear quarter. There was no more speed left in the old hydro to get out of trouble. Drake had to time this to perfection and kept his focus on the red car, watching its trajectory toward them. Luckily, Jimmy was curled up into a ball, and Drake had an unobstructed view of the red hydro.

With five meters to go, Drake yanked as hard as he dared on the emergency brake and turned the steering wheel as quick as he could. The old hydrocar rocked to the side, throwing Drake against Jimmy, and Jimmy against the door, as it slid sideways down the road. The red car, tires still screeching, came to a standstill as it gently touched a wall. Drake stopped watching the red car, released the emergency brake, and did a quick counter-steer. The hydrocar fishtailed violently from side to side, and for a moment it looked like the pendulum effect was getting worse, but it calmed a bit, and within a few meters, the hydro was speeding along in a straight line.

"Let's hope that doesn't happen again," Drake said, as he wiped his hands on his legs.

"You are THE MAN!" Jimmy yelled as he uncurled himself. "That was fucking amazing!"

"What would be amazing would be if we never have to do that again."

"What are you talking about? You had that under control the whole time! I knew you had it."

"How about you show me some of that confidence next time?" Drake said, feeling his heart rate normalizing.

"I was just staying out of the way, letting you do what you do best, ya know?" Jimmy replied.

Drake let it go and went back to concentrating on the green line on the road.

***

Almost an hour later, they arrived at their destination. Once they left the dimly lit area of the pickup, they drove through some very well-lit areas of New Franco, but found themselves back on the fringes now. Drake pulled over to the side of the road where the green line ended and a red marker hovered in the air. He kept the hydro running and looked at the small building next to them. Most of the buildings in this area seemed recently abandoned, as their windows were still in place and the doors not kicked in. The only big difference to the one in front of them was that this one had lights on. All the other buildings sat empty and dark.

Drake turned to Jimmy. "Okay, you're up. Please make it quick, and don't fu—"

"I got this, ya know?" Jimmy replied hastily, jumping out to prove his point, almost running toward the door.

Drake watched on, waiting for him to turn around before reaching the door. Ten steps, eight steps, six steps. Five steps to go. Jimmy froze on the spot, dropped his shoulder in defeat, and shuffled back to the hydro.

"Here you go!" Drake said through the open window as he handed Jimmy the package.

"I think the almost crash gave me PTSD or something, maybe. My head is not where it should be, ya know?" Jimmy offered an excuse.

"Sure, buddy, let's just try again. Clock is ticking."

This time, Jimmy made it all the way to the door. He pressed some buttons on a small DDU. Shortly after, the door opened. Drake could only make out a silhouette in the doorway and squeezed the grip on his pulse gun a bit for reassurance. If anything went wrong, he would fire a few shots at the building to give Jimmy time to get away. Hopefully, it wouldn't get to that, but better to be prepared.

The door slid shut, and Jimmy started back to the hydro.

"We good?" Drake asked, as Jimmy closed his door.

"We good, partner," Jimmy replied, showing Drake his arm. They were good.

| two |

The door creaked as Drake pushed it open and banged it against something inside. Taking a deep breath, he entered the small room. Jimmy brushed past him and jumped onto an old couch that seemed on the verge of collapsing.

"What a night, huh?" Jimmy said, stretching out on the derelict piece of furniture.

Drake took another deep breath.

"It was, Jimmy. We need to be more careful with the promises and timelines we give people, okay?" *We* meaning Jimmy.

"Yeah, yeah, but I knew we could get over there and back in time, ya know? But sure, I hear what you're saying."

"Are you, Jimmy? I mean, yes, we made it, but we almost had a crash, and if the hydro gets damaged—"

"I know, I know, partner. Without the little, red rocket, we can't run parcels, and if we can't run parcels, we can't make credits."

Drake looked at Jimmy, all relaxed on the couch, just happy to be here with no big ambitions weighing him down. He motioned for Jimmy to scoot over and make space for him on the couch.

"We can't be running parcels forever, Jimmy. We barely make enough credits to live off. And it's not much of a living," Drake said, waving his hand across the one bedroom without a door, the kitchenette in the corner, and the bathroom, thankfully with a door. The wave was short.

"What do you mean? Running parcels is the best job I ever had! Almost nobody shoots at you, and we get to hang out all day. What more do you want?" Jimmy asked.

Running parcels was the only thing Drake could think of doing after losing his Hydrostar. Once Penta cleared them on all charges, they were free to go, but they'd had to give up all items or any credits they gained by illegal means. That included the Hydrostar he bought. No truck meant no hauling, so Drake had to come up with something to do. Jimmy had a thousand hairbrained schemes straight off the bat. Most of them were barely legal. Drake needed a clean start, and that meant staying legit.

Every day that became harder and harder to do.

"Don't think I don't know tonight's parcel was some illegal crap, Jimmy," Drake said.

"What do you mean?" Jimmy protested with the worst poker face Drake had ever seen.

"Deliveries have been scarce lately, yet you seem to get these last-minute calls almost daily to get us by. And I've been keeping quiet since god knows we need them, but don't think I don't know what's going on," Drake embellished. He had a hunch, but knew Jimmy would crumble under the lightest of pressure.

"Now hold on, partner," Jimmy started his defense.

Drake waited patiently, but the rest of his case never materialized.

"It's not that I'm not grateful, Jimmy, but I need to keep things on the up and up. If we want to set ourselves up to be haulers again, we have to stay clean."

"'Cause haulers are all angels," Jimmy muttered.

"No, they're not, but getting your licenses, buying a truck, all these things will go so much easier with a clean record. Or at least a clean*ish* one."

Drake knew that getting back on the road, hauling again, was his dream and not Jimmy's, but he also knew that Jimmy longed for a better life than the one he had before.

"It's you and me now, buddy. All I'm saying is, run jobs past me before you just say yes, okay?"

"You're the boss." Jimmy was clearly still sulking.

"How about we do the responsible thing and go waste these credits at the nearest bar?" Drake offered, and the look on Jimmy's face sealed their fate.

***

"Good evening, lads. Let's see those arms and I'll get you your usual," the heavily tattooed barkeeper said as Drake and Jimmy sat down. They obliged, and once the barkeep was happy they had no serious warrants out on them, he poured two beers from the unmarked tap. "Enjoy."

"Should we worry that we have a usual?" Drake asked Jimmy as they both sipped on the cold, tasteless beer.

"What do you mean? It means he remembers us, ya know?"

"Exactly, Jimmy. Maybe we are spending—"

"Well, well, well, if it isn't the world-famous Benjamin Drake himself," a voice said next to him.

Drake turned his head, hand gripping the glass, ready to smash it against whoever was clearly looking to get their head smashed with a glass. And he was right. If ever someone deserved a glass, brick, or any hard, unforgiving object smashed against their head, it was Sammy Sanders. Sammy Sanders, who stole a contract right out from under his nose and changed the course of his life. The only thing keeping the glass safely on the counter and away from Sammy's deplorable face was the beer inside of it.

Drake really wanted that beer.

"What the fuck do you want?" Drake was polite for now.

"Yeah, what do you want?!" Jimmy jumped off his chair, ready to bark from a distance instead of biting.

"Slow down, boys. We're all friends here, right? I just thought I'd come over and buy the most famous hauler in New Franco a drink." Sammy smiled, testing Drake's resolve to the limit.

"Never said no to a free drink, ya know?" Jimmy piped in.

"Three of whatever they're having," Sammy yelled at the barkeep.

The three of them sat in silence as they watched the golden liquid fill three glasses, which heavily tattooed hands then put down in front of them.

"To Mars!" Sammy raised his glass.

"Get fucked, Sammy," Drake spat out the words. "What the hell are you doing?"

"Drake, relax. I'm just saying, thanks to you, Mars is now an independent planet with boundless opportunities. Once shuttles start going there, I'll be first in line."

"That's if Santo can keep control of it," Jimmy offered.

"True, but he's been alone up there for months now. After Penta completely missed the plot with that lame retaliation of theirs, no one has even spoken of going again. And you know why?" Sammy took a long sip of his drink, waiting for someone to ask him.

Drake replied by taking an even longer sip of his beer. Jimmy took a very short sip.

"Why?" Jimmy asked.

"Because he's awaiting on Shangcorp to make an offer or an alliance. It's the only smart move to make. Take the planet and sell it to the highest bidder."

Drake hated Sammy, but had to agree. Penta's impatience and arrogance resulted in an under equipped team of shuttles being sent and getting defeated within days. The victory established Raymond Santo as the undisputed ruler of Mars, and everyone has been waiting for his next move.

"Thanks for the beer, Sammy, but I'm afraid you're vastly overestimating my role in all of this," Drake said.

"Maybe, but you ruffled enough feathers here in New Franco to last two lifetimes," Sammy replied.

"Want to join to that list?"

"Three more beers, please!" Sammy yelled over to the barkeep again. "I feel we are getting off track."

Drake didn't feel the need to reply, and since a fresh new beer was on its way, he dutifully finished his.

"Ahh, that's better. Cheers!" Sammy only half lifted his glass this time. "Things have been pretty hard since Mr. Turner disappeared."

Bob Turner. Drake's old boss. The man who always looked out for Drake and made sure he had a contract. Until the day Sammy Sanders stole that contract, and Drake learned that Mr. Turner had played him all along. Bob bloody Turner.

"Yep, just vanished," Sammy continued.

"Good." Drake took another sip of his free beer.

"You two were pretty close, though, weren't you?"

"Almost like his dad," Jimmy answered for him.

"Thanks, Jimmy." Drake wondered why he ever told Jimmy anything.

"That's what I heard. So, I guess you must have some idea where he would be?"

Nothing was ever really free.

"Someone put you up to this, huh? Convince you to get me to talk so you and whoever it is can find him and claim a bounty or something?"

"No, Drake, you got this all wrong. I just want to reconnect and try to get the hauler network in New Franco going again. It's a bit every man for himself at the moment."

"Jimmy, look up on that fancy new HIC of yours to see what bounty Penta put on Mr. Turner's head." Drake hated that he still referred to him as mister.

Jimmy got to work on the Human Interface Console on his arm, the only thing that stayed with them after their release.

"Wow! A cool one million credits," Jimmy said, not taking his eyes off all the zeros.

Drake figured that Turner would have a bounty out for his involvement in procuring the stolen Bismuth that he hauled to

Zuma and lead to Santo taking Mars, but a million seemed crazy. He tried to hide it from Sammy.

"And there it is. The only reason we're enjoying these refreshingly cold beers."

Drake looked on as he saw Sammy struggling to get his lies in order.

"Okay, so there is a bounty out on him. Everyone knows that. And rumor is it's doubling next week. So yes, Drake, you got me. Guilty as charged. I'm trying to find him and cash in. And besides, you owe me."

Drake almost choked on his beer.

"I fucking what?" The glass in his hand was almost empty enough. Almost.

"If you didn't double cross everyone and work with Penta to save your own skin, then we'd all still have contracts to haul. So yes, you owe me—big time."

"Fu—" Drake felt a hand gripping his tensed glass arm. A quick glance revealed it to be attached to Jimmy Something.

"Thanks, Sammy. If we hear from him we'll let you know, okay?" Jimmy said as he got up and steered Drake with him.

"Be sure you do!" Sammy yelled after them as Jimmy dragged Drake out of the bar.

| three |

It was Drake's favorite time of day. The sun was still rising, painting everything in hues of orange and pink. Most people were still asleep, making New Franco appear abandoned. Sand was lazily twirling over the road. Soon the traffic would push it back toward the desert. For a tiny window every day, he felt like the only person alive.

"We need to at least talk about it, ya know?" Jimmy broke the spell.

Personal space did not exist in the small cabin of the old Nikolatec MK2 sedan. Jimmy and Drake were shoulder-to-shoulder, legs bumping together continually, body odors indistinguishable. Right now, Jimmy's face and breath were only inches away from Drake's.

"Sammy wasn't wrong when he said you were the closet person to Mr. Turner. If anybody could—"

"I told you last night already. I'm not interested in going after him. He is the past. I need to move forward, Jimmy."

Jimmy turned his face forward and chewed on his bottom lip. Drake waited for him to try another angle.

"Okay, but Mr. Turner trusted you more—"

"Jesus, Jimmy! You're not even trying. Nothing that you can say will make me chase after Mr. Turner."

Jimmy started on his lip again.

***

New Franco was divided into sectors. The higher the number of the sector, the farther away from the center. The smaller the numbers became, the bigger the houses got, and more security patrols lined the streets. If you lived in a single digit, life was good. Single digits hardly ventured out of their zone and lived oblivious to the rest of the populous. They had the best jobs, most of the money, and all the power. Most people hated them, but without them, the city would stop.

Drake had never even been to a single digit sector. Mid-twenties was his high score. He had no desire or any need to go there. Haulers did most of their trade on the fringes and had no place in the inner city. But Drake was not a hauler anymore.

Sitting in front of the gate, flanked by walls on either side, he knew they had arrived. The walls were only three meters high, but had armed drones perched every ten meters, ready to deploy if anyone or anything jumped the fence. The only way into the single digit sectors was through gates like this one. Gates with heavily armored personnel.

"Hey, buddy. Got a package here for a Mr. Bush," Drake told the officer, who stared at him through the open window of the hydro.

"Identification, please," came a monotonous reply.

Drake stuck his arm out the window, and the security officer scanned his HIC. After staring at his small handheld DDU for an excessive amount of time, he tapped on it once, and the gate opened lazily.

"You have a thirty-minute permit. Please ensure you're back at a checkpoint in time, or face expulsion and a fine."

"Sounds a bit over the top, but sure, we'll try our best," Drake said, and drove off before he could get a reply.

"I'd like to see them try to expel us, ya know," Jimmy said right next to Drake.

"Well, let's try to not test their resolve, okay?"

They drove in silence for a while, taking in their surroundings. The road underneath them was flawless, no potholes, and smooth as butter. It reminded Drake of the highways he used to live on. Next to the road, on both sides, were houses, each with its own lawn and flowers. It all looked fake to Drake, but it impressed him. The houses all looked identical—clean and bigger than any he was used to. Only newer model hydrocars sat outside on the curbs. The entire scene reminded him of a town he once saw called Proteus.

The delivery was for a house in the seventh sector, and Drake felt relief when no more checkpoints popped up between sector nine and eight. Travel between the single digit sectors seemed to be free.

How nice for them.

Drake followed the green line on the road, but still noticed how everything—the road, the sidewalks, the houses—just kept getting bigger and bigger.

"Funny to think we live in the same town, huh?" he said to Jimmy.

But Jimmy was elsewhere, his initially wide-eyed amazement replaced by something darker.

"You okay, buddy?" Drake asked.

"Yea, I'm fine. It's just, ya know?"

"Overwhelming?"

"Yes. No. I guess. My mom worked for a while as a house assistant in sector eight."

"Oh, I didn't know that," Drake replied.

"The family was really nice to her and always gave her old clothes and toys to give to me, but she would always sell them when she got home. Sometimes, if I was quick enough, I would snag something, ya know? A toy car. Or a clean shirt. Just something nice."

Drake wished he could drive faster so they could get out of sector eight as quick as possible, but he dared not risk a drone disabling his hydro for speeding.

"Hey, we're almost in sector seven, buddy. You ready?"

Drake kept looking on the road as he heard Jimmy swallow hard, centimeters away from him.

"Fuck yeah, let's do this!" Jimmy replied half-heartedly.

***

Sector seven did not disappoint, and the houses, the yards, and even the cars were bigger again. Drake could not imagine how things could get any more indulgent as the countdown continued to sector one. The deeper they went into the sectors, the less it looked like the New Franco he knew. Up ahead, Drake could see the inverted red teardrop hovering on the road, showing the end of the green line and their destination.

"You got the parcel?" he checked with Jimmy.

"Yep, ready to go, partner." Jimmy sounded like himself again.

"Okay, we have plenty of time left till the next pickup, but let's hurry and get out of this place, yeah?"

"No need to tell me, ya know," Jimmy said, already opening his door as Drake bought the hydro to a standstill.

The house looked like all the others on the street. Everyone tried to make theirs stand out, with a few quirky or individual items, but even those looked strategically placed or sized. Most likely approved by a council vote as to not disturb the aesthetic of the sector or downgrade it to a higher number. Drake envied these people less and less.

Drake watched Jimmy as he ran up the steps, tap on the Data Display Unit next to the front door, and then suddenly vanish into the house the moment the door opened.

"What the," Drake muttered to himself, already dialing Jimmy on his Augmented Retina Projector.

As he watched the house, three white dots floated in front of him, projected via his ARP and only visible to him. ARPs used to be bulky glasses with an earpiece, but the popularity pushed the tech companies to make them smaller and cheaper at an exponential rate. Now, ARPs comprised a small neuron connection to the retina and a cochlea implant. The three dots danced in circles, and Drake tapped his foot as he waited for them to join in one big circle.

"Answer, you little shit." Drake's foot upped the tempo.

The three circles joined, and Jimmy's face popped up in front of him.

"Jimmy! What's going on? Are you okay?" Drake blurted out.

"Can't talk now—"

"Jimmy, wait!" But Jimmy was no longer in front of him.

What the hell are you doing?

Although he cut Drake off, Jimmy didn't seem stressed or in danger. Drake did not know what he was up to, but waited it out. At least for another five minutes. Drake's foot kept tapping away as he sat staring at the closed door, the small hydro feeling smaller than ever.

With no warning or fan fare, the front door opened, and Jimmy came running back.

With a bigger parcel.

"What's going on?" Drake asked, looking at the parcel in Jimmy's hands.

"We need to go, right now!" Jimmy tried to catch his breath.

"Okay, but where to?"

"Just go! Get to the checkpoint as fast as you can, and I'll program Yolanda."

Drake did as he was told and watched on as Jimmy fumbled on the hydro's Data Display Unit, nicknamed Yolanda. A green line projected onto the windscreen of the hydrocar, giving the impression of it being on the road. Drake followed it, keeping the hydro as close to the speed limit as he dared.

"Buddy, talk to me. What happened back there?"

Drake turned to look at Jimmy and was greeted by an enormous smile.

"Oh, nothing. Just got us a thousand credit delivery, that's all," Jimmy boasted.

"What? A thousand? Who would pay a thousand credits for a delivery?"

"I dunno, but that guy did, so let's get going," Jimmy replied.

Drake snapped his head, almost hitting Jimmy's.

"Jimmy, what happened in there?"

The checkpoint was coming up, so Drake slowed down, stuck his arm out the window to have his Human Interface Console scanned, and sped off, uncharacteristically not saying a word. Jimmy waited until they were up to speed again before talking.

"So, when I got to the door, I tapped on the DDU to let them know I was there, ya know. And as quick as I did, the door whooshed opened and someone pulled me inside." Jimmy looked at Drake, completely perplexed.

"This guy stood in front of me, looking a bit bewildered, ya know? Also, he smelled really nice. So the nice smelling guy says, 'I need to get this to sector forty-five in the next twenty minutes. Can you do it?'" Jimmy looked at Drake with total disbelief, as if he'd just heard the story for the first time.

"So, I know we have some time and I say to him 'Fuck yes' only I think I used the word hell. I hope. Shit, I might have said fuck. Sorry, Drake, I know you don't like it when I swear in front of customers, but it sort of just blurted out. Yep, the more I think about it, the more I'm sure I said fuck. Fuck."

"Jimmy. It's fine. Just tell me what happened."

Relief washed over Jimmy's face.

"So, as I was saying, the nice smelling man asked me if we could deliver something quickly to sector forty-five and I said," Jimmy paused for a second, "yes, and then he brings over this box. He asked me how much it would be, and you'll like this ..." Jimmy waited dramatically. "I just said one thousand like it was nothing!" Jimmy's smile was as infuriating as it was infectious.

"Just like that, 'one thousand credits,' and he swiped over the details and gave me the box. I ran out as fast as I could just in case he changed his mind, ya know?"

Drake glanced at the telemetry on the screen. They were in sector twenty-six. Once they got to thirty, he would start pushing the hydro slightly over the speed limit.

"Jimmy, a thousand credits for a quick job like this is great, but it's also not so great," Drake said. "There is no way the contents of that box are legal, or that we are dealing with at least one criminal party here."

Jimmy's face turned from defeated to determined.

"Okay, so what if it is? All we are doing is moving a parcel between two points. That's what we do, ya know?"

Drake knew Jimmy was right, in a very simplistic black and white way, but nothing was ever that clear cut. Knowingly transporting something illegal differed from turning a blind eye to what might be illegal. The two were close, but not the same. Drake realized he was avoiding what had been going on for weeks now. Trying to justify their normal runs over this one was hypocritical. He just couldn't admit to himself that he was sliding further away from his old life and more toward Jimmy's life. He always skated on the edge of the law, but he could feel himself drifting further and further away from it.

"You're right. As long as we don't know what's in the box, we have done nothing wrong. Right?"

"Right!" Jimmy agreed.

They crossed over into sector thirty, and Drake pushed the hydro to a little over the speed limit. The bridged DDU on the hydro would warn him if a drone approached, and in these sectors, they usually overlooked small indiscretions.

"This doesn't mean I want you to go all out and start looking for dodgy jobs, you hear?"

"No, but I have been saying no to a lot of jobs, thinking you might get angry, ya know?"

"As long as we don't know what is in the parcel, we're good."

Slipping further and further away.

| four |

Drake opened his eyes, and for a second thought that Jimmy had bum dialed his ARP. He closed his eyes and Jimmy disappeared, meaning he was, in fact, hovering over him. Drake kept his eyes closed for a second longer before facing Jimmy.

"Hey, you're up," Jimmy cleverly observed.

Drake's head was throbbing. He recalled delivering the thousand-dollar package and celebrating later that night. Not sure what there was to celebrate.

"Yes. My head—" Drake sat up.

Same shirt as yesterday, same pants, one foot still with a sock and boot on, the other with nothing. At least he tried.

"Did we miss a job?" Drake asked, reaching for a bottle of water on the floor. Furniture was not one of the apartment's selling points.

Jimmy stopped hovering over him and sat down on his own bed, a few feet away. He grabbed a white box meal next to him and handed it over to Drake.

"It's a breakfast one. I checked," Jimmy said as Drake took the meal from him.

"Thanks," Drake replied. He opened the box and started eating the brown mush. Nestem, the producers of the white box meals, claimed there was a vast difference between the individual box types, but to Drake, they all tasted the same. At least Jimmy heated it up. Good old Jimmy.

"So, partner, what do we have today?" he asked after another mouthful.

Jimmy scooted forward on his bed.

"Well, last night when we were celebrating, ya know, I sent out a message to my old crew saying that we are now running parcels in all sectors." Jimmy winked at Drake.

Barely twenty-four hours had passed since Drake agreed to be less particular on the packages they collected, and already Jimmy was advertising it to the world.

Specifically, the underworld.

"That's great, Jimmy, but don't you think that might have been a bit, I don't know, pre-mature?"

Jimmy leaned forward, lifted his arm, and showed Drake his HIC.

The display on his arm showed thirty odd unread messages.

"What am I looking at, buddy?" Drake asked.

"That, partner, is jobs waiting to be grabbed." Jimmy smiled wider that ever.

Drake grabbed another mouthful of mush. The last few months they'd lived day to day, barely scraping by. After the whole Santo Zuma fiasco, he wanted nothing more than to lie low, stay out of trouble, and get his life back to where it was. Not that it was in a great place before, but it was a comfortable place. He had to swap his freedom and the small living compartment of his Hydrostar for an apartment that was barely bigger and filled with another person: his new ally, friend and business partner. He'd lost everything and would do anything to get it back.

"Let's have a look then," he finally said.

Jimmy went through the messages, using some selection criteria Drake was not privy to. He made a lot of *ooh* and *ah* sounds and finally looked up.

"I think I've found one!" Jimmy said.

Drake finished the last of his breakfast and looked at Jimmy's arm. The apartment did not come with a built-in DDU, as advertised.

Drake read the message, felt his connection with the lawful world snap, and put his sock and boot back on.

***

The pick up was in one of the higher numbered sectors, close to where they lived. Drake recalled hearing an old expression once about shitting and your food and knew it related to this, but couldn't recall the right phrasing. *What was that saying?*

The green line on the road pointed the way, and Drake obediently followed it. Jimmy was way too quiet for Drake's liking.

"You okay?" Drake asked.

"Bit nervous, ya know?"

"Why would you be nervous? You most likely know the person who sent you that message," Drake pointed out.

"I do. That's why I'm nervous."

Drake felt a knot tying itself in his gut.

"Jimmy, I'm all in. I told you. So please, no more secrets. Just tell me who it is."

Jimmy mulled it over for a second. Drake noticed they were almost at the pickup coordinates.

"No one you would know, I'm sure, but he has a bit of a reputation in these parts," Jimmy said.

The green line ended, and Drake stopped at the red marker.

"I'm the driver, you're the grab it and give it guy," Drake reminded Jimmy of their roles. "Chances are you are going to have a history with most of our new clientele. If we want to do this, we need to accept the risks."

"You're right. I got us into this, this is my role, and I will do it!" And with that, he flung the door open, and off he went.

"I hope I see you alive again, buddy." Drake watched Jimmy disappear into the building.

Drake made himself as comfortable as he could in the small hydrocar, not knowing how long it would take Jimmy to grab the parcel or get himself killed. Either way, it might take a while.

But it didn't.

Drake almost found a semi-decent comfortable spot when he saw a rare sight—Jimmy actually walking out of a building. As he got closer to the hydro, Drake noticed the red around his eye. The size of a fist. Soon it would be black and blue. Jimmy gave him a sheepish smile.

"Seems he remembered me."

***

Hector Delgado ran a large operation out of sector fifty-nine, close to the edge of town. Nothing illegal went down without his approval. Even legitimate dealings usually went through his hands first, ensuring he had total control of the sector. Most of the sectors in the lower numbers had someone like Hector running things, and Penta Security was more than happy for them to do so.

New Franco was in a Penta Corporation territory, which meant the city had the newest and best security tech available to keep it safe and functional. And mostly Penta did just that, especially in the lower sector numbers. But in the overcrowded sectors, on the fringe of town, it was easier to supply weapons and tech to people like Hector Delgado, and let them sort things out. And if they got too powerful, Penta would step in and let a successor take over, reminding everyone who was actually in control.

Hector and Penta had a great relationship, and he never tried to overreach or grab more than was available to him. He stayed in his sector and did no business elsewhere until the deal of a lifetime came to him. Hector had never given into temptation for business out of his sector, but this was too good to pass on.

Not willing to risk one of his own men, he sent for Jimmy Something. He'd never dealt with him before, but got his name from a colleague who used him from time to time. The job was pretty straightforward and risk free, but Hector needed to have no ties to it. So he used friends of friends and made an untraceable connection to Jimmy. Jimmy agreed to do the job immediately, and within a few days, Hector got word back that he'd completed the job. Only problem was, Jimmy Something accidentally shot his contact in the process and was now in possession of the files that Hector needed, with no idea who to return it to. Hector would need to send someone to get Jimmy, bring him in, and then transfer the files. Obviously, he would then need to kill Jimmy, which would be a problem. If he let him go, there was no guarantee he wouldn't snitch, and Hector could not have that uncertainty hanging over his head. Jimmy had a record with Penta, and if he got killed in Hector's sector, it could expose the entire job. If that happened, relations between Hector and Penta would surely sour, or at best, put an unnecessary strain on their arrangement. Hector regretted ever taking this job or using Jimmy.

He put the word out on Jimmy.

The word never got out.

Moments after Hector decided Jimmy Something's fate, a knock sounded on his office door.

"What!" Hector yelled at the closed door.

"Sir, you'd wanna see this," came a reply he heard ten times a day.

"Come in, for fucksakes," Hector said and leaned back in his oversized chair.

The door slid open, and one of his men walked in, followed by a scrawny, little man with the wildest red hair, followed by two more of his men.

"Who's this?" Hector always sounded annoyed, and currently he was.

The three men shared a quick, puzzled glance at each other, and then the first one to enter the room walked closer to Hector's desk.

"Sir, this is Jimmy Something," he whispered.

Hector Delgado grinned from ear to ear. He leaned forward against the substantial belly in front of him and reached for a bottle of un-synthesized whisky. He poured himself a glass and sat back, surveying the tableau in front of him. He took a leisurely sip of the whiskey, savoring the taste of it, before swallowing. The little man in front of him could be no one else than Jimmy Something. The unruly red hair, small wiry build, and beady eyes that never stopped dancing around, always moving, assessing the situation. Hector had never seen him before, but heard enough to assume that this was indeed the man he was about to kill.

"Where did you guys find him?"

The three men looked baffled again.

"Sir, we didn't. He just, well, showed up at the front door," the same guy replied.

"You came here, to me, by your own will?" Hector asked Jimmy.

Jimmy Something looked at him as if he just asked him if he believed the Earth was flat.

"Yes, Mr. Delgado. I have your stuff. So I thought best I bring it to you. Since the guy I was going to give it to—" Jimmy stopped himself.

Hector Delgado starting laughing, making his chins wobble. The three men chuckled along nervously.

"Your reputation precedes you, Something. I've heard people call you The Eel, 'cause no one can ever catch you or get a grasp on you, and I have to say, it's true! Who else walks into *my* office moments after I decide to kill them? Who does this?" Hector started laughing again.

"Well, since you don't have to kill me now, I'd rather just transfer the files and take my credits now, ya know?"

Hector stopped laughing, and the wobbling subsided. He let out one more snort and took another sip of the whisky.

"I guess you are right, Something. How can I kill you now?" Hector replied. He winked at one man, who dragged Jimmy over to the desk. "Whenever you're ready."

Jimmy lifted his arm and swiped it. Delgado saw the files appear on his HIC and swiped his arm as well. Jimmy looked down at his arm again and saw the credits appear in his Human Interface Console.

"Consider us partners now, Jimmy. If I need something, I expect you here immediately."

Hector didn't need an answer and waved Jimmy away. His men knew what to do and escorted him out.

A few weeks later, Hector needed someone to do an errand and sent for Jimmy Something. But Jimmy never showed up.

Hector did not like that.

| five |

"Shit, Jimmy, you okay?" Drake asked as Jimmy shut his door.

"It could have been much worse, ya know?" Jimmy replied. "I was expecting to get shot, to be honest."

Drake felt lightheaded for a second, and his heart skipped a beat.

"You went in there, knowing you could die?"

"Like you said, I'm the grab it guy, you're the driver," Jimmy said calmly.

"Jimmy, that does not mean you have to put your life on the line." Drake felt like the biggest prick. "Why would you think you need to do that?"

"It's all good, Drake, honestly. We need to get going, though. Believe me, we do not want to miss this deadline."

Drake looked at Jimmy, slouched in the seat next to him. He would die for Drake, and Drake hated that.

"You're right, buddy, put the details in Yolanda."

Jimmy punched in the coordinates while Drake got the little, red hydro up and running. By the time the green line was on the road, most of the shuddering had settled.

Once they were on the road, Drake turned to Jimmy.

"Care to tell me what actually happened in there?"

***

Walking up to the door of Hector Delgado's warehouse, Jimmy felt his stomach cramp. It had been months since he'd been this nervous. His last meeting with Hector went pretty well, he thought, but then he made a crucial mistake. Hector contacted him for a job, and Jimmy ignored him. He had no choice. He finally got in with a crew and had a steady life. Steady for a small-time criminal. He was still low on the food chain and to rock the boat by suggesting they take the Delgado job, or worse, do it himself, would be suicide. No, best to ignore Hector and just stay clear of sector fifty-nine.

And he did. Until today.

Scanning his palm on the DDU outside the warehouse, Jimmy took a deep breath and waited for the door to open and someone to shoot him in the face with a pulse gun. The door slid open, and Jimmy closed his eyes. Instead of a shot to the face, he was pulled inside, violently enough for him to lose his balance and topple over. He quickly jumped up and assessed the situation. He was standing in the enormous warehouse, filled with boxes, crates, and hundreds of other items. Four heavily armed tough guys surrounded him. He remembered that Delgado's office was in the loft against the back of the warehouse. Jimmy turned around to see Hector Delgado leaning against the railing in front of his office, grinning at him.

"Welcome back, Jimmy!" he said, and the four guys ushered him closer to Delgado.

Delgado waited for Jimmy to be standing right underneath him before he spoke again.

"I'm glad you took my call this time, little eel. You surely have a set of balls on you. Maybe I should call you the badger instead?"

Delgado started his cumbersome descent on the metal staircase and walked over to Jimmy. Jimmy wondered what a badger was and if it moved him up or down Delgado's shit list.

"Usually I forego these little talks and let my men handle people like you. People who disappoint me, Jimmy. But, yet again, you wiggled yourself out of the situation."

Delgado stepped even closer to Jimmy. He wasn't much taller, but his sheer bulk made him dwarf Jimmy. Jimmy knew he was only alive because Delgado deemed it so, and decided, against all of his instincts, to keep his mouth shut and wait for Delgado to speak again.

"As I prefer to stay in my kingdom, I need someone that can easily transport things for me from time to time, no questions asked and no fear over their loyalty." Delgado stared at Jimmy.

Jimmy wondered if he needed to say something now, or kneel, or kiss Delgado's hand.

"Do not cross me again, Something," Delgado said and walked back to the stairs.

One of the tough guys grabbed Jimmy by the arm and dragged him back to the door. When they got there, he slammed a small parcel into Jimmy's stomach, hard enough to take the wind out of him.

"Fuck you," Jimmy muttered, doubled over.

"Fuck you!" the tough guy replied and punched Jimmy in the eye just as he stood up. "Get lost," he said, and shoved Jimmy out of the door.

Jimmy's head was throbbing, and he could feel his eye swelling up. His breathing was still labored but getting better.

He had never felt so good before in his life.

***

The green line on the road made a turn, and Drake followed it around the bend. The telemetry on the screen showed their destination to be a few minutes away.

"So what now?" Drake asked.

Jimmy's story of Hector Delgado sounded like a lucky escape, but Drake knew they were now in the pocket of a very ruthless man.

"Well, the next pickup is in sector thirty-three, so I'm thinking—"

"Delgado, Jimmy! What do we do now about Delgado? I'm happy to run a dodgy job now and again, but not work for a crime boss full time."

"I'm sure he'll only use us once or twice, ya know?" Jimmy's answer did not fill Drake with confidence.

"How scared should we be, Jimmy? Be honest. Are we in trouble?"

"Nah, I've known Delgado for years, and he's always liked me. He even has nicknames for me. We'll be fine!" Jimmy said.

Drake wished he had Jimmy's unwavering confidence. Once you worked for someone like Hector Delgado, you lost all free will. Saying no to any of his offers was to sign a death warrant. From now on, when Hector Delgado said jump, they'd have to jump.

Drake hated being told when to jump.

| six |

Drake did not use the Autodrive often and preferred to drive manually. Most people found it strange that anyone would bother to do something a program could do for them. But Drake loved it. It wasn't just the feeling of the steering wheel and the physical act of it. He loved to be in charge of where he was going and how he got there. Fate was not something that he put much faith in, but right now he was driving toward the drop off, in charge of the hydro, but he did not feel in control.

Drake was trying his best to just focus on the green line and not think about anything else. He hardly took notice of where they were going. He just stared at the green line and followed it until he saw the red inverted teardrop hovering in the road.

"I'll be quick," Jimmy said, and disappeared.

"Cool," Drake said to the empty seat.

Drake's thumb found the crack in the wheel, and slowly he observed his surroundings. Sand was everywhere, as the sector was right on the edge of town. The highway was behind the buildings in front of him, and he knew there must be an on ramp nearby. In fact, he knew exactly where the entry to the highway was. Drake turned his head and looked at the abandoned lot across from their drop off. The fence was still up, but pushed down in places, leaving it useless. Most of the lot was just open dirt, with one small office building almost right in the center. The door was open, and the windows shattered—looted a long time ago. Drake's eyes followed an imaginary driveway to the gate that stood wide open. The sign above it had no power to make it readable. But Drake knew exactly what it used to say: Turner Haulage.

∗∗∗

Three dots danced across the broken sign hanging over the entrance to Drake's previous life. A quick glance at his arm showed Sammy Sanders' name on his HIC. The three dots merged, and Drake realized he'd missed his chance to reject the call.

"Drake! Glad I got you. Wasn't sure you'd take my call." Sammy smiled his practiced smile.

"I wasn't. But I decided it would be more fun to hang up on your face. I was right. Bye, Sammy." Drake's finger moved to his HIC to swipe Sammy away.

"Two million!" Sammy yelled at Drake.

"Two million what?" Drake hated getting reeled in so easily.

"Two million credits for the capture of Bob Turner, Drake."

Turner Haulage. The sign was going to fall off its hinges any day now and crash into the ground below it.

"And I was thinking a generous twenty percent for you to point me in the right direction. Payable once I get the bounty, of course."

Hydrostars and Hydrocomets compacted the ground, and it was rock solid from years of the trucks going back-and-forth hauling cargo all over the territories. It would shatter the sign on impact, removing all traces that Bob Turner was ever there.

"But as an entrepreneur, I'm willing to negotiate."

Even if the sign never fell, Bob Turner had already stopped existing to Drake.

"Good for you, Sammy." Drake swiped him away.

***

"Who you talking you?" Jimmy asked as he jumped back into the hydrocar.

"Sammy."

"Sanders? Going on about Turner again, I bet."

"Yep."

"And you told him to get lost, yes?"

Drake's thumb massaged the crack in the steering wheel. A slight wind picked up and made the broken sign swing.

"Drake?"

"Yes. I mean, I hung up on him. He was right, though."

"Right about what?"

"The bounty. It's two million now."

Jimmy processed this information with all the zeroes in it.

"Wow, that is a lot of credits, ya know?" he finally spoke up.

"I know. And I know it's tempting, Jimmy, but we can't do this," Drake said, facing Jimmy and taking his eyes off the sign. "I need to move forward, not run in circles."

"Damn, Drake, two million credits, ya know?"

"Yes, Jimmy, I know."

With no green line pointing the way, Drake took off.

***

Sammy Sanders watched as Drake's face disappeared in front of him. He did not really expect Drake to just say yes and give him the coordinates to Bob Turner's hideout. He knew he would have to work for it. All he had to do was plant the seed and let it grow. No one, not even holier-than-though Benjamin Drake, could refuse that amount of credits. It was going to take some time, but if anyone could catch Bob Turner, it would be Benjamin Drake. Drake always had his head up Turner's ass. All the haulers knew Drake was Turner's favorite, even though things went south after the bismuth ordeal. Drake was the one who indirectly put Penta on Turner's trail and sent him running, but Sammy knew Drake was still the key to unlock Turner's whereabouts. All he had to do was find an angle. Someone or something he could manipulate into making Drake talk.

Someone or Something.

| seven |

Drake couldn't stand the small apartment, so most nights, they went to the closest bar. It wasn't the worst bar Drake had ever gone to, but it was far from the nicest. The floor was clean, the tables not too sticky, and most of the clientele kept to themselves. It wasn't located close to a factory or a highway, so most people were just ordinary folk from the surrounding living complexes. Just normal people, living normal lives, having a normal night out. Drake liked not having to hang around haulers for a change.

"Here we go!" Jimmy placed a beer in front of Drake and pulled a chair up to the small table.

"Thanks, buddy," Drake said, and took a sip.

The bar was always busy, no matter the time of day. New Franco's outer sectors were a hard place to make a living in, and people needed an escape. Not everyone had a job, and the lucky ones that did barely made a better living than those on the Basic Citizens' Income.

Drake looked around at all the faces and saw little joy.

Except for the face in front of him.

"We killed it today, partner!" Jimmy said, smiling over his beer. "You drove like a maniac, ya know!"

"Really? Felt like I was on Autodrive, myself."

"We almost made more today than we did all of last week!" Jimmy was ready to celebrate tonight.

"I hate to admit it, Jimmy, but we'll get to our goal of buying a Hydrostar much quicker now." Drake knew if he kept his eyes on the prize, he could stomach running illegal parcels for a short time. Just long enough to save up enough credits.

"I've always said, as long as you don't think about it, it won't hurt, ya know?"

Drake loved Jimmy's simple view of life.

"To not thinking!" Drake raised his glass.

"I never do!" Jimmy laughed and downed his beer.

***

"Time for a piss," Drake announced and staggered off to the restrooms.

The moment Drake left, boredom set in, and Jimmy looked at his HIC to distract himself. An unread message notification blinked in the screen's corner. He'd somehow missed the vibration and noise when it got delivered, but sitting in a noisy bar, fairly intoxicated, it didn't surprise him. All messages relating to deliveries went straight to a separate folder with a separate notification, but this one was in his personal folder. Maybe one just slipped through. Since Drake was taking his sweet time, Jimmy read it.

Jimmy, you might not have this number in your HIC, but it's Sammy Sanders, Drake's friend. I have been working on a proposal for him that would be very lucrative, but thought it best to run it past you first, as you are his right-hand man. Let me know when we can talk.

Be best if you did not mention this to Drake, as the proposal is still in the developmental stages and I would hate for all of us to miss out on a MILLION credit deal.

Sammy S.

Jimmy reread the message two more times before Drake returned.

"One more before we hit the road?" Drake asked, holding on to a chair for balance.

"Sure thing, partner," Jimmy replied, and moved the message into a new folder.

***

Like everything in their lives, their sleeping arrangement was in a small, confined space. Something both of them were used to. Drake had spent most of his adult life sleeping in the small living cabin of his Hydrostar, and Jimmy was used to squeezing into whatever bed, hydrocar, or hole he could to find some rest. Stretching out on their own beds was a luxury.

Drake's breathing was slow and steady and accompanied by the occasional snore. Jimmy was sure he was asleep. With the covers pulled over his head, he swiped his HIC and found Sammy's message.

I would hate for all of us to miss out on a MILLION credit deal

If they kept delivering parcels, even with their new business model, it would take years before they would have enough credits to pay for a used Hydrostar. And that was the dream, right? Getting back on the road hauling. Or, more correctly, it was Drake's dream, but he included Jimmy when he talked about it.

How they were a team now, partners, and they were going to make an honest living being haulers. Drake was looking out for him, so he had to do the same for Drake.

Fearing he might bump the front door against the table, or the light from the hall might shine on Drake, Jimmy climbed through the window onto the small landing that used to serve as a fire escape. The ladder had long since fallen off, and most people used the area outside their windows to dry their laundry, storage, or just sit and enjoy the view of the building next to theirs.

After the Zuma fiasco, Drake went paranoid for a while, so Jimmy installed a rope ladder on the landing for them to use in case someone came knocking on the door. No one ever did, but tonight Jimmy was glad they'd put it there. He carefully unrolled the coil of rope and plastic rungs and lowered it to the ground. After confirming Drake was still asleep, he climbed over the railing and descended.

Jimmy walked to the edge of their building and turned the corner. He wanted to be a hundred percent sure Drake would not see or hear him. He looked up the message from Sammy again, and after reading it, he swiped it, and in doing so, made a call to Sammy via his Augmented Retinal Projector. Three circles danced and danced in front of him, and Jimmy wondered if Sammy was asleep. It was pretty late. Scared he would not have the courage to go behind Drake's back again tomorrow, he patiently waited for the circles to merge. And they did, blending together and fading away to reveal Sammy's face. He clearly just woke him up.

"Jimmy! So glad you called. I was waiting for your call."
Sammy smiled.

Jimmy was used to conmen and sleazy characters like Sammy,
and the smile did more harm than good.

"Sammy. I'm a very busy man, so this better be worth my
time, ya know?"

"Hey, I know the feeling, right? So here it is. Your partner,
Drake, is the only person left that had any close ties to Bob
Turner. And as we all know, he has a million-credit bounty
out, so—"

"I thought it jumped to two million?" Jimmy corrected him.

"Ah yes, it changed so recently, it slipped my mind. But yes,
two million credit bounty. As I was saying, Drake is the only
person who stands a chance to figure out where Turner might
be. He had a relationship with him that no one else had. So if
anyone stands a chance to get to Turner, it's him."

"Okay, so what's the deal?"

"Straight to the point! I like it. Okay, since we all know Drake
is a goody two shoes, that only got into trouble because of you,
no offence ..." Sammy paused.

"I gave him the contract, that's true. Go on," Jimmy replied
with pride.

"Yes, that's what I meant. You were the one doing all the
work, and he just tagged along. The Drake I know prefers other
people to do his dirty work for him. People like me ... and you."

Jimmy knew exactly what Sammy was doing, trying to play
on his emotions and manipulate him into helping him. And he
had to commend Sammy on doing an outstanding job.

"So you want me to talk to him to help you," Jimmy said.

"You make it seem so simple, Jimmy, but yes. And in exchange for any information, I will give you guys a cut of the bounty. I was thinking something like twenty percent?" Sammy sounded eager to seal the deal.

"Forty percent, but there is no guarantee I can get Drake to tell me anything."

"My expenses on this is going to ruin me, with no guarantee of a bounty, so let's settle on thirty?"

Thirty percent of two million credits would go a long way in securing a Hydrostar, Jimmy thought.

***

"Boss, we have most of the components ready. All we need is the last piece."

Delgado sat back in his chair and looked at the young man with the big numbers of five and nine tattooed on his face. Such loyalty. To completely devote your life to something that is not even your own was beyond the grasp of Delgado. To die for something you believed in and worked for, he understood, but to do it for another man's vision? Still, without devotees like this man, standing proudly in front of him, he would not have an empire.

"Outstanding work, soldier. I'm expecting a delivery soon." Delgado dismissed the man.

Besides, he had enough ambition for all of them.

| eight |

Drake closed the door of the hydrocar and initiated the startup procedure. Jimmy was still on the outside fiddling with his HIC, organizing today's deliveries. Sitting down on the front of the hydro, Drake watched Jimmy's lips move as he read the messages and allocated their priority and times. Once done, he jumped down and took his seat next to Drake.

"So, let me have it, partner. Where is our first stop?" Drake asked.

Without Jimmy, Drake knew he would struggle, living on the Basic Citizen's Income and waiting for a miracle. Jimmy gave his all every day, made sure everything ran smoothly, whilst Drake just followed the green line. He was more than just his partner now.

"Well," Jimmy started as he typed the coordinates into Yolanda, the hydro's DDU. "Our first stop today," he kept typing, "is a delivery for Delgado's." He stopped typing. The green line appeared on the screen, and Jimmy was already back on his HIC, clearly avoiding eye contact with Drake.

"Already! Fuck, Jimmy, I knew it. He owns us now. We should never—" Drake didn't bother finishing his sentence. He knew nothing he would say would change the fact that they were now firmly in Delgado's pocket.

"If getting paid four times our normal rate for a job is owning us, it might not be so bad, ya know?" Jimmy replied.

"It's not all about the credits." Drake paused. "Four times?" Drake had to admit, earning that amount of credits by running parcels for Delgado would expedite their plans to get back to hauling exponentially. "It's just hard for me to accept that we are running parcels for criminals now."

"Drake, I know these people. Heck, I am these people. We'll be fine. Besides, it's only temporary, ya know?"

Drake stepped on the accelerator, and the little red hydrocar shuddered forward.

A light dusting of sand covered the deserted streets, no one around to disturb it yet.

This used to be Drake's favorite time of day.

***

The pick up for Delgado's parcel was on the other side of New Franco, which meant the green line took them to the highway that ran around the outskirts of town in a big loop. People simply referred to it as the loop. From the loop, other highways branched off to connect New Franco to multiple cities and territories. Most people used the Hyperloop train to travel longer distances, but trucks still used the highways, making it their domain. Hydrocars seldom ventured out onto the highway, and haulers rarely made them feel welcome when they did. Having a huge Hydrocomet follow you at speed, a mere one meter behind you, was normal for Haulers as they formed giant autonomous caravans, some stretching for kilometers. But having them on your tail in a hydrocar was a nightmare. Most caravans reached speeds way over that of a normal hydrocar, so if a hydrocar did not move out of their way quick enough, most haulers just locked on to them and pushed them along for a while. Although it was illegal to do so, haulers did this all the time to scare hydrocars off the road. Most, if not all, hydros took the first exit of the highway when the caravan released them, their driver scarred for life, never to use the highway again.

Drake knew his little, red hydro would most likely rip to pieces if it reached the speeds of the caravans, so he kept a close eye on his radar and telemetry to ensure he was always in an empty lane. It was exhausting driving on the loop, but would save them an enormous amount of time.

Drake wiped his hands on his pants, realizing how sweaty they had become, when he saw the green line veer off the highway and back into a sector. As much as he loved to be on a highway, he hated being there in a hydrocar.

He dreaded the return trip to Delgado's.

Arriving at the pickup, Drake parked the hydro, and Jimmy jumped out to retrieve the parcel.

"Jimmy, wait!" Drake called out.

"What's wrong?" Jimmy asked.

"Switch on your ARP. If anything happens, I can call for help or do something."

"Smart idea. Not the calling for help part, but switching it on. Calling security out here would not do much, ya know?" Jimmy said and walked off. He switched on his ARP and turned it to broadcast, allowing Drake to see his point of view.

Drake watched as Jimmy reached the door and pressed the communication button on the DDU mounted on the wall. A few seconds went by, and then a face appeared on the screen.

"Pick up for Mr. Delgado," Jimmy said to the face on the wall.

Drake heard a buzzing sound, and the door slid open.

From the outside, the building looked ready for demolishing. The rusted roof, cracks in the walls, and broken windows all showed it to be a building past its usefulness. But once Jimmy stepped inside and his ARP adjusted to the light, a different scene took place.

The inside of the derelict building was clean, modern, and very well equipped. It seemed to be a housing unit, with huge DDUs on most walls and sleek furniture everywhere. None of the walls had cracks, and the roof was intact. Clearly, the outside was a ruse to keep attention away.

Jimmy walked over to the eating area and picked up a fresh, red apple. Drake watched via his eyes as he turned it over and over, admiring it and taking in a deep breath of its aroma.

"Have it," a voice said behind him.

Jimmy almost dropped the apple and turned to face the voice.

"Um, sorry, I was just—"

"Have it. Go on, take a bite. Please." The voice now had a face, and Drake liked the face.

A woman, maybe in her forties or fifties, stood in front of Jimmy. Her warm smile and bright eyes made Drake feel at home, even remotely via Jimmy's ARP.

"I know a guy who can get me more. You really should try it," the woman said to Jimmy.

Hesitantly, Jimmy took a bite, and Drake could hear the crunch.

"Oh my god," Jimmy mumbled as he took another bite. "This is so good."

Drake tried his best to imagine how good it tasted and wondered if he should fake an emergency and go in as well.

"Thank you so much. That was just—" Jimmy finished the apple instead of his sentence.

"It's my pleasure. Now, I believe you are here to collect a parcel for Hector. Yes?"

Drake watched as Jimmy looked at the apple core, then at the table, then back at the lady.

"Don't leave it there," Drake wished out loud.

"Um, yes. The parcel for Mr. Delgado," Jimmy said.

"Give me one second," she said, and left the room.

Jimmy stood there, looking at the core and the table again. Drake knew he was just going to leave it there.

The woman returned with a fist-size parcel.

"How about we swap?" she said, holding out the parcel and reaching for the apple core.

"Oh, thanks. Didn't know what to do with it, ya know?" Jimmy said as they made the exchange.

"Not a problem, Jimmy. Now, best be on your way. We don't want to keep Hector waiting."

"Guess not," Jimmy replied.

Drake watched him retrace his steps through the house, and as he stepped through the open door, Drake saw the red hydrocar from Jimmy's POV. He disconnected the feed.

"Let's go!" Jimmy was all smiles, getting back into the hydro.

"That apple looked pretty good. Saved me some?" Drake started the hydro and waited for Jimmy to program the DDU. He knew the way to Delgado's, but Yolanda would ensure they reached it the fastest possible way, avoiding any accidents, road blocks, or any event that might slow them down.

"Oh, shit, Drake, I'm so sorry, but I didn't. I wanted too, but then—"

"Relax, buddy, I'm just kidding. I mean, it looked delicious, but I didn't really expect you to save me some." The start-up process was complete. "Your turn," he motioned toward the DDU.

"Oh, yes, sorry, Drake. Man, that apple was good, ya know?" Jimmy shook his head in disbelief and programmed Yolanda.

The green line appeared, and they were off.

"So, who was that?" Drake asked once they got back on the loop. He could feel his palms getting sweaty already.

"The apple lady?" Jimmy asked.

"Yes, Jimmy, the apple lady. Who else?"

A caravan of Hydrocomets appeared in Drake's rearview monitor, and an alarm went off to warn him of the impending doom. He quickly changed lanes, seconds before it came speeding past them. Drake waited for it to disappear in the distance before he repeated himself.

"So, who is she?"

"I don't know," Jimmy replied straight-faced.

"She called you Jimmy," Drake refreshed his memory.

"Most people do, ya know?"

Drake felt his muscles tense up in frustration. He gave them a quick flex and let it go.

"Of course, Jimmy. I just didn't recall you introducing your-self, that's all."

"Huh," Jimmy replied.

"So, you don't know her then?" Drake asked yet again.

"Let me think," Jimmy said, and Drake settled in for the long haul.

The green line kept guiding them forward, and only two more caravans came speeding past before Jimmy stopped think-ing about it.

"No," Jimmy finally said.

In the distance, Drake could see the green line veer off to the left, and a red arrow on the screen confirmed the change in direction approaching. After taking the turn and entering a sector, Drake turned to Jimmy.

"She sounded like she knew you?"

"I guess, but I swear, Drake, I do not know who she is."

Drake believed him.

| nine |

Drake stopped under the red inverted teardrop in front of Hector Delgado's warehouse. He left the hydrocar running. Two of Delgado's men guarded the door. Both had the same tattoo on their faces. The number five under the right eye and the number nine under the left. Big, black numbers, running from under the eyes, down to the jawline. No other tattoos were visible on their faces.

Jimmy watched Drake, making no attempt to go into the building.

"It's part of the initiation, ya know?"

"What is?" Drake asked.

"The numbers. The tats. They have to get it done to be in the organization."

Drake looked on as the two numbered men shifted their weight around and repositioned their pulse guns. They were clearly not happy being observed like this.

"Better be going then," Jimmy announced his departure.

"ARP on!" Drake yelled after him.

Jimmy nodded, and after a swipe on his HIC, Drake had a front-row seat to Jimmy's world.

***

"Hey, fellas! Got a parcel here for Mr. Delgado," Drake heard Jimmy say to the guys at the door.

The guard in front of the wall mounted DDU stepped aside. Jimmy walked up to it and scanned his hand. The door slipped open. Clearly, he was on the day's list of people not to shoot.

It took a second for the ARP to adjust to the darkness of the warehouse, but once it did, Drake had an unobstructed view of what was inside. Which wasn't much. A few boxes stood on a pile in the middle of the floor, and the rest of the space was empty. Jimmy turned his head around, and Drake noticed that there was also a lack of people in here. Must be a busy day somewhere else for the Delgado empire, Drake thought.

Jimmy started walking toward a set of stairs that lead to an office set up in a loft in the back of the warehouse. Drake appreciated his initiative. Jimmy made his way up the yellow steel stairs, walked down a short catwalk, and stopped in front of the door. He pressed his hand on the DDU next to it. Drake saw the screen turn red. This time, he was not on the list. Unsurprisingly, as Delgado would have a very short list of people that can just walk into his office.

Still, seconds later, the door slid open.

"Something, get in here," Delgado's voice boomed out from somewhere in the office.

Jimmy quickly stepped inside.

Most people in these sectors of New Franco were skin and bones, always on the edge of starvation, barely hanging on. Clearly not Hector Delgado. From the top of his shiny bald spot to where he disappeared under his desk, were folds of skin and fat covered in a shiny film of sweat. He glanced up at Jimmy, his chins firmly tucked against his chest, ready to resume whatever had him so occupied.

"Be quick," he snapped.

Drake watched as Jimmy walked over to the desk.

"Here you go, Mr. Delgado. Seems like you guys are busy today."

"We are. Leave it on the desk, and go." Delgado's eyes were already down, back to work.

"Okay, well, if you need us, ya know." Jimmy walked backwards to the door. "Anytime, any day," he advertised, before turning around and exiting the room.

***

"Anytime, any day?" Drake greeted Jimmy back at the hydro.

Jimmy got in and made himself comfortable.

"Yes, ya know, letting him know we are the best and that he can trust us."

"Jimmy, he is already using us. We do not have to work on the relationship. At all!"

Jimmy squirmed around in his seat.

"I know. He scares me, ya know? I just sort of blurted it out."

Drake saw Jimmy shrinking away, Hector Delgado still in his head.

"Can't harm to stay in his good books, can it?" Drake backtracked. "Okay, put the next job into Yolanda, and let's get the hell away from here."

Jimmy typed in the new coordinates, and Drake fell in behind the green line.

"The place looked pretty deserted, ay?" he said once they left the warehouse behind.

"The only people I saw were Delgado and the two fellas at the door. You think something is going down?"

"Without a doubt, buddy. And with everyone gone, it has to be big. Did you see Delgado?"

Drake looked at the telemetry on the screen to confirm everything was in order and took notice of the ETA to the next destination. The streets were still pretty quiet, and he didn't foresee any problems getting there on time. Once the roads filled up, however, it was every man and woman for themselves, and deadlines became much tighter.

"Yes, I was in his office." Jimmy looked quizzically at Drake.

"I know, I know. I mean, didn't he look a bit stressed to you? All the sweat on his face?"

Jimmy seemed to reflect on his encounter with Delgado five minutes ago.

"He looked angrier than normal, now that I think about it."

"That's what I mean. He usually looks composed and in charge, but I thought he looked a bit flustered. Whatever is going on today has to be huge," Drake said.

The green line ended, Jimmy got out, came back with a box that barely squeezed into the back of the hydrocar, and they were off again, chasing a new green line.

The road was much busier now, with people driving their beat up hydrocars to the factories and even more taking the hydrotrams. Drake hated the trams, with their seemingly random stopping and stupid right of way. If it wasn't for his highly illegal DDU in the hydrocar, he would forever sit behind them or waiting for them to allow him to overtake them.

All the people in the trams looked dead to Drake, and he did not envy their lives.

His chest tightened just looking at them, and he knew that only the open road could free it up again.

"You okay?" Jimmy spoke up next to him.

"Yes, just looking at those poor souls on the trams."

"Just being alive is not enough, ya know?" Jimmy said.

Drake agreed.

***

The big box's destination was in the inner circle of sectors. According to the telemetry, they had a bit of a drive ahead of them. Caravans of trucks would litter the highway by now, so Yolanda put them on a course through the city.

"Lunch before or after the drop?" Drake asked. He missed having a heating unit in his vehicle.

"You read my mind!" Jimmy replied enthusiastically, as always.

"Great. So? Now or after?" Drake asked again.

Jimmy looked at the windscreen that was filled with data about speed, location, and many other things. He made a face, showing him to be in great pain. Or thinking.

"If you go a bit, and I mean just a tiny bit faster, we could save about ten minutes of our time."

"Go on." Drake wanted to see where this was going.

"Which means," Jimmy typed on his HIC and then swiped it to the screen, "we could grab something from here."

On the windshield, an advertisement appeared for a small diner in the same sector they were heading to. Not only did they serve colored box meals, but also fresh items. Jimmy's excitement was palatable.

"You know those colored boxes are just—" Jimmy's face dropped a fraction of the enthusiasm. "They are just the best. Let's waste some money!" Drake amended.

"Yea!" Jimmy yelled and punched the air.

Drake just shook his head and smiled.

***

"Jimmy, no fucking around when we get there, you hear? This is a simple grab and go mission. You understand?"

They were cutting it close. A few times on the way to the drop off, Drake swore he heard drones following them, but nothing showed up on the screen, so he kept the speed up and pushed on. The customer was so happy with the speedy delivery, they even paid them a few credits bonus. Now, heading to the dinner, they only had twenty-one minutes left on their inner sector pass.

"Got ya!" Jimmy said, focused and ready.

The green line took them right to the diner, with fifteen minutes to go.

Drake looked over at Jimmy, who gave him a nod, and they were off.

The diner was brightly lit to showcase how clean it was and to ensure that people didn't get too comfy. The longer they lingered, the fewer people they could serve.

"Okay, Jimmy, I'm grabbing a red box and some fruit. That apple you had made me crazy for one," Drake said, sticking to the plan of being quick and decisive.

"Mmm, it all looks so good, ya know?" Jimmy said, ogling all the possibilities on the menu, forgetting that there was a plan.

Eating authentic food was a rare pleasure, one Drake did not want to take away from Jimmy, but time was not on their side.

"How about you just grab the same as me?" Drake prompted him.

"I was thinking that, but then ..." Jimmy lost himself in thought.

Drake looked at his HIC. Ten minutes before their pass ran out.

"Go with your gut, buddy. Whatever you think looks good, just go with it."

"Yeah, you're right, ya know? It's going into my gut, so why not listen to it?"

Eight minutes.

"Let me, get a—" Jimmy almost got there.

"Jimmy, please, we have seven minutes left to get the fuck out of this pretentious sector. Let's go, buddy!" The woman behind the counter gave Drake the stink eye. "No offense," he mumbled in her direction.

"Sorry, yes, you're right. Just make it the same as his, please. To go." Jimmy smiled at Drake.

Drake left Jimmy to pay and went out to get the hydrocar started. He did this to save time and the friendship. With three minutes to spare, Jimmy came running out of the diner, finally on board with the time schedule.

"Let's go, let's go! Time's ticking," Jimmy yelled, getting into the hydro.

Drake slammed the hydro into drive and left the diner as quickly as he could. The cabin filled with aromas he hadn't smelled in a while, and he could feel his mouth watering already.

"Hang on!" he yelled to Jimmy.

The closest checkpoint was six minutes away, and the time left on the pass showed four on screen. If Drake broke the speed limit in a low sector, drones would immediately deploy and shut his hydro down, followed by a security patrol who would not be interested in anything he had to say.

If he missed his check out time, drones would immediately deploy and shut his hydro down, followed by the same security patrol who would still not be interested in anything he had to say.

Drake knew he had to choose one, so speed it was. He hoped the brief window of time would allow him to get to the gate before the drones did. So far, so good.

Drake heard the distant buzzing sound of a drone.

"No, no, no, come on," he said to no one.

The time to the gate was now only three minutes, and the pass had two minutes left.

The buzzing grew louder, but still not near enough for a warning from Yolanda. Drake pushed the little hydrocar even harder, making the tires squeal and the body shake.

One minute to go. The times were tied.

"You got this, Drake!" Jimmy yelled as the gate came into view.

The DDU and windscreen flashed messages in red, warning Drake to slow down and pull over. He could see the eyes of the guards at the gate, wide and panicked. They raised their pulse guns, ready to fire. Drake slammed on the brakes, trying to push his foot all the way to the floor. The hydrocar skidded uncontrollably toward the gate. The guards exchanged looks, not sure whether to shoot or run. Drake was pulling on the steering wheel and pushing on the pedal, trying to get the most leverage. The drones buzzed right above them now.

And then everything stopped.

"Hey, guys. Looks like we just made it." Drake smiled at the guard closest to his window.

Everyone was quiet. Jimmy opened his eyes, still clutching their valuable cargo. The guards just stared at the red hydrocar in shock. The drones buzzed off, their programming telling them their job was done.

"Mind if we get going? Don't want the food to get cold." The guard slowly raised a hand and swiped this HIC to let them through.

"See ya!" Drake waved them goodbye.

***

"This is sooo good," Jimmy said through a mouth full of food.

Drake watched him take another bite, although his mouth was still full from the last one.

"Slow down there, buddy! It's not going anywhere." Drake laughed.

Sector ten was still high enough in the hills to give them a panoramic view of New Franco. Behind them was the wall, keeping everyone safe from everything that lay in front of them. New Franco stretched from horizon to horizon.

Drake had pulled the hydrocar over to the side of the road almost immediately after they left the checkpoint. Now, sitting on the roof of the hydrocar, not caring that it popped in when they sat down, they could enjoy their colored box meals.

"I know we spent almost all the money we made today, but damn, it's worth it, ya know." Jimmy spoke through his food again.

"It wasn't quite that expensive." Drake laughed. "You are right, though. It's pretty good."

"Pretty good? It's the best!" Jimmy kept talking and eating.

Drake took a few bites of his meal, enjoying every bite, before turning to Jimmy.

"I can't stop thinking about that woman knowing your name," he said.

Jimmy nodded and kept eating.

"It's not just that she knew it, but she said it like she knew you. Didn't you get that feeling?" Drake asked.

Jimmy was still nodding and eating. Drake had another bite too, allowing Jimmy some time to mull it over.

"I guess. But before you met me, I was up to some sketchy stuff, ya know?"

"I know."

"All I'm saying is I might have run into her, done something for her, and just couldn't remember. I'm not that good with names and faces, ya know?" Jimmy used his finger to get the last scrapes of food out of the box.

"I should just let it go, I guess," Drake said.

| ten |

Rain poured down for the first time in months. No one, least of all Jimmy Something, expected it to be this wet tonight. Standing on the corner, two blocks away from their small apartment, Jimmy was shaking. He rubbed the skinny arms sticking out of the sleeveless shirt, to no avail. Why, on all the nights, did it have to rain tonight?

To make things worse, he didn't even want to be there. He hated being there, rain or no rain. Standing there, on the corner, made his stomach hurt. It felt like he was trying to get into a new gang again. He wished his feet would just move and take him home.

A dark hydrocar stopped at the curb, and a door swung open.

"You're a mess! Try not to make it too wet in here, okay?"

Jimmy tucked his head in and climbed into the hydro. It was much nicer than the shit box Drake and he had. The console was intact, it didn't smell, and everything seemed to be from one hydrocar. The only bad thing was the driver.

The driver who looked very pleased to see Jimmy.

"So? Any news?" Sammy Sanders asked.

Jimmy wanted to be home. Warm and in bed, listening to Drake snore.

"I told you. When I get a chance, I'll talk to him. And so far, we've been way too busy."

"Jimmy, I trust you, I do, but the longer we wait, the further Bob Turner is getting away."

Jimmy rubbed his arms again, but the cold and wet clung to him.

"I know, Sammy. It's just not that easy, ya know?"

"I do, that's why I'm talking to you, Drake's right-hand man." Sammy smiled.

"I'll try tomorrow, but no promises."

"That's all I wanted to hear, Jimmy."

Jimmy's feet finally took him home.

***

When Jimmy woke, he still felt damp and cold. Shuffling over to the heating unit, he placed two white box meals in it and waited. Once done, he took them to Drake's room.

"Rise and shine," Jimmy said, holding one meal out to Drake.

"Thanks, buddy. Smells good," Drake mumbled.

Unlike Drake, Jimmy was a morning person, always the first to rise and get the day started. He wasn't like that as a kid, but living on the streets, he soon realized the sooner you were ready for the day, the better chance you had of making it. No goon was going to stab him still lying in bed.

"Today looks like another busy one. Business really picked up, since ..." Jimmy paused and looked at Drake.

"It's okay, you can say it. Since we started to run parcels for undesirables, like Hector Delgado." Drake was sitting up now and poking at his meal.

"Well, yes, since then," Jimmy replied.

They ate in silence.

Jimmy's arm vibrated, and a message alert came through. He swiped his HIC and read it.

"Looks like we are going back to apple lady again."

"Huh?"

"The lady, the one I got the apple from, she has another pick up for us."

"Since we only deal with lowlives now, I assume she must be some sort of apple thief or something," Drake said.

Jimmy tried his best to place her face, but he just couldn't. A memory was floating on the fringes of his mind, but it just didn't want to appear and make itself visible. It was driving him nuts, but he didn't want to bother Drake with it.

"I guess so. Delgado also has a pick up for her, so we'll go there first and then her place?" Jimmy asked. But it was just a formality, as Drake's only care was the driving.

"Sure, buddy, whatever you say."

Jimmy made the notes on his HIC and went to his room to get dressed.

***

Today was going to be a very busy for Hector Delgado. Life in New Franco had become very stale and predictable. Everyone was keeping to their sectors, and things were getting very monotonous. The biggest problem for Delgado, however, was the lack of growth for his sector.

He had a steady income, protection, and could do whatever he felt like in sector fifty-nine, but all that freedom was an illusion. He was the king, untouchable, surrounded by kings and queens that felt the same. And they all lived under the all-seeing eye of Penta. He needed to branch out. He needed to get bigger and stronger than any other sector boss. Penta needed to fear him, and not the other way around. But he would have to be very careful. He had to do it without Penta getting wind of it. The moment they did not like the way he operated, they would cut him off and let a replacement take over.

Delgado did not know who that might be and had no desire to find out.

If today went to plan, he would never have to find out.

***

The warehouse was full of boxes and personnel. Everywhere Jimmy looked, there was action. Everyone that worked for Delgado seemed to be here, loading and unloading crates. Jimmy felt invisible in the sea of activity.

He walked over to the stairs leading up to Delgado's office, no one giving him a second look. He placed his hand on the DDU next to Delgado's office and again got a red screen. But like last time, the door slid open.

"Something. Come here," Delgado greeted him.

"Mr. Delgado," Jimmy said as he approached the desk.

"Take this and give it to that bitch, and make sure you get there fast. Understood?"

Delgado pointed to a parcel sitting on the corner of his desk.

"Yes, sir. That's what we do, fast and …" Delgado was already back to work, so Jimmy just backed away and left the room.

***

"What do you think is in here?" Jimmy asked Drake, gently shaking the package from Delgado.

"I don't know, and I do not want to know, Jimmy," Drake replied.

"I know it's part of your *as long as I don't know* policy, but surely you must be curious, ya know?"

Drake just stared at the green line ahead of him.

"There is no way for us to find out, so guessing would be harmless, right?" Jimmy persisted.

"A head," Drake replied.

"What the hell? You think there is a head in here?" Jimmy dropped the box on the floor between his legs.

"You said guess, so I did."

Jimmy looked at the box at his feet. He wished he never asked.

"Whose head do you think it is?"

"Jimmy, I was just kidding. I don't really think it's a head. I mean, it could be, coming from Delgado, but I'm sure it's not."

"How can you be sure?" Jimmy asked, his heart racing, his chest squeezing his lungs.

"You started this, buddy. Besides, why would Delgado send the apple lady a head, huh?"

That was a good question. Why would Delgado feel the need to intimidate apple lady? But what if apple lady ordered the beheading, and this was her trophy? Jimmy wished he'd gone first in guessing the contents.

The green line stopped. Drake put the hydrocar in park and looked over at Jimmy.

"Time to deliver that head, partner." Drake smiled at Jimmy, who was on the verge of throwing up.

***

"Ah, thank you so much," the lady said as Jimmy handed her the parcel.

He wondered what a cold-hearted person she must be to be so delighted in receiving a head. He had to make sure not to screw up any of her deliveries.

Jimmy watched her place the box on a countertop and walk over to a drawer that she pulled a knife from. She was going to open it in front of him. Why? What did he do? Was she punishing him? Or was it a threat?

The knife went into the box and easily slid to the side, exposing its contents to her. She smiled.

"Would you care for another one?" she asked, holding up a fresh new apple from the box. "I told you I had a guy."

| eleven |

"Your face." Drake felt the tears roll down his cheeks.

When Jimmy got out of the hydro, he looked like a condemned man. Drake couldn't be a hundred percent sure it wasn't a head, but he also didn't think they would find out if it was. Jimmy was so rattled when he got out, he forgot to switch his ARP on, but the look on his face when he returned told Drake it was not a human head, or any other body part, in the box.

After Jimmy told him what happened and Drake couldn't help but laugh. Jimmy still looked like a man who'd just dodged a pulse bullet to the head. Sweat pearls clung to his forehead, and the little color he usually displayed had disappeared.

"Apples," Drake snorted, and burst into another fit of laughter.

"Could have been a head, ya know?"

"Sure, buddy. Oh man, that made my day." Drake finally got control of himself.

In typical Jimmy fashion, he had already moved on and was typing away on Yolanda, setting the fresh course, the last few minutes already behind him. He looked at Drake.

"Ready when you are."

"You are one of a kind, Jimmy. One of a kind," Drake said, still smiling.

***

The package the apple lady gave Jimmy was the same size as the small box they took to Delgado, but this one had a different destination. Sector thirty-four.

"Guess what I saw on the news today?" Jimmy asked as they entered sector forty-one.

"Penta failed again at dethroning Santo?" Drake guessed.

Since Captain Raymond Santo took control of Mars, Penta embarrassingly could not oust him. They sent a small, heavily armored squadron on outdated slow shuttles to overthrow him, but failed miserably. The soldiers that didn't die in battle had the choice of joining, or trying their luck in the Martian wilderness. It was a simple decision, and now Santo's force was even bigger.

Penta had since completed building shuttles based on the design Santo used to get there and was on their way to try their luck again. The catch—so had Shangcorp. No one knew how they'd gotten a hold of the intellectual property, but they did, and within a few days of Penta launching their new shuttles, Shangcorp did the same. The race was on. War was eminent, both on Mars and Earth.

"No, they're not even halfway there. Aren't you following the mission?" Jimmy asked.

Drake was not. He wanted nothing to do with Santo, Mars, or Penta.

"So, what did you read then, Jimmy?" he got Jimmy back on track.

"The bounty on Turner went up to two million credits." Jimmy sounded way too surprised at this.

"Okay. Sammy said it would. Big deal." Add Turner to the list. Drake wanted nothing to do with Santo, Mars, Penta, or Turner.

"It means," Jimmy continued, "that no one has caught him yet."

Drake knew what it meant, and he knew where Jimmy was going with this.

"No," Drake said.

"No, what?"

"No, we are not helping Sammy Sanders to catch Mr. Turner. I have no fucking idea where he is, and I don't care. We are doing great here, Jimmy, we don't need to go chasing after him."

Drake was focusing on the green line, but could feel Jimmy's eyes on him.

"I said no, Jimmy."

"Okay," Jimmy mumbled.

***

Somehow, an accident occurred at an intersection, and drones filled the sky, capturing footage and securing the area. Small traffic control bots were on the ground, signaling the new direction for people to take. Drake obeyed their commands, and the green light on the road readjusted itself.

"Wonder what happened there?" Jimmy said, craning his neck as they drove past the scene.

"Just some idiot with bridged hydros who doesn't know how to drive," Drake replied.

"Yeah, that's what I thought, ya know?" Jimmy turned back in his seat.

Drake could feel Jimmy looking at him. He knew without looking what expression he would have on his face—the one where he looked like a child ready to ask for permission for something he knew he wouldn't get.

"Jimmy, if it's about Turner, I will throw you out of this hydro and deliver that package myself, you hear?"

Jimmy said nothing, confirming to Drake that he was right.

They passed over to a new sector, but in the lower sectors, things changed gradually. There was no sudden change in housing unit sizes, or the state of the hydros on the road, or the poverty of the people on the streets. Things seemed to blend all together in the lower sectors, but the people knew and respected the boundaries. Mostly out of fear of the local gangs or crime bosses running the show.

Drake saw another accident ahead of them, drones buzzing overhead, bots directing the traffic.

"Strange to see two crashes in one day," he said.

Jimmy was straining his neck to see the carnage.

"Wow! It looks like it's blown up. Awesome!" Jimmy exclaimed.

"Really? It's a dodgy sector, but that's rough."

"I know, same as the other one," Jimmy said.

"What? The other one was blown up too?" Drake took his eye off the road and looked at Jimmy.

"Oh, yeah. No way anyone inside got out alive, ya know?"

"And you said nothing when you saw the first one?"

Jimmy looked offended.

"Well, it just looked like a burned-out wreck, but seeing the second one, I realize they kinda looked the same, ya know?"

Drake shrugged off Jimmy's skills of observation, but something didn't sit right with him. Seeing two crashes, or exploded wrecks, in one day, only one sector apart, felt like more than a coincidence.

"Jimmy, look up to see if there are any reports on more of these crashes. Or explosions."

"I'm on it," Jimmy said and got to work on his HIC. Instantaneously, he got something.

"There have been five more reports of hydros blowing up, all in the neighboring sectors."

Drake was right. This was no coincidence.

"That's seven in seven sectors. Best we get moving and get out of this trigger-happy area," Drake said, and sped up a bit.

| twelve |

Jimmy knew Sammy would call again soon. He had to get something out of Drake to give Sammy. If he could help Sammy catch Turner, he could buy a Hydrostar or even a Hydrocomet and get Drake and him back on the road hauling.

Drake parked the little, red hydrocar in front of their building and shut it down. Night had fallen a long time ago, and the few streetlights that weren't broken tried their best to illuminate the area.

Getting out of the car, Drake stretched himself out next to it before he closed the door. Jimmy got out too and mimicked him.

"That was a long day!" Jimmy said, mid-stretch.

Drake looked at him. He seemed tired, but relaxed. Now or never.

"Sammy asked me to help him catch Turner," Jimmy blurted out.

Drake looked less relaxed.

"I told him I would, because he offered me a lot of credits, ya know, and I want to help buy a Hydrostar," he kept going.

Jimmy wished Drake would say something, but he just stared straight ahead.

"If we have the Hydrostar, we'd be back on the road, no more deliveries. No more people like Hector Delgado."

Jimmy walked around the hydro to face Drake.

"Drake, I know you hate this. Sitting in that small hydro day in and day out. All we need to do is think about where Turner might be, and if we're right, then we get a shitload of credits. If not, well, fuck Sammy, ya know?"

"Let's talk about it tomorrow, okay?" Drake finally replied.

"Sure, of course, let's get some sleep, and we'll chat tomorrow."

He didn't say no.

***

"Drake, you need to see this!"

Drake rubbed his eyes and sat up.

"Look!" Jimmy said and shoved his arm in front of his face.

Jimmy woke up earlier than usual. The excitement of finally talking to Drake about Sammy, and not having to go behind his back anymore, was too much to bear. Since Drake was still snoring away, he checked out the news. A few headlines in, he saw one that grabbed his attention.

City Rocked by Multiple Sector Attacks

The article stated multiple bombs exploded in neighboring sectors, destroying hydrocars and killing their occupants. Penta Security was on the case and declined to answer any questions.

With his interest piqued, he delved deeper and found more information from less mainstream sources. One big detail that the major news sources omitted was that the victims of the explosions all belonged to organized crime groups, and all of them were high ranking. No leaders or bosses, but still high enough on the ladder to be significant.

Someone was sending a message.

Drake read the articles on Jimmy's HIC. Jimmy wished he would hurry, as his arm was getting tired.

"That explains a lot," Drake said, and Jimmy dropped his arm.

"That's what we saw yesterday. Must be a turf war or something, ya know?"

"Or something. Do we have anything in that area today?" Drake asked.

Jimmy never thought of checking that.

"Good call," he said, and started on his HIC. "Nope. Not today. Mostly twenties and thirties today. Nice and clean."

"Good. It'll give us time to talk then," Drake said, and went to the toilet.

***

For once, Jimmy knew not to push, so he kept the conversation light at breakfast and on the first two deliveries. The third one was longer, and after the pickup, Drake got to it.

"What did Sammy offer you?"

"Thirty percent. That's six hundred thousand credits, Drake."

Drake went quiet again, but Jimmy stayed patient. He had to bite his tongue, literally, and he could taste the blood, but he kept quiet.

"What makes him think I can help?" Drake continued.

"You know Bob Turner best. If anyone can find him, it's you."

"Knowing him, doesn't mean I'm psychically connected to him. He could be anywhere."

Jimmy knew he had Drake's attention, and might not get this chance again, so he kept pushing.

"True, but he might have said something. Talked about his plans for when he stopped working or maybe some family he had somewhere."

Drake went quiet again, and Jimmy nibbled on his lower lip.

"So all Sammy wants is information, and we'll get thirty percent?"

"That's all, partner. He'll do the hard work, ya know. You just have to point him in the right direction."

The green line ended under a red marker.

"You're up, buddy," Drake said as he stopped the hydrocar.

***

Getting back in the hydrocar, Jimmy sensed a change in Drake. He couldn't tell what it was.

"Ready to go?" he asked Drake.

Jimmy realized the car was not running. Drake always kept it going so they could save time and get to the next job quicker.

Drake made no attempt to get going.

"Set up a meeting with Sammy. Tonight." Drake broke the tension.

"Yes, of course. I'll do it right now," Jimmy said, and got busy on his HIC. "He'll get back to me soon. No way he's going to sit on this, ya know."

"Let's get going. We still have work to do," Drake said.

"I'm all over it," Jimmy agreed, as he put the next coordinates into Yolanda.

***

Phase one was complete.

Hector Delgado looked at the DDU on his desk. All the news sites were reporting on the random hydro explosions. They had by now, to their credit, worked out that all the deceased were high-ranking members of organized crime groups in their respective sectors. They ruled a turf war out, since it happened in multiple sectors, and there was no history of conflict between all the connected sectors. The only thing they had in common was that they were all sectors in the fifties. Most of the sectors in the fifties, the sites reported, had multiple groups running and not one controlling group like in the slightly higher numbers. Delgado laughed when he read this.

"Not yet, they don't," he said to the screen. "Not yet."

| thirteen |

Drake was a creature of habit, so he told Jimmy to set up the meeting in the bar they went to sometimes. Most nights. Truth be told, nightly. He wanted to be somewhere of his choosing, not Sammy's. Drake didn't think Sammy would pull any silly stunts, but better to be safe than sorry.

Jimmy and Drake entered the bar roughly the same time they did every night. Drake noticed a few familiar faces around, but he never found out the names.

The bartender gave them a familiar nod and scanned their HICs. Regulars or not, rules were rules.

After ordering and grabbing their beers, they walked over to a vacant table. It was still early, and half the tables were open. Soon it would become crowded for an hour, and then it would quiet down again.

"So, where do you think he is?" Jimmy asked.

"Sammy? Who knows? Probably trying to screw a widow out of her inheritance."

"You think he'd do that?"

"Yup."

"Wow. What a lowlife, ya know. But I actually meant Bob Turner."

"I don't know, Jimmy. Not a clue." Drake took a sip of his beer.

"Oh. So, what are you going to tell Sammy then?" Jimmy looked worried.

Drake took another sip. A few more tables filled up. Tonight was a rowdy crowd and noise filled the bar.

"I'm not sure, to be honest, but I thought I'd hear him out first. See what he knows."

Jimmy's look changed from worried to perplexed.

"I thought we are going to tell him where Turner is, not the other way around?" Jimmy said.

Drake nodded his head toward the door, and Jimmy followed his gaze.

Sammy Sanders, dressed in his finest, came slithering over to their table.

"Evening, Drake. Jimmy." He gave Jimmy a brief smile.

"As I promised, Benjamin Drake," Jimmy said, pointing both hands at Drake, as if revealing a prize.

Drake mouthed, *what the fuck* to Jimmy.

"Never doubted you, Jimmy. Not for a second," Sammy said.

"So, who's going to go first?" Jimmy asked.

Sammy shared Jimmy's confused expression of minutes ago.

Drake leaned forward and put his elbows on the table.

"What do you know, Sammy?" he asked, staring Sammy down.

"The same as you, Drake. Turner is on the run, and there is a bounty out on him."

Still leaning on the table, Drake said, "Why don't you humor me, and tell me anyway."

Sammy leaned back in his chair, looked at Jimmy, and then back at Drake again. He shrugged.

"Okay. After you went rogue and picked up the contract from Jimmy, we all knew that you and Turner were done. It meant more work for us, so at first, everyone was pretty happy. Then, once the story broke, that Santo took Mars, and that McKenna spilled his guts to everyone, Turner shut shop overnight and disappeared. Just left in the night, not even locking the gates." Sammy took a sip of his beer.

"We showed up one morning and found the place deserted. He must have tried to cover his track, as we found all the DDUs smashed, which meant we couldn't access his data bases to get to the contracts. So we all had to look elsewhere for jobs. Which was difficult, I tell you." Sammy paused for effect.

"There are some angry haulers out there, Drake. The only reason they have done nothing is they think you're still working with Penta."

Sammy stared back at Drake, waiting for him to defend himself.

"So, you have been running around, chasing your tail, and now you want me to offer Turner on a plate to you. Is that right?" Drake said.

Drake watched as Sammy clenched his jaw. He had him. Sammy Sanders was nothing more than a vulture, circling and waiting to profit from someone else's hard work. He didn't want help or advice about where to get Mr. Turner. He wanted a hand-drawn map to the exact spot where he was hiding, so he could rush in and claim the bounty. Minimal effort from him. Drake could see that Sammy knew he knew this.

"You make it sound so easy, Drake," Sammy fired back. "While you had an adventure across the world, we were struggling back here. It's because of you that Turner ran away. You owe me something."

"I guess you're right, Sammy, I do owe you something."

Drake got up, walked over to the bar, ordered a beer, and returned to the table.

He sat down at the same spot, lifted the glass, and drank most of it. Using the back of his hand, he made an exaggerated movement to wipe his mouth.

"Here," he placed the half empty glass in front of Sammy, "is everything I owe you, Sammy. Never ask me or Jimmy for any fucking thing again, you understand?"

Drake got up and left.

***

"Drake, wait up! Drake!" Jimmy called after him.

He stopped, and Jimmy caught up, placed his hands on his thighs, and tried to catch his breath.

"Damn, Jimmy, that was barely a jog," Drake said.

"What? I was full out! Whatever." He stood, hands on hips, still huffing away.

Drake gave him another minute to recover.

It was getting late, but in these sectors, the night had just begun. The shadows embraced the poor souls who tried their best to survive. Sometimes they got desperate and ventured into the light. Sometimes people got desperate and ventured into the shadows. Here, anything was possible and anything could happen. The street looked calm, but Drake knew it was bubbling with life just a few steps away.

"Okay, so what now? I really thought we were going to help him, ya know?"

"How much did he offer you, Jimmy?"

"I told you. Thirty percent."

"And why did he need us?"

"'Cause you are the only person who might know where Turner is," Jimmy replied.

"So, why then, do we need him?"

Drake looked on as Jimmy's face went through all the motions of him hearing the words, dissecting them and figuring out what it meant.

"Are you saying we are going to go after Turner ourselves?"

Drake smiled at Jimmy.

| fourteen |

"What should I pack?" Jimmy asked Drake as soon as he opened his eyes.

"How long have you been standing there?"

"Not long. Maybe a minute. Twenty max." Jimmy was all energy this morning.

"Pack for what?" Drake asked.

"The trip. Remember, we are going to catch Bobby Turner."

Drake sat up, barely awake, and tried to catch up to Jimmy. The events from the previous night slowly played out in his head, and he smirked when he remembered his exit.

"Sammy's face," Drake said, still smiling.

"Yeah, you surprised both of us, ya know?"

"To be honest, Jimmy, I surprised myself. I wasn't sure if I was going to say yes or no to him when I got there. But when he started with his *you owe me* crap, I just couldn't help myself."

"Yea, the entitled prick," Jimmy chimed in.

"Anyway, best we get going with today's jobs then." Drake got up, grabbing a pair of pants.

"But aren't we going to chase Turner?" Jimmy asked.

Drake finished getting dressed and turned to Jimmy.

"How about we get a plan first, before we go headfirst into the unknown, huh?" Drake never thought he would say those words. "I haven't given it any thought yet, Jimmy. I need to do some thinking first." Who was this person?

"Sure, yes, makes sense, ya know? Okay, let's get rolling!" Jimmy said and started for the door.

***

Hardly a day went by without a pickup or a delivery between Delgado and the apple lady. At least three or four times a week, they had to go around to their places to pick up and deliver parcels. Delgado's workshop seemed much busier since the attacks in the surrounding sectors. Drake and Jimmy knew he had to be behind it, but kept their thoughts to themselves. Delgado was clearly capable of murder. As long as they didn't know what was in the parcels, they could keep their conscience clear. Or so they told themselves.

"First stop, apple lady," Jimmy announced as they got into the hydrocar. He programmed Yolanda, and once the green line appeared, they were off.

Drake could've driven there blindfolded by now, but Yolanda had a connection to the hauler network, scanning for anything that could slow them down, like roadblocks, patrols, or drones.

"Let me guess. Off to Delgado's?" Drake said. Lately it felt like they were employees of Delgado's.

"You bet!"

"Ugh," Drake replied and put the hydro in drive.

***

"Welcome, Jimmy, always a pleasure to see you. Apple?"

"Don't mind if I do," Drake heard Jimmy say via his ARP. Drake watched him grab a shiny, red apple and immediately take a bite.

"I'm going to miss these," Jimmy said through pieces of apple.

Drake flinched. *Shut your mouth, Jimmy.*

"Oh? Why is that?" apple lady asked.

"We, that is, Drake and I, are going to hunt down a fugitive. Big bounty too, ya know?" Jimmy kept talking and eating. Drake decided to call him and get him out of there. The fewer people knew what they were up to, the better.

"That sounds very exciting, Jimmy. And who is this person you're after, if you don't mind me asking?"

"I doubt you'll know him. It's Drake's old boss. A guy called Bob Turner." Jimmy had almost finished the apple.

"I thought you might say that, Jimmy." apple lady replied and walked closer to Jimmy. "Would you mind asking Mr. Drake to join us?"

***

Drake was about to press the connect button when he heard her words.

He saw Jimmy look down at his HIC. All it took was a quick swipe to change the live feed into a call, and Drake would see his face, instead of his point of view.

"Hey, Drake," Jimmy said once the cameras changed. He finished the last bit of the apple.

"Jimmy," Drake replied, knowing what was about to happen.

"So, apple lady wants to meet you," Jimmy said.

"I know, Jimmy. We're connected, remember? Also, I'm sure she just heard you call her apple lady."

Jimmy didn't seem too fussed. "I guess, ya know. So, you're coming in, right?"

"Yes, but we need to make this quick." Drake was already out of the hydro and walking to the fake dilapidated front door.

As he reached it, it swung open for him, and he stepped inside.

Seeing the interior firsthand blew him away.

Jimmy always walked quickly and directly to the kitchen area, rarely looking around. The first half of the interior was dimly lit, which didn't help either. Drake never noticed the plush carpets, paintings, or the antique furniture. Everything he saw had color and texture. The kitchen area was all white and stainless steel, but the rest was almost a sensory overload. He felt like he was back in Shamo.

In the kitchen, Jimmy and apple lady stood, both looking at Drake as he entered, wide eyed.

"Family collections and heirlooms," apple lady said.

"It's beautiful," Drake replied. And he meant it.

"Thank you, Drake," she said with the same familiarity she had with Jimmy.

"Do I know you?" he asked, not able to help himself.

Apple lady smiled.

"Would you like something to drink or eat?" she asked as she motioned for him to sit down at an old, wooden table.

Drake accepted the invite to sit, but declined the offer of food or drink.

Apple lady motioned for Jimmy to join Drake, and he did.

"So," she started while pouring them all some water. "You don't remember me?" She placed a tall glass of ice-cold water in front of everyone and took a seat.

Drake exchanged looks with Jimmy.

"No. Should I?" Drake replied.

"We've only met once or maybe twice, and it was a few years ago. Different hair color and so forth." She drank some water.

"I'm sorry, but I cannot place you. No offense," Drake offered.

"That's fine, Drake. Like I said, it was years ago. Back when I was still married to Bob."

| fifteen |

Suddenly, Drake remembered the face. The hair was different, and a few summers had passed, but he could clearly picture it now. A small picture, in fact, taped against the wall of Bob Turner's office, behind his desk. A tiny, little scrap of paper, the colors faded, and a corner torn. Most people spend very little time in Bob Turner's office, and had no time to find, let alone inspect, the forgotten photo on the wall.

But Drake did.

Mr. Turner's pet, everyone called him. Always hanging around, waiting for Mr. Turner to feed him some extra little scraps. Drake just ignored them. There was some truth to it, but why would he turn down the extra jobs Mr. Turner threw his way? He spent more hours in that office than anyone else and knew it by heart. Including the little photo. He asked Mr. Turner about it once and almost got his head ripped off. He never dared bring it up again and, in time, he forgot about it.

Until today.

"Mr. Turner never spoke about you," Drake finally said.

Mr. Turner's ex-wife smiled at him.

"You can call me Lucy," she simply replied.

"Okay, he never mentioned you, Lucy."

"I doubt he would have. I broke his heart when I left him." Her voices sounded sincere, but her smile remained.

"You said we met?"

"Yes. I had to go to his office once or twice for," Lucy smiled at Jimmy and returned her gaze to Drake, "business, and you were there."

Drake had a hard time processing all of this.

"I'm sorry. Sounds like I had a bigger impact on you than you did on me."

Lucy laughed, loud and uninhibited.

"I'm sure you did, but I kept tabs on all of Bob's employees, since I own sixty percent of his business."

Drake had no words. For years he worked for a man he thought he knew, only to be betrayed by him and now to discover he wasn't even the boss?

"I can see this is all a bit much for you to process right now, Drake. So how about you two go about your business and come back tonight? I'll have dinner ready and we can talk business then."

It was clearly an instruction and not a request, so Drake motioned for Jimmy to leave.

"See you later!" Jimmy said as they left apple lady's house.

***

The green line was patiently waiting on the road, ready to lead them to Delgado, but Drake just sat and stared at it.

"I guess now we know why she knew our names, ya know?" Jimmy said.

Drake snapped out of his trance.

"Bloody hell, Jimmy. I thought by chasing after Mr. Turner I would get some control back of my life, but—"

"But we are still going after him, right?"

"I don't know, buddy. I mean, she's his ex-wife. And now she wants to discuss business with us, right after you told her we are going after him?"

"Just bad timing, ya know?"

"I doubt it, Jimmy. It will be one hell of a coincidence if she wants to talk about anything else but Mr. Turner tonight."

***

Sammy sanders sat outside the warehouse, looking at the two men guarding the door. They looked mean as hell. Both had the same face tattoos. The number five on the left cheek, and the number nine on the right one. Sector fifty-nine. Everyone knew Mr. Delgado's crew, and no one Sammy knew was dumb enough to cross them. They ran the sector with no opposition. They were the law.

The door to the little, red hydrocar, parked right in front of the building, opened up, and Jimmy Something got out. The two guards greeted him and they all had a chat, ending in every-one laughing. Jimmy slapped one on the arm, proceeded to the DDU, and scanned himself into the building.

"Just as I thought," Sammy said.

***

"Why are you so fucking late!" Delgado greeted Jimmy.

Jimmy Something scampered over to his desk and placed the parcel on the corner.

"Crazy morning, Mr. Delgado," Jimmy said, shaking his head.

"Not my problem. You better step up your game, Something. Things are about to get much busier around here."

"Great, that's so good, ya know?" Jimmy was all nervous energy.

"What the fuck is going on with you, Something? You are more spastic than normal!"

Hector looked on as Jimmy shifted from one foot to another, then stopped as he caught himself being erratic, and folded his arms to contain himself.

"Just ready to go to the next job and satisfy another customer, ya know?" Jimmy could not lie to save his life.

"I don't like it when people hide things from me, Something." Hector watched him wriggle.

"No, sir. Nothing to hide. Mind if I go now?"

Delgado observed the strange, little man in front of him. He clearly didn't want to be here.

"Go. But be ready and quick when I call." Delgado watched him run out of his office.

Delgado motioned to one of his men to come over.

"Do me a favor. Follow that little piece of shit and let me know what he's up to."

Hector Delgado was a very busy and powerful man, but he always made sure that he never missed out on an opportunity.

And right now, Jimmy Something was hiding one from him.

| sixteen |

Jimmy stood in front of Drake in his best clothes. It was only fractionally better than his normal clothes. At least he had shoes on, with no holes in it, or a jacket covered in dust. He also looked like he had his second shower for the week.

"Trying to impress Mr. Turner's ex?" Drake asked.

"Says you!" Jimmy spat back.

Drake did not need to impress anyone, but he gave his boots a quick wipe, grabbed a clean pair of pants, and a shirt he rarely used. He even looked in a mirror for once and ruffled his hair in roughly the same direction. The week-old stubble could stay. Not because they were running out of time, but because he liked it.

Maybe he wanted to impress after all.

"She's a nice lady, and I'm sure she'll appreciate us to try, that's all."

"Sure," Jimmy said and winked.

"Just get in the hydro," Drake said, and pushed Jimmy out the door.

***

"Nah, I've got this," Drake said as Jimmy entered the coordinates into Yolanda. The night was warm, the stars were almost visible through the smog, and Drake felt good. Maybe it was the prospect of being on the road soon, or just getting away from Delgado, but he wanted to drive full manual tonight. No assistance.

"Cool. Could probably get there blindfolded anyway," Jimmy said. He relaxed back into his seat as Drake got the hydrocar up to speed and swiped around on his HIC.

They drove in silence, Drake enjoying the sensation of the hydro, and Jimmy swiping away. Drake imagined this to be the life when they were hauling again. For a moment he was back in his Hydrostar, crossing the country. Jimmy sitting next to him talking nonsense and playing on his HIC. It felt good.

"Anything on that fancy HIC of yours?" Drake asked after a while.

Jimmy got to keep his expensive Human Interface Console after Penta released them, since they would have to pay for the procedure to have it removed. They decided it was too much effort. Drake didn't pay it too much attention as it brought up too many memories.

"Looks like Shangcorp is ready to land on Mars. They somehow got the jump on Penta. It's going to be ugly."

For months, Drake carried the guilt of helping Captain Raymond Santo take over Mars. The lives lost, the future implications, all felt like his fault. His doing. But having Jimmy Something by your side had its benefits. Jimmy never let him wallow in his sorrows for too long, and he always had a unique take on things.

He told Drake many times that he was just a pawn and that Santo could easily have used someone else. Jimmy kept reminding him he was nothing special and that it was just chance. Conveniently, Jimmy always forgot to mention his part in all of it, but Drake didn't care. The Jimmy from then wasn't the person sitting next to him now.

"I hope it doesn't end up with a war here, too," Drake replied. The stars weren't visible anymore.

"I'm sure they'll just negotiate a deal. There hasn't been a major war in decades, ya know?"

Jimmy was right. There was too much at stake, too many credits involved, to start a war on another planet.

"I sure hope you're right," Drake said.

***

By the time they got to apple lady's house, Drake was back to his optimistic mood. Jimmy was dreaming big on the drive, telling him about all the adventures lying ahead once they were hauling. Drake decided not to fight it, and went along, believing all the tales Jimmy told. It was better than thinking of war.

Or causing it.

When they stopped in front of the house of Mr. Turner's ex, Lucy, Drake turned to Jimmy.

"Thank you, buddy. You always get me out of my funks."

"Hey, we're partners. What else do you expect?" Jimmy said, and exited the hydro before Drake could answer.

Jimmy was already scanning his palm by the time Drake caught up. The DDU flashed green, and the door slid open.

The house was even more welcoming at night.

Lamps of all designs and origin illuminated every room. Their yellow glow warmed up the entire house. Drake had to stop himself from touching everything he saw.

"Hello, Jimmy. Drake," Lucy greeted them, as warm as the lamps themselves.

Lucy was standing in the kitchen working on something. As they approached her, Drake could see that it was a variety of vegetables she was cutting up. He could only identify one or two.

"Hey, Mrs.—"

"Lucy is fine, Drake. Besides, I dropped Bob's last name ages ago."

"Okay then, Lucy. So this is how the other half eats?" Drake said.

Lucy's laugh filled the entire room.

"I wish I ate like this every day," she said, resuming the chopping. "I came across these by sheer luck."

Lucy dropped the chopped vegetables into a container and placed it in the heating unit.

"Would you care to join me in the lounge?" Lucy said and led the way.

The lounge immediately became Drake's favorite room. Soft carpet, rich brown and red colors, and the softest couch he had ever sat on.

"I like your chairs, Mrs. Lucy, but they seem very, um, old, ya know," Jimmy said as he shuffled around to get comfy.

"They are very old, Jimmy. Most of them are handmade," Lucy replied.

"But surely you can afford new ones, ya know?" Jimmy was still trying to get comfortable.

"They are lovely," Drake jumped in. He gave Jimmy a look. "They feel so—" Drake couldn't find the word.

"Authentic?" Lucy offered.

"Yes! They just feel like this is how things were meant to feel like. If that makes any sense?" Drake felt like an idiot.

"It does, Drake, and that's why I have them. Although I have embraced technology and immersed myself in it, I find it refreshing to break away from it too."

All three took a moment to soak up the moment.

"Not to be too forthright, Lucy, but why are we here?" Drake asked.

Lucy shifted around a bit, looking mildly uncomfortable for the first time.

"As you know, Bob Turner and I were married, years ago. In fact, by the time he set up his hauling business, our marriage contract had already expired. It was a mutual agreement not to renew it."

Lucy kicked her shoes off and folded her legs underneath her. Instead of making her look vulnerable, it made her look calm and confident.

"We were both from poor families in the lower sectors. I grew up in this very house," Lucy said.

"Wow," Jimmy muttered.

"I can assure you, Jimmy, only the outside still looks the same. So, when I met Bob, he was still a Moon miner, all muscle and no brains," Lucy said, and a faint smile appeared on her face.

"Some things never change," Drake quipped.

Lucy didn't reply, but continued, "We got married quite young, and in the beginning, he would still do stints on the

Moon. I stayed back home and started a business. Eventually Bob decided it was time to quit the mining and became a hauler."

Jimmy smiled at Drake.

"So, once again, he left me home alone. First the Moon, then the road. My business was doing well, so I suggested we start another business, together. Our own hauling company. That way, he could be home. Bob agreed, and so we did."

A noise from the kitchen informed them that dinner was ready.

"Shall we?" Lucy said and led the way back to the kitchen.

***

After one of, if not the best, meals Drake had ever eaten, they all returned to the same room with the antique couches. Jimmy got comfortable much quicker and quieter this time.

Lucy indulged them in small talk at the table, but now it was time to get back to business.

"Okay, so I told you about him hauling and us starting our own company, yes?" Drake and Jimmy nodded.

"As the years went on, our businesses grew stronger, but our marriage became weaker. We both felt it, so when our marriage contract ran out, we both agreed not to renew it. We parted as friends and kept in touch. Mainly because of the business. But also nostalgia."

Drake loved to hear about Mr. Turner's past, stories he never knew about the man, but he still couldn't figure out why Lucy invited them over.

"Lucy, I, we really enjoyed dinner and the stories you've told us, but I'm still unsure why we are here?" Drake said.

"You're right, Drake. I have dragged this out for far too long. I want to you to find Bob and bring him back."

"And," she continued, "I'm willing to match whatever the bounty is."

| seventeen |

The three dots kept dancing in front of Jimmy's face. He could see the caller's name on his HIC and refused to answer. Unfortunately, they refused to give up too, so now they were in an ARP standoff. Jimmy watched the little circles run around, chasing each other. They had been going at it for so long, they were hypnotizing Jimmy. Frustration got the better of him, and he swiped.

"We told you, no!" Jimmy answered.

"Hey, settle down. Glad you finally answered. Still figuring out how to use that overpriced HIC of yours?"

"Did you call just to insult me?"

"No, just a perk. So, I've got a new proposition for you and your boss," Sammy Sanders said. Jimmy did not like the confidence in Sammy's voice.

"Whatever it is, count us out. Like Drake said, we don't need you."

"Oh, but you've not even heard my offer yet, Jimmy," Sammy replied.

Jimmy had a bad feeling about this.

"Well, we're not interested, but just to please you, what is the offer?" Jimmy asked.

Sammy ran his tongue over his teeth as if cleaning them.

"I think it's better if we meet face-to-face. The three of us. Because, believe me, you can't say no to this deal."

Sammy gave Jimmy a time and place and hung up.

Jimmy felt an ache crawl into his belly.

***

"What took you so long? I almost pissed myself," Drake said, shoving Jimmy aside as he exited the bathroom.

"Sorry, Drake. Got distracted."

Jimmy sat down on one of the two chairs in the unit and waited for Drake.

"Ah! That was close," Drake said as he came back out.

"Sammy wants to talk again," Jimmy blurted it out.

"What now?" Drake said and flopped down on the other chair. "What could he possibly have to say to us?"

"I don't know, but he said it's a deal we can't say no to."

"First, fuck him. Second, Sammy does not have the credits to even come close to Lucy's offer. And third, fuck him."

"But—"

"What, Jimmy?" Drake was running out of patience. He made his mind up to go after Mr. Turner, but obstacles kept popping up.

"I don't know. It's just…" Jimmy shook his head, as if to shake out the words he couldn't find. "He was so confident when he called, ya know?"

Drake saw the worried look in Jimmy's eyes.

"Okay, Jimmy. If you think he has something to say, we'll go. But I swear, if it's just another sales pitch, I'll put a pulse bullet right between his eyes."

"Sounds fair," Jimmy replied.

***

Delgado did not book in any pickups or deliveries, so Drake told Jimmy to not book any other jobs and set up the meeting with Sammy. The sooner they got it done, the better. Lucy said there was no hurry to get back to her, but as they all knew, the longer they waited, the bigger the odds grew of someone else finding Mr. Turner.

Drake had already made his mind up to find him. He wanted to catch him and turn him over to Penta. Let him rot in some basement somewhere.

But it all changed after Lucy got involved. Not because of the credits. Four million were more than Drake knew what to do with, but the way she humanized Mr. Turner. Drake had turned him into a villain, but he forgot who he used to be to him.

If he took Lucy's offer, and captured and returned Mr. Turner, then what? Would they have a heart-to-heart and bury the hatchet? Could Mr. Turner somehow convince him that what he did was not personal? That he never intended for Drake to get shot at, lose everything, and live with the guilt of starting a war?

"Hey, he's here!" Jimmy said, and Drake snapped out of it. He was holding a full beer, and Jimmy had an empty glass in front of him.

"Sorry, Jimmy," Drake said, "my mind was somewhere else."

"I noticed. All good, though. Lots going on, ya know?"

Drake just nodded.

Sammy reached the table, and Drake saw the confidence Jimmy was talking about.

"You have exactly five minutes, Sammy."

"Okay, but I'm sure you'll be happy to give me more," he replied with that smile of his.

Drake did not like this at all.

Sammy rolled up his sleeve and accessed his HIC. After a bit of swiping around, both Drake's and Jimmy's HIC vibrated.

"I've just sent you some files. Go on, have a look."

Drake and Jimmy exchanged looks and did as they were told.

The files Sammy transferred to them were all video files, and Drake and Jimmy both started watching them.

"Be right back," Sammy said, getting up. "You boys want anything?" he asked. No one answered.

The footage was all shot via an ARP and gave them the observer's point of view. Clearly, someone was following them, recording them going from Lucy's place to Delgado's and a few more runs to Delgado and back. They recorded it over a few days, maybe a week or two. Drake forwarded through most of them, as he knew what would happen.

Sammy returned to the table.

"What do you think?" he asked.

"Not much. Someone with too much time on their hands has been recording two honest, hardworking guys go about their business," Drake replied, playing it cool, but fearing what Sammy was up to.

"I guess that's what it would look like to the untrained eye," Sammy said. "But anyone that knows anything about what I know, knows what it is."

"What the fuck, Sammy? What are you rambling on about?" Drake felt some relief, as Sammy was clearly not as coherent or organized as he thought. He was just fishing, trying to get an angle to get their help.

Sammy produced a small, brown box and put it on the table. Drake did not know where he'd been hiding it till now. It was the same size, style, and color as the ones they'd been transporting between Mr. Delgado and a few other places. Including Lucy's.

"Sammy, can you get to the point?" Drake said.

"Do you want us to deliver that?" Jimmy asked.

"I don't think so, Jimmy," Drake said, watching the confidence in Sammy grow.

"Oh."

"Would you mind opening it, Jimmy?" Sammy asked, but kept his eyes on Drake. This was not good.

"Sure," Jimmy said and eagerly tore into it. He grabbed something out of it and put it on the table. He shrugged.

Drake looked at the small item. He'd hauled some before and knew what they were. He never even made the connection between the box and the content, till now.

"What is it?" Jimmy asked.

"It's a device used on the Moon." Drake was talking to Jimmy, but staring right at Sammy.

"It's very expensive, and quite hard to get, as it is heavily regulated," Drake continued.

"I see. What do you do with them?" Jimmy asked.

Sammy's stupid smile grew bigger. Drake wanted nothing more than to wipe it off his face.

"Only one thing," Drake said. "Blow shit up."

| eighteen |

The three men sat around the table, with the small explosive device between them.

"Um, so, can it blow up now?" Jimmy's voice trembled.

"No. This one's not activated. It should be safe," Sammy replied.

"Should be!" Jimmy shoved his chair back.

"It's fine. See, the pin is still intact." Drake lifted the device up to show Jimmy. He seemed to relax, but kept his distance.

"So, it seems we've been transporting some explosive devices. Worst case, we get a fine for not having the right permits or licenses or whatever you need to carry these things around," Drake tried his best to sound unimpressed. "So, another failed attempt to get us to help you. Don't contact us again, Sammy."

Sammy sat smiling. "You guys saw the news? About all those hydro explosions?" he asked. Drake's heart picked up the pace.

"Guess what they found at all those sites?" Sammy continued.

"What?" Jimmy asked, scooting his chair back.

Drake refused to answer. He would not give Sammy the satisfaction.

"C'mon, tell us!" Jimmy pleaded.

Sammy's face told Drake that he could sit here all night.

Drake picked the device up and placed it in front of Jimmy.

"They found the devices we've been delivering to Delgado and all his goons," Drake said, fearing Sammy's next move.

"Oh shit," Jimmy caught up.

"Oh shit for sure, Jimmy. So I think we both know where this is going," Sammy said to Drake.

Drake knew.

"You are going to blackmail us into helping you get Turner," Drake surrendered.

Sammy laughed too loud and too long. A laugh as fake as his teeth.

"No, no, no, Drake. Why would I want to do that?" Sammy looked at Jimmy, shaking his head. Jimmy slowly shook his in unison, as if hypnotized.

Drake knew exactly what Sammy was about to say.

"Why chase after him, if I can get you to do it all for me?"

***

Jimmy quietly waited for Drake to finish punching the steering wheel of the hydro. It took him a while, but eventually he ran out of steam. Drake dropped his hands, and his shoulders relaxed.

"Dammit, Jimmy," Drake said.

"So, what now?" Jimmy asked.

Drake had no answer for him. Plan A was to go after Mr. Turner themselves and turn him over to Penta, which turned into Plan B, which included Lucy and no Penta, and now Plan C was no Lucy but Sammy Sanders.

If they went after Mr. Turner and just turned him over, it would be over, and they could move on. It would upset Lucy, but he could handle that. Except Sammy would then do his best to implicate them in the explosions out of shear spite.

If they helped Lucy, they would make loads of credits. Turner would still be free, and Sammy would screw them over.

If they helped Sammy, he would shoot himself in the face.

Drake felt like punching the steering wheel again.

"Do you think Sammy would risk going to Penta and rat us out?" Jimmy asked.

"I honestly don't know. He is pretty deplorable, Jimmy. I wouldn't put it past him."

"I guess, but if he does, wouldn't Delgado go after him?"

Drake never even thought of that. If Sammy tried to turn Drake and Jimmy in, he would also have to implicate Delgado. And Hector Delgado did not take kindly to people telling on him.

"He could still make it an anonymous tip?" Drake thought out loud.

"True. So what are you going to tell Lucy? She seemed very keen to get Turner back."

"I know, Jimmy. Until Sammy showed up, I was going to ask you if you wanted to help her."

"And now?"

"I do not know, Jimmy," Drake said. "No idea at all."

Drake initiated the startup procedure for the hydrocar. Once all the telemetry displayed on the screen, he switched on Auto-drive. All he wanted to do was get home.

"Let's get out of here, buddy," he said to Jimmy.

"Yes, let's," Jimmy agreed.

Drake released the brake, the hydrocar crept forward, and three circles appeared in his view.

***

Lucy Hughes, the name read on Drake's HIC. He looked up at Jimmy, who offered no help. He swiped.

"Hi, Drake. You working?" Lucy asked.

"Hi, Lucy. No, just going home."

"Everything okay?"

Drake took a deep breath and put on a smile.

"Always. Just a long day, I guess."

"I know the feeling," Lucy replied. "I'm sorry to be harassing you already, Drake, but have you given any thought to my offer?" Her warm smile radiated through his ARP and made him feel better.

"We were just discussing it, in fact," Drake said. Jimmy looked at him, a big frown creasing his forehead.

"Oh. And how did this talk go?"

The little hydrocar hummed along, following the green line. Traffic was light, and the drive home went faster than normal.

"We'll do it," Drake heard the words leave his mouth.

"We will?" Jimmy said next to him.

"You will?" Lucy said in front of him.

"Um, yes, we need to discuss a few things, but—"

"You don't sound too sure, Drake," Lucy accurately observed.

"No, I am. We'll do it. Can we come over tomorrow and talk?" Drake was running in circles.

The green line ended, and the hydro stopped.

"Drake, getting Bob back means everything to me. I hate to put this all on you, but there is no one else that I trust to do this. I'll see you tomorrow." She disconnected.

Drake sat in the hydro, looking out at the street in front of him. It stretched out for a while and then curved around a bend and disappeared.

Drake wished he could do the same.

| nineteen |

Lucy Hughes was waiting for them in the kitchen. She seemed to always be there when they arrived.

"Good morning," she greeted Drake and Jimmy as they approached.

"Morning," Jimmy matched her energy.

Drake gave her a smile and a nod.

"Have you eaten already? I have some white box meals ready to go."

"You eat white box?" Jimmy asked.

"Yes, Jimmy. I'm afraid getting fresh food is a treat, even for me."

Lucy turned to Drake. "So, you sounded unsure last night?"

Drake wished he could teach his mouth to wait its turn. Give his brain first crack at it and then have a go. Instead, it always jumped the cue and went first.

"Yes, I was, but like I said, we'll do it."

Lucy's face lit up.

"Oh, Drake! That's just wonderful."

"There are a few things first," Drake pumped the brakes.

Lucy didn't lose any of her optimism. "Tell me what it is, so we can get you on the road."

Drake pulled a chair over and sat down. Jimmy copied him.

"We've had another offer," Drake confessed.

"Oh," Lucy seemed surprised. "Who else would have an interest in Bob?"

"They are doing it for the credits, the bounty, nothing more."

"Okay, so how is their offer better than mine? It can't be more credits?"

Drake looked over at Jimmy, who seemed also to wait for the answer.

"It's complicated and ..." Drake paused. He wasn't sure how to proceed.

"Drake, please, just tell me," Lucy said.

"The parcels we've been picking up from you and taking to Delgado."

"Yes?"

"What do you know about it?"

Lucy didn't answer immediately, but studied Drake's face for a second.

"Delgado and I have done business in the past. He asked if he could use me as a middleman for a deal with a mining company he had going. As I've still got connections to some of Bob's old mining friends, it would make it less suspicious if this venture went through me first. It was a simple way to make some extra credits."

This time, Drake took a second to study her face. Lucy looked as calm and sincere as always.

"And the contents of the parcels?"

Lucy smiled and shook her head.

"It was a need-to-know basis, and I did not see the need to know. I was merely a name and an address for the deliveries."

Drake wanted to push her more, but saw the irony. Jimmy and he had been following that exact need-to-know philosophy.

"Okay, well, the contents of those parcels could get me and Jimmy in trouble. Possibly you too," Drake said.

"Delgado assured me it was purely mining equipment, and I have a trading permit that allows me to buy and sell mining inventory, so unless it wasn't—"

"No, it is mining equipment." Drake realized how smart Delgado had been. Using Lucy as a middleman, he could obtain the explosives legally through a shell corporation and then make them disappear in paperwork. Or report them as stolen. Either way, Drake was sure Delgado had no trail that led back to him.

But Sammy didn't care about Delgado or Lucy. He would be more than happy to put all the blame on Drake, and see him rot in detention if he refused to help him.

"I'm sorry, Drake, but I'm not following you," Lucy said.

"Yeah," Jimmy mumbled.

Everyone was pulling Drake in different directions. He'd have to choose which direction he wanted to go in.

Or risk being torn apart.

"Nothing. Just nerves, I guess. Never chased anyone down before. But don't you worry. We'll bring him home."

Drake gave Lucy the biggest smile he could fake.

***

"Okay, that's it then! When do we leave?" Jimmy asked once they were back in the hydro.

Drake didn't start the hydro, but turned to Jimmy.

"Contact Sammy. Tell him we need to talk right now. Same bar we always go to. Tell him to be there in ten minutes." Drake didn't wait for an answer as he started the hydrocar.

"Done!" Jimmy said after sending the message on his HIC. "So, are we going over to beat Sammy up or something?"

Drake did not switch on the Autodrive this time.

"Something like that," Drake said and sped up, pushing the limits of the hydrocar.

It only took them a few minutes to reach the bar. As they pulled up, Sammy got out of his hydro. Drake stopped next to Sammy and rolled down his window.

"Ah, seems we—"

"We'll do it. We'll get Turner for you. But you'll need to get us some credits upfront to set us up for the chase."

"Give me one day. I'll send some credits to you tomorrow."

Drake rolled his window back up and drove off.

***

"Um, Drake?" Jimmy said as they left Sammy standing in the parking lot.

"Sorry. I've not been a very good partner," Drake said in the way of an explanation.

"That's fine, ya know, but what exactly is the plan here?"

Drake took a corner too fast, and the wheels squealed. It fish tailed slightly, but Drake caught it in time.

"No plan, Jimmy. But since everyone is keen to send us out to get him, let's get him, and make some credits. What do you think?"

"Sounds good, but won't you upset Sammy?" Jimmy pointed out.

"We'll use the credits we get from Lucy to give Sammy his cut. Plus extra credits to appease him. Means we'll get a shit load fewer credits, but we'll be free and hopefully on our way to be on the road. It's so simple, I don't know why I didn't think of it earlier." Drake was smiling and driving way too fast. He felt like someone had lifted a weight off his chest. He could finally see an outcome to all of this. An outcome that he liked.

"That makes sense, ya know," Jimmy agreed.

"Right?" Drake was beaming.

All they had to do now was pack the hydro, get their credits from Sammy in the morning, and be on their way.

On the road.

Free.

Drake looked over at Jimmy, who was swiping away on his HIC.

"Just canceling the rest of the week's pickups, I hope," Drake said. "Because we are done with that life, buddy!"

Jimmy looked up.

Drake didn't like what he saw.

"Someone died?" Drake asked.

"Not yet," Jimmy replied. "Delgado wants to see us. Right now."

| twenty |

Hector Delgado had eyes and ears everywhere. Mechanical, electronic, human. If it could capture information, he had it. Nothing happened in his sector, or the neighboring ones, without his knowledge.

So when word got to him that Sammy Sanders was trying to secure a loan for a secret mission involving the famous Benjamin Drake and his sidekick, Jimmy Something, he needed to know more. He sent some of his men to grab him and bring him in. Easier to communicate with people face-to-face, Delgado believed, especially if they might need some convincing.

Once he put word out to get Sammy, it took less than an hour before he stood in front of him.

"Mr. Delgado, it's so nice to meet you, finally. I've actually done a few hauls for you in the past. You might remember?" Sammy said, as he was shoved into Delgado's office.

Delgado didn't. Sammy looked and acted like any small-time hustler, and Delgado immediately perceived him as expendable.

"Why are you trying to get hold of all this money?"

"With all due respect, Mr. Delgado, I don't see how it's any of your business."

Delgado didn't move. But Sammy did. He could not stand still or stop fidgeting.

"That's where we disagree. I think it has everything to do with me. Since you are trying to poach two of my employees, I think I have the right to know."

Delgado watched Sammy's resolve crumble.

"Two of your employees?" Sammy tried once more.

"Something and his friend ..." Delgado lifted his palms up and looked at his men.

"Drake, sir. Benjamin Drake," one quickly responded.

"Yes, that's it, Drake. So, I heard you are trying to send them off on some mission. Sounds very exciting."

This had nothing to do with credits, but everything to do with power. Delgado could not afford to have someone undermine him by taking someone who worked for him and use them for their own profit. He had a reputation.

"It is, sir. I just need ten to twenty thousand credits to fund this little project. That's why I was trying to secure a loan."

"And what is this little project?"

Sammy shuffled around some more. "I'm chasing a bounty. Bob Turner."

The name sounded familiar to Delgado, but not enough that he should care why he was a wanted man.

"And what is the bounty on this Turner guy?"

Sammy had to swallow twice before the words came out. "Two million."

Delgado had no interest in chasing after a bounty. As a business proposition, the return on investment was almost zero. Bounties hardly ever got paid out. Penta always found some loophole to avoid paying the full amount or anything at all. They set the bounties crazy high to attract losers to go chasing after the person of interest, flushing them out and allowing Penta to scoop them up. No payout necessary.

But this was about power, not credits.

"Okay," Delgado said.

"Um, I'm not following." Sammy looked around nervously.

"I'll loan you the money. If you catch Turner, half the bounty is mine. If you don't, you owe me double of what I loan you."

Sammy looked terrified. "Thank you, sir, I really appreciate it."

Delgado's men ushered him out.

Now to have a chat with the little eel.

***

"So, what do we do?" Jimmy asked.

Drake pulled the hydro over and switched it off.

"Did he say why?"

"No. But the timing is suspicious, ya know?"

Drake agreed. The second they got momentum and had a plan to get out, Delgado popped up. Delgado had them pick up unscheduled parcels all the time, but this felt different. Jimmy was right. The timing was suspicious.

"No point in guessing. We'll have to go and face him. Did you say anything to him last time you saw him?"

Jimmy bit his upper lip in full thought mode. "No, I don't believe I did, ya know?"

Drake was unconvinced, but had to give Jimmy the benefit of the doubt.

"Okay then. Let's get this done."

Drake started the hydro back up again and raced to meet Delgado.

***

"Little eel!" Delgado greeted them as they entered his office.

Drake had seen him before, via Jimmy's ARP, but this was his first time standing in front of Hector Delgado.

"Little eel?" Drake whispered to Jimmy, who just shrugged.

"And this must be the infamous Benjamin Drake!" Delgado stayed seated and gestured for them to sit down.

"Without going into details or revealing my sources, I learned that the two of you are planning to leave town."

Drake shot Jimmy an angry look.

"Don't blame your partner, Mr. Drake. I have eyes and ears everywhere. So tell me, is it true?"

"Yes," Drake replied. "It's just a quick contract we picked up and we'll be back to normal in days, a few weeks tops."

"I see, Mr. Drake. And who will courier my parcels in the interim?"

None of my damn business, you fat bastard.

"Not sure. But I'm confident you'll find someone. People in New Franco are always eager to work."

"Ah, but it's not that simple. See, I need someone I trust, and you and the little eel have been very trustworthy indeed."

Drake knew a shake down when he saw one. Dealing with corrupt power hungry officials was a part of the hauling game. Delgado didn't care about them going, he cared about losing control over them.

"How could we help to make this transition easier for you, Mr. Delgado?" Drake asked.

Delgado pursed his lips and nodded.

"Quite the savvy businessperson yourself, Mr. Drake. So, let's talk numbers. I think it'll take me at least a month to go through various people and trial them out. Most won't make the cut. So there will be retraining and so forth, plus the undelivered parcels ..." Delgado did some math on his HIC. Made up, on-the-spot, bullshit math. "I think we can agree that two hundred thousand credits seem fair?"

Drake knew there was no point in arguing the point. Delgado had six guards in the room. This was not a negotiation, it was a robbery. They were contractors to him and owed him nothing. But this was a power play to let them know who ran the show in sector fifty-nine.

And to make them rethink leaving from underneath his control.

"Sounds perfect to me," Drake said with a big smile on his face.

| twenty-one |

Got the money, but the deal has changed. Twenty percent or I go to the authorities.

Jimmy felt his tummy tie itself in knots. Since they'd left Delgado's office, Drake had been even quieter than before and just stared straight ahead, driving to who knows where. If Jimmy read Sammy's message to him now, he might just drive into a wall. Twenty percent. So, that means Sammy would get 1.6 million credits, and leave them with 400 thousand. But Drake said yes to Lucy and told him they would give Sammy an extra 200 thousand to shut him up. That means they would take Lucy's two million, and pay Sammy 1.8 million, leaving them with 200 thousand. The exact amount Drake agreed to give Delgado. So, if he did his math correct, they would leave with nothing?

"Um, partner, Sammy says it's now twenty percent, and I did some numbers, ya know, and I think we're screwed," Jimmy said, as slowly and calmly as he could.

Drake clenched his jaw and nodded.

"Fuck, why not? Everyone else is squeezing us dry."

"Hopefully we find Turner quick and we can get back to parcels and save up for that Hydrostar, ya know." Jimmy tried his best to see the bottom half of the glass.

Drake stayed quiet and kept driving. Jimmy felt uncomfortable and had to do everything in his power not to keep talking and upsetting Drake. Drake looked very determined, albeit just driving aimlessly around New Franco. Jimmy wondered what was going on in his head. They had been working together for almost a year, and sometimes they felt like brothers, other times strangers. He knew they were from different worlds, and that they had less in common than he wanted to admit, but he could not imagine a life without Drake. His partner. His first real friend. He couldn't stay quiet anymore.

"We'll figure this out, ya know," Jimmy said.

Drake turned his head and smiled at Jimmy. "We will, buddy, and I think I know how."

***

"Okay, like I said, it's twenty percent, or I—"

"Whatever, dickhead. We said yes already. Where's my credits?"

Drake had no time to listen to Sammy or watch him try to play tough with new demands. All that mattered right now was that they got their credits and got out of New Franco.

Jimmy stepped up to Sammy and held his HIC up, ready for the transfer.

"Wasn't easy getting the credits," Sammy mumbled.

Jimmy saw the credits appear in their account and nodded to Drake.

"We'll let you know when we get him," Drake said, and turned to walk away.

"I expect daily updates!" Sammy yelled after him.

Drake stopped. "What was that, Sammy?"

"I, I said, daily updates, so that, you know, I know what's happening."

Drake turned back and walked up to Sammy. He was no giant, but he towered over Sammy.

"And I said we'll let you know when we get him."

"Yes, but—"

Drake punched him in the face. No warning, no last chance. Sammy opened his mouth, and Drake closed it.

"We'll get Turner, and you'll get your bounty." Drake walked away, leaving Sammy holding his bleeding mouth.

***

"And then you said," Jimmy replayed the entire scene back to Drake, word for word, action for action.

It's been a while since Drake had been in a fight, and he flinched at the pain in his knuckles as he gripped the wheel. He forgot the adrenaline wore off so quick.

Jimmy was still going on, and he let him be. He knew there was no stopping an excited Jimmy Something. Plus, it was good having the positive energy in the hydro.

"Are you almost done? I need to call Lucy," he eventually said.

"Yeah, yeah, sure. Got a bit excited, ya know?"

"No need to apologize. I did too, that's why I punched him!"

"Yeah, you did!" Jimmy laughed and reenacted the punch again. It made Drake laugh.

"Okay, I'm dialing her now," Drake said. He switched over to Autodrive and had his ARP display on the windscreen instead so Jimmy could take part.

The three dots bounced around on the screen and quickly merged to show Lucy's face.

"Hey, Drake. Jimmy. I assume by the look on your faces that everything is ready to go?"

"Yep. Just had to tie up a loose end." Drake winked at Jimmy. "We'll leave in the morning."

"Thank you again, guys. I cannot even begin to express my gratitude."

"Two million credits is gratitude enough, thanks," Drake said.

Lucy thanked them again, and they broke the connection.

"What happens if she finds out about Sammy? Or Sammy about her?" Jimmy asked.

"Stop worrying over what might or might not happen, buddy. Tomorrow morning we'll fill this bad boy up to the brim and hit the open road."

Drake still had no ambition to see Turner again, but once the talk about hitting the road started, he could feel himself breathe again. All he wanted was to be out there, on the road.

And tomorrow morning they would be.

| twenty-two |

Drake could barely sleep. He kept waking up from dreams of Penta forces chasing him. He knew it was just terrible memories and not a premonition, but every time he woke up, it still unnerved him. Eventually, he gave up and packed a bag. He heard noises from Jimmy's room, only a few feet away.

"You awake?" he whispered loudly.

"Couldn't sleep, ya know?"

"I know."

"Should we just eat and go?" Jimmy asked.

It sounded like the best plan in the world to Drake.

"I like the way you think, Jimmy!"

When they finished packing up, they sat down in the kitchen area, which was a shared space with the living room area.

"I'll miss this dump," Drake said through a spoon of white box.

"You mean home?" Jimmy sounded sincere. Drake felt like a prick and changed his tone.

"Just calling it names so I don't feel too bad."

He had a few more names for the little shoebox Jimmy called home, but kept it to himself. They finished up, grabbed their gear, and headed outside to the little, red hydrocar.

"You reckon it's up for the trip?" Jimmy made a valid point. This hydro was one of the earlier model hydrogen fueled cars. Its economy was average, its speed was average, its comfort was average. And that was when it was new.

"It'll be fine. Besides, it's all we have." Drake opened the back door and threw his bag on the back seat.

A box of red apples sat there.

"Do you know anything about this?" Drake asked Jimmy.

Jimmy ducked his head into the cabin. "Oh yes, Lucy, sent them over yesterday. Such a nice lady, ya know?"

"A tank full of hydrogen would have been nicer, but sure," Drake said and got into the hydro.

Jimmy joined him, and they started their individual pre-drive rituals. Drake initialized the startup procedure, and Jimmy programmed the DDU.

"Um, Drake," Jimmy said.

"Yes, buddy?"

"Where are we actually heading to?" Jimmy asked.

Drake did not know. All this talk about him being the only person who could find Mr. Turner and then all the deals that were struck. He never actually sat down to come up with a plan. Not really surprising, though. Drake had always been a firm believer in leaping before looking.

"Shit, Jimmy, I don't know," he said and leaned back in his seat.

"Okay, so, let's say you were on the run, and all you knew was mining and hauling. Where would you go?"

Even when Penta was chasing Jimmy and him, he never contemplated running away. He just always looked ahead and followed the road. Eventually, it always took him somewhere.

"I don't know, Jimmy. I guess, maybe ..." He had nothing.

They sat in the red hydro, listening to its little engine converting hydrogen to electricity.

"So, maybe that's what we should do, ya know?" Jimmy eventually said.

Drake just looked at him. Had he been thinking out loud?

"Just drive. Do what you said you were good at, ya know. Go to Turner's truck yard, and just see what feels right."

Drake had no argument against Jimmy's plan. Yes, it was dumb, most likely a waste of time, but at least he had an idea.

"Well, driving around in circles it is then," Drake said and put the hydro in drive.

"First stop better be a refueling station," Jimmy said and pointed to the telemetry on the screen. They were almost out of hydrogen.

"Bloody hell, Jimmy. How are we ever going to do this? We can barely get out of town?"

"Nah, you're just rusty, ya know. We'll be fine," Jimmy said.

Drake let Jimmy's confidence fill the cabin and soak into his skin. He was right. He belonged on the road, and once they were there, he would find his way.

***

The hydrocar finally stalled about a kilometer from the refueling station. Just before the inevitable happened, and as the telemetry counted down, the tension in the cabin rose.

"Why didn't you warn me we were almost empty?"

"I did! Plus, your eyes are also on the screen, ya know?"

"Do I have to do everything around here? Drive and plan?"

"No, but maybe you should listen more, ya know?"

"If we run out of fuel, so help me."

"Oh, so you want help then?"

In the last stages of the countdown, total silence fell in the cabin as hope rose that maybe, just maybe, they would make it. These things were always out by a few kilometers, anyway.

Then they saw it. The hill. Drake could see the signs for the station on his screen, and knew it was just beyond the crest. They only had a few hundred meters to go to reach the summit. Then they would be safe.

Jimmy shut off all non-essential programs, including the climate control, music, and verbal communication. They were down to prayers and angered looks.

Drake felt the first surge of the hydro, with fifty meters to go to the crest of the hill. He closed his eyes and kept his foot steady. "C'mon, c'mon, c'mon," he whispered under his breath.

The hydro lost momentum. Twenty meters.

A red warning filled the screen. Ten meters.

Everything died. Right on the crest. About a kilometer in the distance, they could see the bright lights of the hydrogen refueling station. Instead of a slope down to the station, there was instead a perfectly flat plateau.

Not a loss, but a draw.

"You push, I'll steer," Drake said.

"Nah ah. We take turns. It'll take forever if only one does it."

Drake knew he was right. Besides, Jimmy had the strength of a six-year-old.

"Sure. Now get pushing."

An hour later, and filled to the brim, Jimmy jumped back into the hydro.

"Grabbed us two boxes for the road." He smiled, already on to the next phase and done with the past.

"Thanks, partner. And sorry if I got a little tense back there. Running out of hydrogen is the biggest blunder a hauler can make. If my old hauler buddies ever got wind of this—"

"It happens to all of us, ya know," was all Jimmy had to add.

"Okay, off to the old depot then," Drake said, as he pulled out of the refueling station.

He knew his way around these parts, but he didn't stop Jimmy when he entered the destination into Yolanda. He had his job and Jimmy had his.

"This is so cool," Jimmy said next to him.

"What is?"

"This! Getting ready for an adventure, not knowing what lies ahead."

Drake wished he shared Jimmy's excitement. He still did not know where they were headed, or how he was going to keep the credits. He knew that without Jimmy, he could not get through this.

"I know, buddy. Scary too, to be honest."

"A little I guess, but you cannot let fear deter you, ya know? It's almost always less scary than you imagined it would be."

Drake looked at the wiry, tooth missing, man-child next to him. The life he must have had.

"Wise words, buddy," Drake said and saw Jimmy's eyes sparkle.

| twenty-three |

It felt familiar, but also strange. Drake had driven into this lot hundreds, if not thousands, of times before. Driving in and passing through under the sign felt normal, but everything looked different. There were no containers waiting to be taken away, or trucks patiently standing by waiting for the go ahead. No haulers hanging around, shooting the shit with each other or getting into arguments. No Bob Turner standing in front of his office, commandeering the entire operation.

"Let's start at the office," Drake said, and parked next to it.

They got out and entered the small, white building.

Dust had blown in through the broken windows and empty door frame and settled on everything. Mr. Turner's office had always been sparsely equipped, and whatever had value had long been stolen.

"Not much to see here," Jimmy said.

"No, you're right. Looks like it's been looted already."

They kept looking and flipping everything they found over, trying to find anything that might be useful. But it seemed the only things left were useless. A few scraps of paper. Empty white boxes. Broken furniture.

"Check it out!" Jimmy yelled after a few minutes of rummaging.

Drake walked over to Jimmy.

"That's her, alright," Drake said.

He took the photo from Jimmy and inspected it closer. In it, a much younger Mr. Turner had his arm around a dark-haired version of Lucy. They were both younger, but clearly identifiable.

Drake shook his head.

"I have seen this so many times. I asked him about it once, and boy, did I regret that! Thought he was going to punch me or something. I assumed by his reactions it was an old girlfriend."

"Well, that's about the most helpful thing in here." Jimmy shrugged.

Drake looked around. Jimmy was right. There was not much to learn from what little the looters had left behind.

"So, what now?" Jimmy asked.

Drake looked down at the photo Jimmy had found. Mr. Turner must have been fresh from the mines. His neck was enormous, and his arms were the size of Jimmy. Like all Moon miners, they shot him full of steroids in order to strengthen him and make him more efficient. Lucy looked slim and fragile next to his bulk, but she had the same warmth radiating from her, even through the old faded photo. Drake could see why Mr. Turner married her.

Behind them was a beach with what looked like an island off in the distance. It was grainy and could have been anything, but Drake thought it was an island. They must have taken the photo on a vacation when Mr. Turner was on Earth for a stretch.

"If you held on to an old photo of most likely the only woman you ever loved, where would you go?" Drake asked Jimmy, pointing to the background in said photo.

Jimmy studied it for a second.

"Nope, still nothing, partner." He gave up.

"Here, dipshit!" Drake tapped the beach with the island in the background.

"Oh, yeah. So you're saying—"

"Jimmy! He had this photo in his office for years, taken with Lucy at this particular spot!" Drake pushed the photo into Jimmy's face. "We need to find this beach," he spelled it out.

Jimmy nodded.

"So, where is that?" he asked.

"That, buddy, I do not know," Drake replied. "But we know someone who had been there before."

Jimmy nodded slowly, showing he did not, in fact, know who Drake referred to.

Drake dialed Lucy.

"Drake. I thought you would be on the road by now?" Lucy answered.

"Hey. We are, but I need your help."

"Okay, what is it?" she asked.

Drake held the photo up so she could see it.

"Oh dear. That bring back some memories."

"We hoped you could tell us where this was taken," Drake said.

Lucy seemed to ponder this for a second, traveling back in time to find the answer.

"I'm sure that was right after we signed our marriage contract, which means it was in the main Shangcorp territory, in the southeast. We traveled a lot that summer, so I can't say where for sure. I'm sorry."

"If it was that easy, you wouldn't need us," Drake replied.

"I'll contact you if I remember anything more specific." Lucy said goodbye and broke the connection.

Drake pocketed the photo.

"Looks like we're off to mainland Shangcorp," Drake said to Jimmy.

"Man, I've always wanted to go there," Jimmy replied with typical enthusiasm.

They gave the office one last look over before heading back to the hydro.

***

"So do I just type in south east Shangcorp?" Jimmy asked back in the hydro.

"We could, I guess, but it's too vague and doesn't guarantee we take the right route."

Drake pulled a map up on the screen.

"Okay, so here we are, New Franco," Drake tapped on it and a little pin appeared, "and here is the southeast region of mainland Shangcorp."

They both stared at the screen.

"I think I've heard of this one before." Jimmy pointed to a name on the map.

"Cathapore?" Drake asked.

"Yeah, that's it. Ancient city, but very modern too. Heard some crazy stories about it. Buildings higher than the clouds, ya know?"

Drake always divided Jimmy's stories by ten.

"Okay, but does it have beaches?" Drake asked.

"I don't know, but," Jimmy swiped away on his HIC, "it is next to the ocean."

"Okay, I guess it will be easy to get lost in a place like that. Especially in a Shangcorp town."

Drake placed the pin on the screen, right in the middle of Cathapore.

"Okay then," Drake said. "Except for one minor problem, I think we have a route."

Jimmy looked at the screen and then back at Drake and shrugged.

Drake scrolled the map across the screen and zoomed in on an area.

"You see this, buddy?" He pointed on the map. "This is where we need to cross water. And lots of it."

| twenty-four |

Flying to Cathapore would have been faster by days. A Sub-Orbital flight would take them an hour, or even less. Driving would take them days, if not weeks, but it made little sense to Drake to fly. Sub-Orbital travel was quick, and although it was the only air travel available, it was prohibitively expensive. Only the rich used it, and Drake doubted that Mr. Turner would waste all his credits on a flight that would get him there quick but also risk him being spotted at the security terminal. He could have asked Sammy for more credits, but it seemed the wrong way to go.

Drake believed that following Mr. Turner on the ground, following in his footsteps, would ensure they were on the right track. Maybe something happened on the way to Cathapore that derailed his plans or he found a place he liked and stayed put. There was no guarantee that he was in Cathapore, only a high probability that he was heading there.

"Okay, I reckon Mr. Turner would have packed up and left as soon as his name got mentioned in the news. Clearly he didn't run the cleanest operation," Drake said.

"You ever going to call him just Bob? You don't work for that son of a bitch anymore, ya know?"

Drake didn't realize he still called him Mr. Turner.

"Just habit, I guess. So, I reckon he would have headed north." Drake pointed to higher on the map.

The logical move would have been to hit the highway and travel north. The higher he went, the closer the gap was to mainland Shangcorp and the less time he would need to spend at sea. Water travel had changed little over the centuries and was extremely slow compared to hydrogen powered road vehicles or hyperloops. Drake was confident Mr. Turner would drive as far as he could before using a boat to cross.

"Pick a town north, and let's go," Drake told Jimmy.

Jimmy studied the map for a while, entered the coordinates into Yolanda, and the green line appeared, pointing the way.

***

"Yes, I got the signal and visual."

"Yes, I know, every day, don't worry, I've got this."

"I'll call you later."

Sammy Sanders watched on as Drake and Jimmy got in their little, red hydrocar and left Turner's old truck yard. Drake drove like a lunatic and left dust hanging in the air, so he pulled out and followed them before he lost visual. He also had them on his DDU, but wanted to keep an eye on them, at least for a while, before he would fall back a bit. He regretted selling his hydrocar and buying a new one, but he could not risk them seeing and recognizing his old hydro. Besides, with the amount of credits he stood to make, he could buy himself ten new hydros.

Drake took an exit and got onto the highway, heading north. Sammy hated driving on the highway in anything else than a truck, like a Hydrocomet, but he had no choice.

"Okay, boys, let's see where this takes us," he said as he entered the highway behind them.

***

"Wow, Porterville, really?" Drake said.

"Hey, it's north from here, and you said to pick a spot, ya know?" Jimmy defended his spot.

"I know, but Porterville?"

"I met a guy from there once and he made it sound like it was the best town on Earth, so why not?"

Drake had passed through Porterville many times before, and even dropped off cargo there, but the longest he ever stayed there voluntarily was for a meal. It was a picturesque town, with a river running through it and trees everywhere. The problem was that it was an independently owned town in a Penta territory. This was not a big deal, as there were hundreds of independent towns in corporate territories. But Porterville, unlike most independent towns, didn't sit on some big natural resource like water or gold. It didn't have a unique manufacturing plant that could sustain the entire town. It had nothing to offer, really. What kept all the people there was their leader, Russel. Just Russel. No last name. A laid back and enigmatic leader. The town had nothing to offer the outside world or its own residents. The motto of Porterville was, "We as one." Which meant everyone shared everything. If you had ten rocks, you kept one and gave away nine. If you had food growing in your backyard, everyone had food to eat. If your neighbor didn't need their hydro today, it was yours to borrow.

Drake, like most people, did not understand how they pulled it off, yet the town seemed to flourish. Whenever Russel was questioned, he answered in metaphors and left people even more confused. Drake found the whole place bizarre, but he also believed that everyone had the right to live the way they wanted. He just chose to not hang around there too long.

***

After an hour on the highway, Drake gave in and switched the Autodrive on.

"Man, this is hard work." He turned to Jimmy.

"A little rusty?"

"No, but driving this tiny death trap on the highway is no picnic."

Drake felt like they had a target painted on them, as single Hydrocomets and caravans of them kept passing by. He barely navigated out of the way of one before another would come screaming down the highway.

"Felt much slower when I was in the Hydrostar's cabin," Drake said.

"Well, they are slower than Comets, ya know?" Jimmy stated a fact. A fact Drake was well aware of, but didn't need to hear. He loved the older Hydrostars and would buy one over a new Hydrocomet any day.

"Whatever. When we're done here, we are getting a Star, not a Comet. Understand?"

Jimmy just laughed. "Whatever, not like you'll allow me to drive it, anyway."

"Damn straight," Drake replied. "Seriously though, I reckon we need to get off the highway. It's only a matter of time before we get taken out by one of these haulers."

Jimmy opened his mouth to answer, but an alarm went off to warn them of an incoming caravan. Before they could brace, it was screaming past them, shaking the little hydro, making the Autodrive work overtime. Multiple warnings flashed on the screen of systems being pushed to their limits. The last truck in the caravan flashed past, and everything went quiet.

"Great idea," Jimmy finally replied.

He leaned forward and entered an alternative route into Yolanda. The green line jumped around on the road, and since the hydro was still in Autodrive, it took the first exit. The exit connected to a smaller rural road that was barely wide enough for one hydro.

"How's that?" Jimmy asked.

"If nothing else, it's quieter," Drake said, quite relieved to be off the highway.

"Do you think Turner would have gone this way too?" Jimmy asked.

He had a valid point. If they struggled on the highway, then they had to assume that Mr. Turner would have too. It was likely that he would have taken the smaller roads as well, and might have done so from the beginning.

Hopefully, in the same direction.

***

Sammy watched as the caravan that almost took him out went past Drake's little, red hydro. The force of the caravan was so great it made the hydro fishtail, and for a moment Sammy thought it was the end of them. It rocked from side to side, but the Autodrive must have been engaged, as slowly and in a controlled manner, the hydro straightened itself out. No way Drake was that good a driver.

The red hydro then veered all the way to the side, and when an exit appeared, it took it.

"Too scared to hang out with the big boys, huh?" Sammy said as he reprogrammed his own Autodrive to keep following Drake's—at a set distance.

The smaller road they ended up on was only a fraction the size of the highway, and empty except for the two hydros. Sammy could clearly see Drake and Jimmy's hydro, which meant they would be able to see him. Unlike on the highway, there were no trucks to keep Drake's attention away from him. Now he would stand out like a sore thumb.

"Time to fall back then. I'll see you boys a bit later."

| twenty-five |

Hector Delgado sneered at the Penta officer standing in front of him. He knew he had to play nice; he knew the game they all played. He would make some big gesture to help the community, and they would turn a blind eye to whatever the complaints against him were. Then they would leave and he would find out who made the complaint. Once he took care of that, it would be business as usual. All would be well until some do-gooder felt the urge to speak up, and they would do their little dance again.

But this officer didn't want to dance.

"We know it was you who planted those explosives. If it happened only in your sector and you killed some of your own people, nobody would give a shit, but you got greedy, didn't you?"

Delgado wondered how much this shakedown was going to cost him.

"Are you trying to expand? Set up little franchises all over New Franco? Have idiots with numbers on their faces run around everywhere?"

He knew they were just trying to assert dominance. All he had to do was play it cool and wait it out.

"Tell me, would they have fifty-nine butchered on their faces or the number of their new sector? Looking around, I don't see too many thinkers in your crew, so I can only assume they might get confused if they had the wrong number on their face."

Delgado was not amused. If this was anyone else, they would die slowly and horribly in a dark room where no one would ever find them. Unfortunately, Penta officials were untouchable.

"I am so sorry that you have wasted your time, but I had nothing to do with those explosions. I am more than happy to use my resources to help bring this terrorist to justice. If there is anything you need from me, please feel free to ask. Anything at all."

Like a new hydro, maybe.

The Penta officer didn't pick up on the hint.

"Leave the security work to us, Mr. Delgado, and make sure you are available for questioning at all times. I'll be seeing you soon."

"Of course." Delgado watched the Penta security team leave his office.

He sat smiling until the door closed behind them. The smile quickly faded.

"Find out who that was and get me everything you can find out on them—now!" Delgado yelled to whoever was brave enough to take on the task.

***

"Have a good nap?" Drake asked a waking Jimmy.

"Um, yeah, good, ya know," he replied, wiping drool from his chin. "I think I dislocated my neck." Jimmy strained to turn his head.

"I don't think that's a thing, Jimmy."

"You sure? How long was I out for?"

Drake looked at the telemetry on screen.

"About two hours. Neither of us slept that much last night."
Drake yawned. "I am pretty tired too."

Jimmy's neck jumped back into position and he sat up
straight.

"Let me drive!"

Drake looked at him as if he'd never seen anything like him.
Which he hadn't.

"No."

"Stop using that word so much! C'mon, look around. There
is no one else here."

Drake had to admit that this road was extremely quiet. A
few times he thought he saw something in the rearview monitor, but it never materialized and must have been local hydros
driving around.

"I have a hydro license, ya know? It's not like the Hydrostar.
I can actually drive this thing," Jimmy pleaded some more.

If they shared the driving duties, it would save enormous
amounts of time. Drake knew it made sense, but hated giving
up control. Especially when it involved driving.

"Jimmy, I swear, if any—"

"Yes, yes, whatever you are going to say, it's all good. I
understand everything. I agree with everything. Now please, let
me drive!"

Drake pulled to the side of the road. He opened his door and
walked around to Jimmy's side to find the door still closed. He
bent down and peered in. Jimmy was already in his seat, pressing

buttons and turning the wheel around. Drake opened the door and got in.

"Buckle up, partner!" Jimmy yelled and pressed the accelerator all the way down.

The little, red hydrocar shuddered a bit and slowly gained momentum.

"What in the hell?" Jimmy looked disappointingly at his feet, as if he wasn't pressing into the floor hard enough. He lifted his foot and stomped down again.

"This thing is ancient, Jimmy. What did you expect?" Drake laughed.

"But you always go like something is chasing you?" Jimmy looked devastated.

For their own safety and Drake's peace of mind, he'd engaged Restrictive Mode as he walked to Jimmy's door. Only the owner, or an authorized person, could engage or disengage Restrictive Mode. Its primary function was to limit the speed and increase the AI safety protocols and was used to teach people how to drive.

"Keep your eyes on the road, don't hesitate to use Autodrive, and wake me up in an hour." Drake reclined the seat as far as it could go and closed his eyes.

"This is bullshit, ya know," Jimmy mumbled.

Drake smiled, eyes closed, feeling the heaviness of sleep approaching.

***

Drake opened his eyes and noticed that night had fallen. Jimmy was gently shaking him.

"Hey buddy, we're here," Jimmy said.

"Here?" Drake was still half asleep.

"Porterville!"

Drake sat up and looked out the window. Jimmy had parked the hydro in a tree-lined street, with soft street lights illuminating the road. Next to it were housing units, all painted different colors and patterns. It definitely was Porterville.

"How long was I asleep?"

"Dunno, maybe three, three and a half hours?" Jimmy said.

"Damn. Well, thanks for getting us here." Drake felt guilty that he hadn't trusted Jimmy enough and engaged Restrictive Mode. It must have frustrated the poor guy the entire drive.

"No sweat. Quite relaxing, ya know?"

"I know the feeling, buddy. I'll see if I can figure out why it didn't want to go any faster in the morning, okay?"

Jimmy's eyes lit up. "I'm sure you'll work it out."

On his last visit to Porterville, Drake had driven straight back to New Franco and risked falling asleep rather than risk getting converted and moving to Porterville. That was not an option today.

"Okay, partner, find us some accommodation. The cheaper the better, and let's get some white boxes into us."

Jimmy immediately got to work on his HIC, and he displayed the results on the screen for Drake to see.

"Strange," Jimmy said as he scrolled through the options.

All the accommodations appeared to be private homes, offering a room or two for the night. No big corporate hotel chains or even local hotels had any listings here.

"I told you, man," Drake started, "this place is weird. What kind of town forces you to share a local's house? Huh?"

Jimmy kept scrolling.

"It's pointless, man. Either we sleep in the hydro, or we buckle up and make new friends," Drake said.

"How about this one?" Jimmy asked and enlarged a picture on the screen.

Room to rent. Travelers and locals welcome. Clean room with a heating and cooling unit. Shared bathroom facilities. Expert knowledge of the area to share. Credits or labor accepted.

"Labor accepted? What the hell, Jimmy? This is the one that caught your eye?"

Jimmy shrugged. "It looks nice, ya know?"

Drake was hungry and knew that all the other listings would have their own quirky Porterville twist to it.

"Fine. Contact them, and let's get some food."

Jimmy swiped his HIC, made the call, and booked the room.

"All done. Seems like a friendly couple, ya know?"

Drake shuddered to think about what lay ahead.

"I'm sure they are, Jimmy. Now, before we get some food, move your ass so I can drive."

| twenty-six |

The young man looked nervous, but eager to please. His tattoo was fresh, the skin around the numbers still red and swollen. Delgado never bothered with their names, as they never lasted long enough.

He looked at the pictures on his DDU. They were clearly taken from a distance, slightly out of focus and awkwardly framed. All showed the same person, leaving a housing complex, arriving at work, and leaving work. Despite the images being pixelated, it was clear who it was.

"You did great, soldier," Delgado told the young man. "Leave your name with Deon. He'll make sure we compensate you."

The young man smiled and left the room, heading straight to Delgado's right-hand man.

Delgado studied the photos some more, watching the Penta officer go about their daily routine.

He reached under his desk, opened a drawer, and took a small item out. He placed it on his desk.

"Looks like we have one more hydro to blow up."

***

Jimmy placed his palm on the DDU next to the headache-inducing, neon yellow door. He gave Drake a nervous smile.

"I'm sure they'll be fine, ya know."

That didn't convince Drake.

A tiny, child-like face appeared on the wall mounted Data Display Unit.

"Oh, hey, you must be Jimmy and Benjamin." The voice was thin and high pitched.

"He prefers Drake," Jimmy quickly jumped in.

"Oh, my apologies! Jimmy and Drake then. Let me open up for you," the child-face said, and the door slid open.

Jimmy and Drake entered.

"Oh, here they are. Welcome to Porterville," the voice now had a face and body. But nothing matched.

Jimmy stood, mouth ajar, and Drake had to catch himself to not mimic him.

The tiny, child-like head sat underneath a mop of golden curls. Underneath the head was the enormous body of a Moon miner. To make things more unbearable, another body entered the picture. This one was better proportioned, and Drake sighed in relief.

"Your head—" Jimmy started, but an elbow from Drake stopped him.

"Thank you!" Drake said as loud as possible, hoping to drown out Jimmy's words.

"Oh, it's our pleasure. My name is Clive, and this is Fred."

Fred just waved his greeting.

"Nice to meet you, Clive and Fred," Drake replied. "We will only stay one night, and then we'll be off again. No need to fuss over us. Just need a place to sleep for the night, have a meal, and we'll be fine."

Clive didn't look too happy about this.

"Oh, but a visit to Porterville would not be complete without a visit to the museum, or the beautiful art district, not to mention—" A stern look from Fred silenced Clive.

"Thank you, Clive, maybe next time. Unfortunately, our business dictates for us to be on the move again early in the morning," Drake said.

Clive looked to Fred for permission to talk again, and apparently he received it, although Drake saw no sign of life from Fred.

"Oh, and what business might that be, if you don't mind me asking?" Clive's chubby cheeks bulged as he smiled at Drake.

"We're bounty hunters," Jimmy said.

"No, we're not!" Drake elbowed him again.

"Ouch! But we are chasing Turner for a bounty. I'm pretty sure that's what bounty hunters do, ya know?"

"Yes, but ..." Drake turned back to Clive, who seemed very interested in the tale of two bounty hunters. "We are after someone who has a bounty out on him, but we are not bounty hunters."

"Oh, so very exciting!" Clive looked at Fred, who didn't seem to share his, or any, excitement.

"Like I said, just a quick stop to refresh, and we'll be on our way again," Drake said, hoping to see the room and the end of this conversation.

"Oh, yes, of course. So tell me. Did this fugitive come through here? Is that why you came to Porterville?"

Drake realized that this would not be a quick conversation.

"To be honest, Clive, we don't know. Mind if I sit down?" Drake gestured to the couch. Might as well get comfortable.

"Oh, yes, let's sit down. Fred, go make some tea." Clive winked at Drake. "the good stuff."

Drake didn't dare ask what the good stuff was. Clive sat down directly across from Drake and Jimmy, hands in his laps, eyes sparkling with anticipation.

"The man we are chasing is my old boss, and we are under instruction from his ex-wife to get him back safely. So yes, there is a bounty out on him but we are not after that."

Clive's face lit up, as if he'd just made a realization.

"Oh my, you are *the* Benjamin Drake! The man who helped Santo steal Mars! Fred!" Clive's voice went even higher. "Fred! Get in here!" Clive clasped his face.

Fred sauntered into the room with a tray and tea cups. He calmly put it down on the table and sat down next to a buzzing Clive. Drake hoped Clive didn't explode.

"Yes, it's me. Seems the news traveled further than I thought," Drake said.

"Oh, everyone knows about that. It was all the news reported on for weeks. Your name only came out later, but by then, Fred was already obsessed with the story." Fred seemed pretty indifferent to Drake.

"We'll that's us," Drake replied.

"Oh, so humble. Here." Clive gave Drake and Jimmy each a cup of the tea.

"Thank you," both said in unison. Drake inhaled the aromas, knowing from experience that tea always smelled better than it tasted.

"Oh my, two celebrities in our home, Fred." Clive beamed. Fred breathed.

Drake ventured a sip of the tea. It tasted half good.

"Nice tea, Fred. Thank you." Drake took another sip.

Jimmy downed his tea in one go, either out of dehydration, or to get it over with. Luckily, he didn't say which.

"Oh, so thirsty," Clive observed. "So tell me, Drake, why Porterville?"

Whatever the good stuff was, it tasted all right to Drake and made him very relaxed too. A glance at Jimmy confirmed he felt the same. Slouching in the corner, Drake hoped Jimmy would stay awake long enough so that he didn't have to carry him to bed.

"No reason. We are just trying to track Mr. Turner down and hopefully follow the same path he took. We're not bounty hunters, so we are just making this up, to be honest," Drake said.

"Oh, if you want, I can make some inquiries and see if any of our friends saw something or heard anything. Would you have a photo of him?" Clive asked.

Drake dug the photo of Turner and Lucy out of his pocket.

"It's a bit old, unfortunately."

Clive took the photo and inspected it.

"Oh, seems like he spent some time in the mines. See, Fred?"

"Yes, he used to work on the Moon, but that was before I worked with him," Drake added.

"Oh, let me scan it, and we'll see what we can find out. No promises, but Fred and I like to keep our finger on the pulse around here. I'm sure one of our friends will have some information. More tea?"

Drake took the photo back from Clive and looked over at Jimmy. He seemed to be asleep, with his eyes open.

"It appears my partner can't handle the good stuff." Drake nodded toward Jimmy. "I think it best if we call it a night."

"Oh, poor little fella. Fred, please show these fine young men to their room, and I'll see if we can't help Benjamin Drake find his bounty."

Drake couldn't wait to put his head on a pillow.

***

Eventually, all the lights went out, without Drake or Jimmy re-appearing. Clearly, they were staying the night. Sammy reclined his seat as much as he could and settled in for the night.

Three swirling dots halted his dozing off.

"Did I wake you?"

"No, no, just setting up for the night. I was actually getting ready to call you," Sammy lied. He was so tired he completely forgot to check in.

"I need to be kept up to date. It was part of the agreement."

Sammy hated being bossed around.

"Sure, sure, like I said, was about to call." He bit his tongue.

"So?"

"Well, I have visual on them and they are staying overnight in Porterville," Sammy said.

"Porterville? Doesn't matter. As long as you monitor them and be ready to execute the plan. Oh, and next time, check in." The connection ended.

"Yes, anything else you'd like me to do, your highness," Sammy said to his reflection on the window.

He didn't need any motivation or reminders to be ready.

He pulled a pulse gun out of a bag and looked at it in the dim streetlight.

He was more than ready.

| twenty-seven |

Drake stared at the wall next to his bed. He had never seen a wall painted with so many intricate patterns and colors. He couldn't even name most of the colors. Even in the sober light of day, it still seemed to be alive and moving. Last night, they definitely moved. Drake was dead tired when he hit the sack, but once his eyes adjusted to the light, the patterns jumped out at him and swirled and danced. No amount of blinking or face slapping could make it stop. He blamed the tea, but now, in the day, they still seemed to move.

"What a night!" Jimmy said and snapped him out of his trance.

"Hey, partner. Clive and Fred are a pair of characters, that's for sure," Drake replied.

"So, grab some food and hit the road?" Jimmy asked.

That sounded like an excellent plan to Drake.

"You throw the bags in the car, and I'll grab some food to go," Drake suggested.

Jimmy stood up, stretched out, and stuffed his things in his bag. Drake did the same and handed Jimmy his bag.

"Okay, I'll meet you at the hydro. Let's see if we can get out of here quickly. Wish me luck!" Drake said, and started for the door.

It slid open, only to reveal a wall of human. Clive.

"Oh, morning there, boys. Hope you had a good night's rest," Clive said. "I made some white box breakfasts and they are waiting for you in the kitchen."

Clive turned around and led the way. Drake was about to protest, but took the route of least resistance.

"Seems we're having breakfast first," he said to Jimmy and followed Clive.

The kitchen was tiny, and like the rest of the house, too brightly colored. Clive's enormous bulk made the room seem even smaller. In the center of the room was a small table with four plates of food.

"You can sit there, Jimmy. Drake, this is yours." Clive directed them to identical meals.

They did as instructed, and only then did Drake notice Fred was already sitting at his spot.

"Oh, how nice is this, Fred?" Clive asked as he made a chair disappear underneath him.

"It looks great, thank you," Drake said and dug into the standard white box breakfast.

Jimmy took his cue and got started too.

"Oh my, so hungry." Clive laughed, cheeks wobbling. "So, after you boys went off to dreamland, I got some information back from my friends."

Drake had completely forgotten about the photo he showed Clive last night. After drinking the tea, he'd lost all concept of time and couldn't recall any conversations they had. He remembered showing Clive the photo.

"It seems," Clive continued, "that a man matching your photo passed through here weeks ago." Clive pursed his lips, the excitement taking control of him.

"That's great. Thanks, Clive. Did your friends have anything else to say?" Drake could see Clive still had much to say.

"Oh, yes. It seems this friend of yours was in quite a hurry, just like you two." Clive giggled. "He stayed one night at one of our good friends, Margie's house. We should have her over for dinner, Fred, it's been a second."

"Did your friend have any more information?" Drake was happy to know they were on the right track, but the more they knew, the easier it would be to find Mr. Turner.

"Oh, how do I say this? Margie found some more information." Clive looked at Fred, who seemed to still be alive. "In the trash he left behind."

"She went through his trash?" Drake wondered what Clive was going to do once they left.

"Oh my, yes, Margie has a bit of a nosy personality. Lovely girl. The best, right Fred? But, quite nosy."

Drake was more concerned with the information than lovely Margie's personality flaws.

"I'm sure she meant well. So, what did she find?"

"Oh, she did. Well, she found a note, and to be honest, who knows with Margie, but it might have been on a table and not the trash like she claims."

"An honest mistake, then. And what did this note say?" Drake had never been so polite in his life. It was draining his will to live.

"Oh yes, just a little slip up, I guess. So the note she found, somewhere, had some names written on it. Paul Sullivan, Major Swanson, and Wallen. Do you know any of these people?"

Drake had never heard of them, and the look on Jimmy's face confirmed he didn't either.

"No, but I'm sure they must be very important. Thank you, Clive, this might just be the break we were looking for."

Clive seemed very pleased with himself.

"Oh, the pleasure is all ours."

Drake noticed Jimmy had finished his meal and took the last few bites of his own.

"Clive, Fred, thank you so much for your hospitality and the help you gave us." Drake stood up and made his way to the kitchen exit.

Luckily, Jimmy got up before Clive could, and they had an unobstructed path to the front door. Jimmy still had the bags with him, and Drake ushered him toward the door.

"You guys enjoy the rest of your breakfasts, and if we come by this way, we'll make sure to pop in." Drake turned before Clive could object or try to keep them any longer.

***

Jimmy threw the bags in the back and jumped in on his usual side. Drake slid in behind the wheel.

"So, what do you make of these names?" Drake asked.

"Never heard of them, ya know. But I'm sure if I search, something will pop up," Jimmy said.

"Okay, let's take five minutes and see what we can find before we go," Drake suggested and they both got to work on their HICs.

Drake's Human Interface Console was outdated. Not by years, but decades. The green pixels were fading, making reading it through his skin hard. Unlike Jimmy's current model HIC that had a full color screen, and actually replaced the skin, Drake's was a monochrome screen, placed under the skin. He had been putting off getting a new one, but knew he would have to soon. He watched as Jimmy swiped his arm, and the faux skin disappeared to reveal the screen. He marveled at how quickly he got results on it. Looking down at his own unit, he saw it had finally returned some results. Jimmy was not only better at research, but he had better equipment too. Drake decided to just leave it to him.

"Got anything yet?" he asked.

"Yeah, sort of," Jimmy said, still swiping away. "Nothing on Paul Sullivan or a Major Swanson yet, but there is a town called Wallen, which seems to be the closets point to Shangcorp mainland."

That meant they were heading in the right direction, and that Turner was most likely on his way to Cathapore.

"You keep working on that, Jimmy, while we keep going," Drake said, and started the hydro.

***

Finally, the red hydrocar took off. Sammy finished his cold, tasteless white box breakfast and threw the empty container out the window. He contemplated going into the house and gaining more information, but decided against it. The chances were too high that the house owners would not like him snooping around, asking questions about their clientele, and they would probably call security. By the time they would finish questioning him, Drake and Something would be hours ahead of him and he'd be playing catch up. No, better just tail them and stick close enough to keep them in range.

Sammy opened his door, got out, relieved himself in the gutter, and got back in.

"Ah, that's better," he said, as he pulled away, following his target.

| twenty-eight |

Wallen was about three day's drive north of Porterville. Maybe more. Looking at the map, it seemed desolate, frozen, and a place Drake would usually avoid. Haulers rarely had to go so far north, and he felt nervous about the journey ahead.

A waiver appeared on the screen of the hydro, informing Drake that he was about to enter a Maplon territory. Maplon's prime territory was vast, and rivaled Shangcorp and Penta for size, but most of it was a barren, frozen wasteland. They had no resources or big industry, and combined with the climate, resulted in a sparsely populated territory.

"Hope we don't run into any bandits," Jimmy said calmly.

"What bandits?" Drake almost yelled.

"Huh, I thought you knew when you chose this place, ya know?"

"No, I didn't, and I still don't. What fucking bandits?"

"Maplon is full of them, ya know? There is almost no law up here. Which means it attracts a very peculiar type of person." Jimmy nodded as if in agreement with his own statement.

"We have no choice, Jimmy. I'm sure Mr. Turner went this way. How else are we going to get to Wallen?" Drake said, unsure of himself.

"No, you're right, I checked. This is the only way. Just thought I'd give you a heads up, ya know?"

"Thanks," Drake said, and turned back to the green line in front of him.

A thin layer of snow covered most of the scenery, and Drake had to concentrate on the slippery road. He realized they might have to find better suited tires for the hydro if the conditions got any worse.

A blip appeared on his radar, and soon he spotted a vehicle in his rearview monitor. He barely took notice of it, as it happened frequently. Some of them caught up and overtook them, some disappeared after a while. Just normal traffic.

Unlike the other blips, this one kept up with them, staying a set distance behind them. Curious, but still nothing to be alarmed by. A winding section of road appeared, and Drake forgot about the blip as he had to concentrate on his driving. Jimmy was awake, for now, just swiping away on his HIC.

The road straightened out again, and Drake had a look over the telemetry. Everything seemed fine. Except the blip was still following them at the same rate. He looked at his rearview monitor, but couldn't make out any details. He monitored it, checking on it every few minutes.

"Jimmy," he said loudly enough to pull Jimmy away from his favorite toy. "Could you try to zoom in on the rearview?"

Jimmy leaned over and zoomed in, using the hydro's DDU.

"What you looking for?" he asked Drake.

"Not sure, but the vehicle behind us has been holding position now for almost an hour. That's strange, right?"

Jimmy fidgeted around some more on the Data Display Unit.

"I can't make out what it is, but it seems to be the size of a bigger hydro. Definitely not a truck though, but bigger than a hydrocar," Jimmy guessed.

"Can you make out anything else?" Drake asked.

"No, but if you slow down, they'll catch up and we can see. If they also slow down, then I guess you're right, ya know?"

Jimmy's insight always surprised Drake.

"Okay, here goes," Drake said and reduced speed significantly. "If they drop their speed this much, something is wrong."

Both men stared at the rearview monitor and radar.

The blip did not slow down. Instead, it was catching up.

Quickly.

"What the—" Drake watched as the hydro came to within a few feet of them and held position.

Now, clearly visible on the monitor, they could see it to be a large off-road hydrocar, typically found in these climates. What was unusual was the paint. Matte black with a logo on the hood.

"Recognize it?" Drake asked.

Jimmy studied the rearview monitor.

"Nah, but I think it's safe to say we have found our first bandits," Jimmy replied.

The speed with which they caught up to them showed a more powerful drivetrain, and as good a driver as Drake was, he would struggle to out drive them. The only option was to stop and see what happened.

The big off-roader was holding position, driving closer than necessary, just stalking them.

"Plan A," Drake started, "we see if we can outrun them. It's unlikely to happen, but worth a shot." He looked at Jimmy to gauge his response. "Plan B, we stop and deal with them. Not something I'm looking forward to, considering we do not know what's inside that hydro."

"I say we stop and fight," Jimmy said, unsurprisingly.

"Okay, I love the enthusiasm, but all we have are two pulse pistols and some apples."

"And the element of surprise." Jimmy smiled at him.

***

"Okay, say when you're ready," Drake said, glancing nervously at Jimmy.

"I'm always ready," Jimmy said, full of confidence.

The plan was simple enough, but they still had to execute it to perfection.

"Okay, here goes," Drake said, and slammed on the brakes.

As the hydro lost traction, Drake snapped the steering to bring the car into a sideways slide. That was the straightforward part. Getting it to slide sideways and hit the snowy embankment was the trick. Jimmy was crouching down, making sure not to be seen, and did not know if Drake was succeeding or not. The hydro kept sliding, and Jimmy wondered if they needed a Plan B and possibly C. A gentle thud, and plan A was back on. The hydro stopped rocking, and Drake gave him a wink.

Doors slammed outside, and Jimmy took his cue to slip out of the hydro. He paused and listened for anyone yelling out from someone that might have seen him. He counted to five and crawled to the side of the road, the hydro hiding him from the bandits. He pushed through the snow, staying as low as possible, and crawled to a tree big enough to hide behind.

"Hey, motherfucker, get out so we can shoot you!"

Jimmy peeked out from behind the tree.

Three men stood in front of the big hydro, pulse rifles drawn. The big off-roader had tinted windows, but luckily, they left the doors open. Jimmy moved to the next tree and surveyed the car. It appeared empty.

"Okay, I would rather not ruin the hydro, but you give me no choice!"

Jimmy switched on his ARP and crawled to the off-roader, the snow crunching under his weight. He took a deep breath, his heart pounding in his chest, and stuck his head inside. No one blew it off. He exhaled.

"Fuck it, let's do this!"

Jimmy heard the sizzling cracks of the pulse rifles go off. Time to get to work. In a flash, he logged himself into their vehicle's DDU, bypassing all the security codes and giving him access. The guns were still going, so Jimmy stayed low and kept hacking.

The guns stopped. He was almost there.

Feet crunched on snow. He couldn't make out if they were walking toward him or away. He resisted the urge to peek and possibly blow his cover. He needed two more minutes.

"What the fuck?"

"It's empty!"

"Quick, spread out! He can't be far!"

Feet crunching snow, quicker this time. Seconds left.

"Nothing here!"

"No tracks!"

"Same—wait, over here!"

The crunching grew faster, but faded away. All access granted.

Jimmy jumped into the driver's seat and saw the carnage. They'd shot the little, red hydro to pieces, and it looked very sad, lying down on its deflated tires, all the windows shattered. Behind it, the bandits had found Jimmy's trail and were circling back to him.

He put the off-road hydro into drive and floored it. As he passed the little, red hydro, he glanced left to see the bandits' shocked faces staring at him. They stood motionless for a second, and then, in the rearview monitor, Jimmy watched them frantically trying to reload, before he disappeared around a corner.

***

Drake stood shivering in the middle of the road. Jimmy stopped the off-roader next to him, and Drake jumped in.

"We did it!" Jimmy held his hand up for a high five.

"Uh huh." Drake was hugging himself, waiting for the heat from the vents to penetrate.

"I knew it would work. Plus, now we have this sweet ride!"

Drake just sat, shaking. He was happy too, but right now the cold was halting any celebrations.

When Jimmy had gotten out of the hydro, he'd followed right behind him, crawling in the same tracks. Once they got to the first tree, they split up. Jimmy made sure he left big, visible footprints. Drake crawled on his belly, making sure he made no marks. Or at least less than Jimmy. He only crawled a few meters, then crouched behind a fallen tree. From here, he could watch and cover Jimmy if anything went wrong. Once he saw Jimmy had access, he crawled further away, and once the bandits stopped shooting, he ran. His HIC guided him back to the road, where he'd waited for Jimmy.

Drake took his jacket off, hoping the heat from the hydro's vents would warm him quicker through just a shirt. It worked.

"Man, I would not want to be caught out here for too long," he said as he thawed out.

"My fingers were numb, ya know," Jimmy said, driving cautiously, with no green line to lead the way.

"Okay then, do you want to stop so we can swap places, or—" Drake was feeling better, but getting nervous about the speed they were going at. If the bandits had any friends in the area, they would surely catch up soon.

"Nah, I got this," Jimmy said, looking very confident, cruising along at this sluggish pace.

"You surely do, buddy, and I'm very impressed by your driving. I thought, maybe I should take over for a while, so you can program this DDU for us so we can get back on track."

"Oh, yeah, of course," Jimmy said and slammed on the brakes.

The off-roader skidded and, luckily, stopped without hitting anything.

"All yours," Jimmy said and hopped out and ran around to Drake's side.

Drake got out and jumped back into the driver's seat.

"That's better," Drake said, and quickly got up to a more acceptable speed, while Jimmy programmed the newly hacked DDU with their destination.

The green line appeared on the snow, and Drake settled into a comfortable pace and rhythm in the tricky conditions. The off-roader was designed for these roads, and Drake loved how much quicker they could travel now.

Jimmy was still playing with the DDU, scrolling through all the files and programs.

"Found anything worthwhile in there?" Drake asked after a few minutes.

Jimmy just kept swiping and reading.

"Jimmy?"

Jimmy looked up. "Jackpot!"

| twenty-nine |

Sammy almost lost track of Drake and Jimmy as he fell farther behind, struggling to keep up in the snow. He was not used to driving in these conditions, and his hydro was ill-equipped for this terrain. His radar picked something up, and soon he had a visual on something up ahead. It looked too big to be Drake's little hydro, but he couldn't be sure. It was too far away, so he sped up as much as he dared to get a better view. As he approached, he could clearly see it was a much larger, darker vehicle than the one Drake and Jimmy were using. His radar picked up a second vehicle, just slightly ahead of the one in front of him. Sammy kept his distance and hoped that the second one was Drake.

With no warning, the hydro in front of him sped up. Sammy struggled to keep up, but eventually he caught up again. Then, suddenly, it stopped. Sammy slammed on his brakes and stayed as close as possible to the side of the road. He switched on his ARP and zoomed in as much as he could. The picture was shaky and lacked detail, but he could see three figures exiting the vehicle and standing next to it. Not long after they got out, the distinct blue discharge of pulse guns was visible as they shot at the little, red hydro in front of them.

Then, catching him and the three men by surprise, the big off-road hydro took off, almost running them over. The men scrambled to get their pulse guns reloaded, but they were too late.

"What the hell?" Sammy said as he switched off his ARP.

He had no choice but to go forward, and only one road to do so on.

He put his hydro into drive and floored it. It made more noise than progress, as the wheels spun on the slippery road, making a racket. He hoped he was far away enough to not bring attention to himself. He eased off the accelerator a bit, giving the AI system a chance to distribute the power a bit more sensibly across all the wheels. The hydro got some traction, and he was off, heading straight for the three bandits. He was almost on top of them before they saw him and reacted. Luckily for Sammy, they were still reloading, clearly taking their time and arguing about who was at fault, not realizing another hydro was approaching. Without slowing down, Sammy sped through the group, clipping one bandit, sending him flying.

"Shit, sorry," Sammy said as he wrestled the hydro around a bend.

His radar pinged again, and he saw the big off-roader way off in the distance, getting away.

"Fuck!" he yelled, as he watched the gap increase between him and Drake.

***

"Spit it out, Jimmy."

"Oh man, this is so good," Jimmy replied, swiping his HIC reading.

"So tell me then!"

Drake was close to stopping the hydro to have a look for himself. No one seemed to follow them, and he felt the risk acceptable. Luckily, Jimmy spoke up.

"They have an entire network, just like the Haulernet—ya know, messages, jobs, you name it. A black market Haulernet," Jimmy finally let Drake in on the secret.

Drake had not been on the Haulernet in months. He used to check it every few minutes, especially when Mr. Turner had no contracts going. It was the place where haulers got contracts, but also a place where they talked, shared information, and interacted with each other when on the road.

"So, anything that could help us?" Drake asked.

"No doubt, but it will also take some time to find it."

"Well, we're still a day or two away from Wallen, so just dig and see what you find."

"Will do, partner. Ooh, you know what else I should do? See if anyone is looking for this hydro, ya know?"

Damn, Jimmy, can you stop outsmarting me?

"Good idea, buddy. I was going to suggest that, anyway."

The snow was getting heavier, but the off-roader was in its element. The road was narrow, but in good condition, and Drake kept the speed up. He hated to think how they would have gone in the little, red hydro.

"Okay, I've searched for a description of the hydro, but no hits. Only found one hit connected to this hydro, or rather the symbol on it," Jimmy said.

"And?" Drake had to nudge him along.

"Seems they are a small group of about seven or so guys, calling themselves Kaos. Not much on the system about them. A few mentions of some hijackings, and some looting, but pretty small-scale stuff."

It relieved Drake to hear it wasn't the biggest, most organized group in Maplon they'd just robbed.

"And," Jimmy continued, "so far, no one from their group has posted anything about them getting robbed by a couple of tourists in a tiny, city hydro. And I doubt they will, ya know."

Putting it that way, Drake had to agree. Most tough guys relied more on their reputation than on their actions to incite fear and respect. Getting your hydro taken from you by the people you were trying to rob was too embarrassing to mention. No doubt they would regroup and come after them, but they would have to do it alone. Drake fancied his chances.

"Excellent work, buddy."

***

The hydro was running low on hydrogen, and neither Jimmy nor Drake had had the chance or the foresight to grab their gear or food from the red hydro. They would have to stop to refuel and resupply soon. Drake asked Jimmy to see what towns or settlements were nearby, and Jimmy got swiping away on his HIC.

The snow cover was getting thicker, but luckily, no snow was falling as they drove. The off-roader reminded Drake of his Hydrostar, and he loved how it ate up the road in front of it.

"So," Jimmy started, "it seems we have two choices. A place called Angon, or Spatsel. Both appear to be dumps."

"Thanks for your objectivity, Jimmy." Drake laughed. Jimmy seemed confused. "Pick whichever one has food, fuel, and a place to sleep."

"Both. Why do you think I gave you those names?" Jimmy asked.

He had a point.

"Sorry. Um, okay then, I pick Angon," Drake said, picking one at random.

"Oof, I would've gone with Spatsel, ya know?"

Drake sighed. "Then why didn't you just say it?"

Jimmy shrugged. "Always nice to have options, ya know?"

"Whatever, Jimmy, you choose then."

"Okay, I definitely choose Spatsel then. Considering the guys from Kaos come from Angon, it might be best to avoid it."

Drake's jaw dropped.

"Why the fuck would you suggest it then?"

"Like I said, it's nice to have choices, ya know?"

Drake took every compliment he ever gave to Jimmy back.

"Obviously, Spatsel then," Drake said, and watched Jimmy program the new destination into the DDU.

The telemetry on the screen changed, and Drake felt relief when it showed they would have enough fuel to reach the town. It was only a couple of hours away, and they would reach it just before nightfall. He was starving and knew Jimmy would be too.

"Okay, buddy, let's get some food and sleep," he said to Jimmy and steered them toward Spatsel.

| thirty |

The Penta security officer marched into his office, pushing the young man with the fresh ink on his face in front of them, and stopped short of his desk. They kicked him behind his knees and sent him into a kneeling position. He looked defeated, arms dangling by his side, his freshly tattooed face beaten to a pulp.

"Really? You thought you could send one of your goons and make me go away?"

Delgado fought the urge to grab the pulse pistol he had strapped to the underside of his desk and simply shoot the officer in the face. Bam, one shot and all this would be over. But he knew protocol would dictate they had their ARP on, and besides, there would be an entire team around or inside the warehouse, standing guard. Diplomacy would have to suffice.

"Good afternoon. And who do we have here?" Delgado smiled from ear to ear.

"Don't play dumb with me, Delgado. You tried to have me killed. I caught this idiot planting the device myself. You're done for."

Delgado's smile never faded.

"I have never seen this man before in my life, I swear. These kids, they get it into their heads if they impress me that I will reward them with some position in my company. But I can assure you, despite his fresh face decorations, that this man is not an employee of mine."

"He already confessed, Delgado."

The officer grabbed the young man by the hair and twisted his head up. "Tell him how you cried when you told us all about it."

Delgado was still smiling, but a sinister look had now crept into his eyes.

"Go on, tell me," Delgado said.

The young man cried. "I just told you I worked for Mr. Delgado because I wanted to be in his favor. He never sent me to do anything. I'm sorry, Mr. Delgado. I lied because I thought they would kill me. I'm so sorry." He fell forward, sobbing.

"Wow, seems you guys really worked him over. Now, since you have your version, and I have my version ..." Delgado nodded toward his right-hand man, Deon, and a video started playing on a DDU on the wall. It showed the young man breaking down in front of Delgado, denouncing his confession to Penta. "I think it's best if we call it a day."

"We have the confession. That's all we need. I'll be back soon."

"I'm already looking forward to it," Delgado said, smiling.

Delgado watched the Penta officer, fury in their eyes, opening their mouth to say something, but then closing it and walking away.

When the door slid shut, Delgado turned to Deon.

"Get this piece of shit out of here and make sure he doesn't bother me again."

***

Jimmy was correct. Spatsel was a dump. No one from the town bothered to program any information for travelers or sold ads for local business. As they drove into town, nothing popped up on their screen, enticing them to see the natural wonders of Spatsel, or go for a walk in the historic part of town, or offering a place to sleep. The only sign that it was a town was the housing units lining the main road, and a small commercial area. They stopped in front of what seemed to be the only bar in town next to vehicles that all resembled theirs. Big, rough, and in need of some maintenance. Drake wagered the drivers of the vehicles would be the same.

Drake got out and met Jimmy in front of the off-roader.

Mud and grime covered every building, every hydro, everything in sight, painting the town in a monochromatic tone.

"Let's see what the inside looks like," Drake said, and led the way into the bar.

The cold and the wet of the outside world was replaced by warmth and comfort. The bar was packed, and Drake guessed it had to be the only place in town to go. Everyone in here seemed to Drake as if they could pass as a bandit. Hard faces and scars were a plenty, but no one seemed alarmed when they entered.

"Oi! All pulse weapons need to be checked," someone yelled off to Drake's side.

A woman, the same height and build as Drake, was standing behind the bar counter serving a patron, but looking at them.

"Lockers are next to you."

Drake turned and saw the lockers.

"Did you bring your pulse?" Drake asked Jimmy.

Jimmy tapped his body, checking himself. "Nope."

"You had to check yourself? How often do you forget you have a gun on you?"

"I dunno." Jimmy shrugged.

Drake just sighed and took out his pulse gun. Each locker had a small Data Display Unit on it, and Drake followed the prompts to open and lock it again.

"Okay," he said once his pulse pistol was secure. "Let's get some beer, food, and find a place to stay."

The woman who instructed them to use the lockers now poured them a couple of beers.

"Thanks," Drake said once she scanned his HIC and handed them over.

"Just so you know, we don't get a lot of fresh faces up here, so whatever it is you are here to do, do it quick," she said.

Drake looked at Jimmy and raised his eyebrows.

Turning back to her, he said, "Just passing through. Just need a place to refuel, eat something, and a bed for the night. Sound like something you might help us with?"

Drake noticed some locals staring now.

"Like I said, just passing through," he repeated, loud enough for them to hear.

A chair screeched on the ground, and a bearded guy walked over to the counter, pulled up a chair next to Drake, and planted himself.

"Another one, Vicky," he said, looking at Drake.

He kept looking at Drake while Vicky poured the order. Jimmy slurped his beer behind him.

"So," he said as he took the drink from Vicky, "you boys are running with them Kaos boys?"

Drake knew things were about to go south.

"No, we just borrowed their hydro. We'll give it back, promise." Drake smiled at the local.

Another man joined them at the counter.

"Like I said. Are you working with them Kaos boys?"

Drake felt movement behind him and assumed more people were lining up for the inevitable ass whipping.

"And like I said, no. We just borrowed their hydro. Look, if they are friends of yours, I'm sure we can come to some arrangement." Drake took a sip of his beer, concentrating with all his might not to shake. The locals outnumbered them twenty to one. Hopefully, some were passivists.

"Where are they now?" the local asked.

Drake felt the crowd moving in. The only advantage he and Jimmy had was the element of surprise.

"Now, Jimmy!" Drake yelled, as he sealed their fate.

Jumping up, he swung at the closest person standing next to him. He missed, but the wheels were set in motion. Jimmy caught on to what the plan was and jumped on the back of the person Drake just missed. Drake quickly regrouped and punched the guy in the stomach, making him doubling over and sending Jimmy scrambling to the floor. Luckily, Jimmy was quick to his feet and charged the next person. Someone tried to grab Drake from behind, but an elbow to the nose stopped them short.

People were yelling now, but the adrenaline buzzed too loud in Drake's ears for him to hear the words.

Jimmy was slapping and clawing at someone, and Drake looked around to see who his next victim would be. So far, so good. No one seemed too keen to have their asses handed to them, so Drake picked one. Locking eyes with a guy, he stepped up and decided a swift kick would suffice. A look of surprise spread across the guy's face, and then a gasp for air as Drake winded him.

Jimmy finished mauling his victim and ran over to Drake. The crowd had now snapped out of their apathy toward the fight and looked ready to join. Drake stepped up to the biggest guy he saw, fueled by adrenaline and confidence.

"Ready for your beating?" Drake grinned as he swung at him.

Then it went dark.

| thirty-one |

"Looks like he's waking up!"

Drake's head was pounding, and his hands hurt. Opening up his eyes and seeing lots of feet, he figured he was lying on a floor. He was not waking up in a bed, hungover as he hoped.

A face appeared in front of him. He vaguely recalled seeing it before.

"If you try anything stupid, Kurt will be more than happy to put you down again, you hear?"

Drake felt his throbbing head nod.

The stranger offered a hand to help him up, and Drake accepted it. As he rose, he saw Jimmy sitting at the bar, drinking a beer and chatting it up with the locals.

"Oh, hey partner!" Jimmy said and waved.

Drake was about to speak, but had to catch himself from falling over.

"Easy there," a voice said next to him, and guided him to a chair.

"Thanks," Drake mumbled. Noises penetrated his head, and his eyes tried their best to focus.

He was sitting at a table in a bar, full of people drinking and laughing, seemingly having a good time. Jimmy walked over and joined him. So did the stranger who'd helped him up.

"How's the head?" Jimmy asked.

"Sore," Drake replied, still adjusting to his senses coming back online.

"Yep, Kurt got you good, ya know," Jimmy said. He shook his head as he took a sip of his beer.

"What the fuck happened?" Drake finally asked.

"I was about to ask you the same question," the stranger at the table said.

Drake recognized the face, but pain clouded the memory.

"You guys were about to beat us up, so we defended ourselves," Drake replied.

The stranger laughed. "We were, were we?"

"Yes," Drake sounded unsure. "You were asking me questions and then suddenly everyone ganged up on us." He remembered the face now and the conversation they had at the counter.

"You sure about that? Maybe Kurt hit you a bit too hard."

Drake admitted he might have jumped the gun a bit. But wasn't the best defense offense?

"Yes, I am. You hassled me about the Kaos gang, and next thing I know, I'm lying on the ground."

Drake looked around nervously, but no one was paying them any attention.

"Mmm, that's one way of looking at it. The other might be I asked you a question, and my friends were merely curious to hear what the stranger had to say. Next thing you went full on berserker and attacked us."

Jimmy was shaking his head disapprovingly at Drake.

"Huh?" Drake uttered.

"Drake, you don't mind if I call you Drake?" He paused for a second. "We've had nothing but trouble from those Kaos boys. They're a bunch of inbred idiots, who are merely tolerated around here. Seeing you pull up in one of their vehicles, we had some questions. Luckily Jimmy here answered them while you had a nap. Having an outsider roughing them up a bit, well, that's just fine by us."

Drake wasn't sure if he heard the man correctly, or if it was the concussion speaking.

"So you are not bandits then?" was all he could come up with.

The stranger and a few others nearby laughed. Jimmy joined them too.

"No one here calls themselves that, but we live here in the wilderness, on the fringes, for a reason, Drake. Jimmy told us all about Zuma and Santo and your adventures, and how you are now chasing a bounty. Which made us realize you are a kindred spirit of sorts."

Drake didn't know if this was a good thing or not. He also wished Jimmy would stop telling people they were bounty hunters.

"Next round is on me," the stranger said. "Let's have a chat."

Drake nodded in agreement, not convinced that it was a request.

Beers arrived, and everyone claimed one.

"So, first thing's first. I'm Frank."

"Frank," Drake acknowledged the introduction.

"Jimmy told us your wild story. If it wasn't for the news clips he brought up, I would have made you two sleep outside tonight."

Drake took it for the thinly veiled threat it was.

"But," Frank continued, "he made an excellent case for you guys being outsiders. Like most of us here in the north."

Drake looked at the assembly in the bar. Mostly men, with only a handful of women thrown in. Mostly burly, bearded, and brash. The men too. It reminded Drake of many truck stops he had been in and thought that maybe Frank was correct—they did fit in.

"I'm sorry, Frank. I thought we were in for a beating and just tried to even the odds," Drake said.

"You were!" Frank laughed, and those nearby joined him. "But luckily your partner has a way with words and saved your ass." The laughter continued.

Jimmy blushed.

"He is full of surprises. I'll give you that much," Drake admitted.

He waited for everyone to settle down again.

"Not to push my luck too far, but where do we stand on the sleeping inside versus outside debate?" Drake asked.

Frank waved someone over.

"This is Trixie. She'll put you up for the night. At a reasonable price," Frank said.

Trixie swiped her HIC toward Drake. "Here are the coordinates, sweetie. I normally charge the rooms by the hour, but we'll work something out." She winked at Jimmy and walked back to her table.

"Do I have to—"

"We'll talk later," Drake stopped Jimmy. "As long as I have your ear, I'll keep going," Drake said tentatively to Frank, who nodded.

"The man we are looking for goes by Bob Turner. Here's a photo." Drake gestured to Jimmy to show Frank a picture of Mr. Turner. It would display much better on his HIC.

Frank studied it for a while before calling Trixie back.

"Is this the man who was here a few weeks back? Fueled up and left here in a hurry?" Frank asked her.

Now it was Trixie's turn to study the photo. Jimmy had to use his other arm to support the HIC arm, as it shook from the strain of holding it up for so long.

"Mmm, dunno. Could be. I only glimpsed him when he asked whose job it was to help him refuel. Seemed rude and bossy." Trixie left.

"Sounds like him," Drake said. "Seems we are on the right track."

***

Sammy stopped outside the bar. The lights were still on, but only a handful of hydros still waited for their owners to return. It took him hours to reach this shit hole, the hydro struggling with the conditions. If the weather and terrain got any worse, he'd have to reconsider or find alternative transport. The drive sapped all his energy; he needed a good night's rest. In a bed, not his hydro. The bar seemed to be the only place open, so Sammy put all his hopes on finding some accommodation in it. He looked around, but couldn't spot Drake's stolen hydro. He decided to take the risk and go into the bar.

The inside of the bar was almost completely empty. Most tables were piled with empty glasses and vacant chairs. The few tables that still had patrons served more as sleeping spots than tables. The woman behind the bar was wiping the counter, clearly in the process of shutting down for the night. She looked up at Sammy, but didn't greet him.

"Wow, so much better in here. I was freezing out there!" Sammy said.

"I'm closing in five. If you want a beer, be quick."

"No, but thank you. Just need a place for the night. I would kill for a nice, warm bed," he replied, rubbing his arms for effect.

"You traveling with those other two?"

"Depends," Sammy replied.

"Tall, decent-looking guy, and a short crazy-looking one?"

Sammy looked around, expecting to see them sitting in a corner, but none of the faces matched.

"You mean Drake and Jimmy? Are they here already? Wow!"

The woman kept cleaning the counter.

"Well, if you wouldn't mind pointing me in the right direction," Sammy said. He had no intention of having them see him, but he needed to know where they were in order to avoid them.

"They went to Trixie's. She's across the road, two buildings down. I think it's a red or brown building." The woman walked to the end of the counter, switched on a vacuum bot, and went over to a sleeping man.

"Thank you, really appreciate it!" Sammy said, and left her to convince the drunks to go home.

Snow was lazily drifting down to the ground, and Sammy pulled his jacket tighter around his body. He crossed the empty street and went looking for a red or brown building. Looking at the first building, he realized they were all some version of faded red or brown. He didn't know which direction Trixie's building was, so he turned right and walked over to the second building. It appeared to be a hydro repair shop, so he went back to the start and two buildings to the left.

The unit was red or brown, depending on the view, and had no trading name on it. Sammy thought it looked more like a housing unit than a hotel. A side alley led to a small parking lot, and sitting there, all by itself, was the hydro off-roader Drake and Something stole right in front of him. They had to be in that building.

Sammy scanned the area. Surrounding the parking space, Sammy saw housing units and maybe a commercial building or two. One unit looked more run down than the others, and Sammy tried his luck. He doubted very much that there were any active security forces in a small isolated place like this, so he grabbed a stone and smashed in a window. He immediately crouched down in the shadows, and sat waiting for a few minutes, making sure no alarm got triggered or anyone heard him. Deciding the coast was clear, he jumped through the window. The building seemed to be unoccupied and empty. It wasn't warm or comfortable, but at least it was dry and better than being outside.

Sammy found some trash lying around, made himself as comfortable as he could, and shivered himself to sleep.

| thirty-two |

The Penta security offices were always busy with officers walking around, announcements blaring over the PA system, and Data Display Units everywhere showing too much information.

All the sounds and commotion was only background noise to the officer examining the small explosive device lying on their desk. The tiny object that had blown up so many vehicles and set off a small intersectoral war.

Looking up at the Data Display Unit in front of them, the only lead in the entire case stared back at them. The only person who might have an answer. The person they should have called a long time ago, but couldn't.

Now time was running out, and pressure from above forced their hand.

It was time for Lt. Lily Wells to call Benjamin Drake.

***

Drake woke up, and for a second, he thought he was back in New Franco. The room was tiny, smelled, and needed a good clean. But the walls were a different color, and the longer he lay awake, the more he saw the differences. One of them being an absent Jimmy.

"Jimmy?" Drake yelled out, not sure if there were any more rooms for Jimmy to hide in.

"Jimmy, you here, buddy?" No answer.

Drake got up, grabbed his pants and jacket, and explored the small apartment. Which turned out to be a room with a bathroom. Jimmy must have gone to his own room last night. Drake's head had been killing him last night after the misunderstanding, so he'd swallowed a handful of painkillers. After that, it was anyone's guess how he got to the room or what happened to Jimmy.

He opened the door and stepped into a hallway. He appeared to be in a housing complex. Doors lined the hallway on both sides.

"Jimmy?" he yelled again.

A door down the hall opened up, and Jimmy staggered out, half dressed.

"Hey, partner!" He sounded very chirpy.

"Hey. Got your own room—" Drake stopped short as Trixie's head popped out from the same room Jimmy had just left.

"We'll make it half price." She winked, and disappeared.

"Anything you'd like to share, Jimmy?"

Drake immediately regretted asking, as Jimmy did indeed, have something to share. In the most graphic detail. When he finally stopped, Drake felt like drinking some more pain killers to black out again.

"And you?" Jimmy asked.

"I passed out, thankfully, and didn't have to work for my room."

"Time to go?" Jimmy pressed on.

"Think so, buddy. You said your goodbyes to your girlfriend?"

"Yup, we good," Jimmy said, smiling, and started for the exit.

Drake followed him out to the black off-roader, waiting outside.

"Hang on. I'll be right back," Jimmy said and ran down the street.

Drake was in no rush, his head still tender. He entered the hydro and reclined the seat. Who knew how long Jimmy would take?

He closed his eyes. His head was better, but not great. Maybe he'd let Jimmy take the first shift today.

Three circles danced in the darkness. They found each other and merged into a bigger circle, which grew to reveal a face. A face he hadn't seen in months.

"Hi, Drake," Lt. Lily Wells greeted him.

***

Drake's eyes shot open. The light hurt his eyes, and his headache flared up again. All the moisture in his mouth evaporated, and his heart worked harder than needed.

"Hey."

The last time Drake had seen Lt. Wells was in the Zuma warehouse, and she'd had a pulse gun pointed at him. Then she shot him.

"Hi, Drake." She smiled at him.

They sat there, looking at each other, no one sure what the next step was.

"How have you—" they started at the same time.

"You go," Drake said.

"Judging by your face, you had a rough night?"

"You know me." Drake heard the words, but felt unconnected to them.

"Why is this so awkward?" Lt. Wells laughed.

Drake had no answer, nor a guard for his mouth. "Because you just disappeared."

Now it was really awkward.

Lt. Wells' smile disappeared, and her face lost some of its softness.

"Sorry about that. The case was not closed at that point, and I had to keep working."

Drake knew he just screwed up. "No, I'm sorry, I was just—"

"We can talk about it later. This is not a social call, Drake." He remembered this tone.

"That's a shame," Drake said. "Unfortunately, I'm not carrying any illegal cargo at the moment, nor am I harboring a fugitive. That I know of. Shit, am I?"

A hundred scenarios ran through Drake's mind, none of them any good.

"Do you know what this is?" Lt. Wells asked. She held up the tiny explosive device.

Delgado. Fuck. He knew they were going to get screwed over working for him. The allure of fast money and getting back to hauling was too great, and now he was on the run again. Idiot.

"Um, maybe?" Drake lied.

"Drake, if you do, you need to tell me. Please."

"I haven't heard from you since you shot me, and now you want me to do what exactly?"

Drake felt a sudden burst of anger. He watched Lily Wells gather her thoughts.

"All I can say is that I'm on a case, and your name, with Jimmy's, came up."

"Lily, if I tell you what I know, I might get into trouble."

Lt. Wells took her time again, not rushing her words. Drake wondered how people did that.

"I'm sorry I haven't contacted you, Drake, but you're smart enough to know that a security officer and someone like yourself do not make an excellent combination."

Drake hated her for talking so rationally.

"Someone like me? You mean a hauler?"

"Drake, when I met you, you were on the run. And right now, you are a suspect in a case. Again."

"Wow, what? How did we go from 'your name popped up' to 'suspect?'"

Three circles, smaller than the previous ones, were dancing in Drake's periphery. Another incoming call. He glanced at his HIC.

Lucy Hughes.

"I got to go, Lily. I'll call you later." He hung up.

Drake took a deep breath and swiped straight into the next call.

"Hey, Lucy."

"Good morning, Drake. Is that a new hydro?" Lucy was as warm and welcoming as always.

"Yes, sort of. It's a loaner," Drake replied.

"I see. I just thought to check in and make sure you guys were still doing fine. Just concerned, not micro managing." She laughed reassuringly.

Jimmy came running around a corner, his breath visible in the cold.

"It's fine. We're fine. Spent the night in," Drake tried to remember the town's name, "Spatsel."

"Glad to hear. I'll assume the black eye is just part of the job then, right?"

He felt like an idiot. Of course she would see the eye and the rest of the bruises. "We are fine, Lucy, I promise. It's not my first beating and doubt it will be my last."

"Well, it seems that you have things under control, albeit in your own way. I'm glad it's you bringing Bob back, Drake."

Drake had conflicting feelings about it, but somehow managed not to share it.

"If anything substantial comes up, we'll contact you, I promise."

"Thanks, Drake."

"Bye, Lucy."

Drake leaned back in his seat and watched Jimmy jump on the hood and squat down.

| thirty-three |

Sammy Sanders saw Jimmy jump on the hood of the off-roader. He squatted down and shook something vigorously. Sammy didn't have the best angle, and things didn't look too good from his point of view. He forced himself to keep watching, but squinted his eyes as much as he could.

"You sick, little man," he whispered through gritted teeth.

Jimmy swapped positions, allowing Sammy to see more.

Sammy let out a sigh of relief. Squatting on the hood of the hydro, Jimmy was spray-painting over some logo or insignia. Sammy couldn't make out what it was. Besides, it was disappearing in front of his eyes.

Jimmy jumped down from the hydro and admired his handiwork. Seemingly pleased, he climbed into the off-roader. Sammy could make out another shape in the cabin and assumed it to be Drake. The hydro's lights went on, and it quietly rolled down the street.

Sammy entered the details of Drake's new vehicle into his hydro's DDU, swiped his HIC, activated a call on his ARP, and selected Autodrive, giving the instructions to follow the off-roader.

Sammy's call connected.

"Leaving Spatsel now. They seem to be on the trail." Sammy jumped straight into the conversation.

"Good. Keep your distance, and report back if anything changes, or tonight at the latest."

Sammy was about to ask about the possibility of some more credits to try a secure a better vehicle, but the call ended.

He had no chance to keep up with Drake and Something in his current vehicle, but he also didn't have the means to buy a replacement. He remembered the sad cases asleep at the bar last night. The bartender did not strike him as the sympathetic type, and Sammy was doubtful if she would have made sure they arrived home safely. He decided to head back to the bar, on foot, as it was only a few minutes away.

The small town of Spatsel was still asleep, or maybe everyone was hiding from the cold, but no one seemed to be up and about. Sammy didn't pass anyone on his walk to the bar or see any vehicles driving around.

Sitting in the parking lot was a trio of hydro off-roaders, covered with a thin layer of snow. One of them had fogged up windows. A sign that there was a breathing body inside. Sammy couldn't see any tracks leading up to or in front of the hydro, implying it had been sitting there for a while. So he had to assume the person inside had been there a while too. And, being in front of a bar, he had to surmise it was one of the drunks from last night.

Sammy walked up to it and cupped his hands on the window to steal a peak at who was inside. The fog was impenetrable. He tried the handles, but the doors appeared to be locked, as he assumed they would be. Once inside, it would be a breeze for him to hack the DDU, but from outside, it was impossible. He had to find a way in.

Having the owner, or at least an approved operator, of the vehicle nearby would make stealing the hydro so much easier. Sammy focused on this one and did not bother with the other two, which both seemed unoccupied. He tapped on the window, softly at first, but gradually louder. Something moved inside the cabin.

The driver must have been half asleep still, as they found it easier to just open the door instead of finding the right button and rolling down the window. The smell that escaped the cabin confirmed to Sammy that it was indeed one of last night's indulgers.

"What?!" The man leaned out and spat on the ground.

"Hey, buddy, sorry to bother you, but I was just walking past and saw that one of your wheels was missing. Crazy, right?" Sammy was relying on the man's hangover and half-awake state to not engage in a logical exchange of words, but hoped for an instinctual reaction. Sammy knew that if someone fucked with his hydro, he would fly off the handle instead of scrutinizing the details.

"What the hell?" The man stumbled out of the hydro and brushed past Sammy.

"Yup, back wheel on the other side." Sammy scanned the area to make sure they were still alone.

The man grumbled something as he moved to the other side of the hydro. The hydro was almost as high as Sammy, and as soon as they rounded the corner, they would be out of sight from the road.

"Huh?" the man said, as he saw the wheel still attached to the hydro.

Sammy had his pulse pistol ready, set on the lowest power, and shot the man between his shoulder blades.

"Sorry," he said as he jumped into the hydro.

The man's HIC was still on, so the hydro's DDU picked it up, and Sammy made quick work of hacking it and transferring permissions to his HIC.

"Good luck, pal." He laughed as he took off, leaving the man face down in the snow.

***

Drake knew that covering the insignia of the Kaos clan would only fool casual inspection and wouldn't do anything to someone scanning the vehicle, but he had to admit it would attract less attention.

Drake waited until they were a few minutes out of town before telling Jimmy about Lt. Wells.

"So, guess who called me earlier?"

Jimmy closed one eye as he pondered it. "Bob Turner."

Drake couldn't stop his jaw from dropping.

"Why would I wait till now to tell you if I had a call from Mr. Turner? Huh?"

Jimmy shrugged it off and seemed to work on an answer again. After a minute, Drake moved things along.

"Lieutenant Wells, Jimmy."

"I was wondering when she would call, ya know," Jimmy answered.

"I mean, yes, me too, but do you know why she called?"

Jimmy's painful thinking face made Drake realize he should stop using questions.

"She is the officer Penta have investigating the exploding hydros case. Which means she spoke to Delgado. Which then also means she knows we transported the parts that made up the explosives."

"Oh shit," Jimmy said.

"Yep," Drake replied.

"Did she sound angry?" Jimmy asked.

"What?"

"She can be scary, ya know?"

Jimmy wasn't wrong.

"No, but she sounded serious. Too serious. Like, 'we're in trouble' serious."

Jimmy grimaced.

The scenery had changed from occasional snow spots, to a light dusting of snow, to thick snow blanketing everything. The road looked like a channel cut into the snow, and Drake hoped the conditions wouldn't deteriorate too much further.

"And, I have to call her back. Soon," Drake said.

***

Lt. Lily Wells' elbows supported all the weight of her head, lying in her hands. Her fingers gripped her hair to prevent it from slipping forward. It also hurt a bit, which helped her stay in the moment.

For months she'd been working herself to death, trying to put the Mars episode behind her, and getting stuck in her work. She preferred it this way. Working was life for her. She took on every case she could and knew she would be up for a promotion soon. The slight hiccup that almost derailed her career was long forgotten.

She even convinced herself that she'd forgotten about Benjamin Drake.

And now his picture was back on her DDU. Stupid smirk and all.

It took her an hour to gather enough courage to contact him. She heard he was running parcels in New Franco and assumed he was still in town. For a split second, she entertained the idea of an actual meeting, but decided against it. A call would have to do. She caught herself steeling a glimpse of her reflection, making sure she looked presentable, just as she swiped her HIC. Was her heart beating faster?

And then disaster. Within a few sentences, she'd reverted to security mode and totally screwed things up. Drake even faked an incoming call so he could escape.

Wells lifted her head and looked at him on her DDU.

The photo was recent. Penta took it when they'd brought him in after Captain Santo occupied Mars to debrief and to clear him of any wrongdoing. He had the smuggest look on his face, like he'd just gotten away with the biggest score, when, in fact, he'd left empty-handed. His stubble was turning into a beard, and his hair looked unkempt.

Lt. Wells knew the photo by heart.

Next to the image of Drake were a few words. Active Case. Person of Interest. Potential Asset.

Underneath it all was a simple command.

Process Bulletin Y/N

All Lt. Wells had to do was press Y and all the Penta security units would receive Drake's file, making him a hunted man. She was running out of time with Delgado, and pressure was mounting from above to get him out of sector fifty-nine. She knew what she had to do.

Lt. Wells took a deep breath and waited for Benjamin Drake to call.

| thirty-four |

The road was getting narrower, and more snow was falling. The off-roader was handling it in stride, but they were not traveling at the same speed anymore. Jimmy was asleep next to Drake, and he figured it was as good a time as any to make the call.

"Hey, Lily," Drake said when the call connected.

It didn't surprise Drake to see she was still in her office.

"Drake! I'm so glad you called." Drake believed her.

"Sorry about that last call. I guess we have some catching up to do."

"We do, but—" Wells looked concerned.

"Delgado," Drake helped her out.

"Drake, he blew up ten hydros outside of his sector. An intercity war is about to erupt. Penta can't turn a blind eye. And I'm the one they've got looking."

"I'm not going to play dumb, although it's easy for me. I ran parcels for him, all over New Franco. I guess that's how you connected me to this."

"Yes, and thanks for being so honest, Drake. Once I dug into Delgado, you and Jimmy came up pretty quick."

Drake knew they had already traveled more than halfway to Wallen. If Penta launched a manhunt now, they should be able to outrun them and reach mainland Shangcorp before Penta reached them.

"Lily, we figured out, after the explosions happened, what we had carried. We never knew that he was going to blow up those hydros." Drake left out Sammy's blackmailing them for now.

"Can you please come in and allow me to question you formally? Maybe you can shed some more light on this?"

Lt. Wells was still in soft mode, and Drake feared flipping the switch.

"We're not exactly in New Franco anymore," he said.

"Oh." Lt. Wells looked surprised.

"Yeah, the parcel thing wasn't really paying the bills, so we became bounty hunters."

"You what?"

Drake could kick himself for saying it, but it was less complicated.

"Yep, and we're after Mr. Turner, no less."

"Uh, wow, okay." Lt. Wells clearly needed a minute. "So where are you?"

Now Drake needed a minute.

If he told her, she would use all her Penta power and intercept them within hours. If he learned anything about Lily Wells, it was that the job always came first. Always. So the moment she had a lock on them, she would swoop. Even it turned out she really just wanted to ask some questions, it would still slow them down considerably.

Lying to her would have future consequences that he didn't even want to consider.

"Drake, you are connected to multiple hydro explosions and deaths. You need to cooperate, for your own good. Please come back to New Franco."

He knew she was right.

"Sorry, Lily. I promise I'll call you back," Drake said, and hung up.

***

Lt. Wells sat for a few seconds and then jumped straight on her DDU. She brought up and signed all the forms she needed. She knew it would take hours, even a day or two, to get the relevant authorizations, so she got up and went straight to the departments. Working in the headquarters had its perks.

First stop was the Vehicle and Transport department. Wells had to book a hydro out of the vehicle pool. She had already done the forms, but a big organization like Penta moved slowly, so she had to speed things up a bit.

The woman behind the counter looked around Wells' age, but double her size. She also didn't seem in a rush to do anything quickly. As Wells entered, she gave her a slow sideways glance, accompanied by a loud breath. *More work.*

"Hey," Lt. Wells said, as friendly as possible, but just shy of patronizing.

"How can I help?" said the woman. The tone contradicted her words.

"Sorry to bother you. I'm sure you've got your hands full, but I need a long-term vehicle. I have already submitted the forms." Wells smiled, but again, kept it shy of being needy.

The woman gave her one last look and turned back to her DDU.

"Name?"

"Lieutenant Lily Wells."

The woman gave her another look before typing away on her DDU. Wells' patience with her glares and huffing was running out, and she had to bite her tongue every time she got a look.

"Request number?"

Wells realized she didn't write it down. Normally she wouldn't need it, as the request would get processed without her presence. But not today.

"Sorry, I didn't think to note it down when—"

"Of course you didn't." The woman spared her a look, but shook her head.

How about you just book out the fucking hydro so I can rid this town of a warlord?

"Sorry."

Wells' arm vibrated. She swiped to see the confirmation of the hydro she booked. The woman was still typing, but seeing that Wells received her booking, she apparently moved on to a new job.

"Thank you," Wells said, as she left with no reply or acknowledgement of existing.

Next stop was all the way down to the basement where the vehicle pool was. Wells requested an Ibex, a small, two-seater hydro used mainly for reconnaissance work. It was an all-wheel drive hydro, light, and would get her anywhere she needed to be, albeit not in comfort. She also made sure it was an unmarked vehicle, as to ensure she didn't attract any unnecessary attention.

The officer recognized Wells immediately, and within five minutes, she was ready to go. She parked the Ibex in an open spot and went back upstairs again. This time, to the armory. She didn't expect she would need any heavy firing power, but didn't want to be left wanting.

Being a regular in the armory helped, as her weapons were already waiting for her when she arrived. A quick inappropriate joke to say thanks, and she was off.

The last stop was at her apartment to pick up an overnight bag, and she was ready to go.

If only she knew where to.

***

"Glad you joined us," Drake said to a waking Jimmy.

Jimmy stretched out, yawned big enough for Drake to see his molars, and wiped the residual drool off his chin.

"Hey, partner. How's the driving going?"

The driving was going smoothly, although at an ever-decreasing speed. The road was barely visible, and Drake relied more on the green line imposed on it than what he could make out to be the road.

"Bit slow, but good, buddy," Drake replied. "So, I spoke to Lieutenant Wells again."

"Cool. How's she doing?"

"Jimmy, she's on the point of hunting us down, again so the call was not so much about her wellbeing."

Usually Jimmy would get all sullen when Drake was mean to him, but the longer they were together, the more he brushed it off.

"Ah, she's most likely okay, ya know. She seems the type to move on quickly."

Drake couldn't tell if Jimmy was being sincere or having a go at him.

"Anyway, she connected us to Delgado and wants us to go in for questioning."

"When?"

How was it possible for Jimmy to always focus on the opposite thing he wanted him to?

"I guess right now. If we had to go back to New Franco, and then wait for them to finish their investigation, it could be weeks before we are back on the road again."

"So what did you tell her?"

"Nothing. I said I would call her back."

Jimmy sat pondering for a while.

"You sure you're not juggling too many balls?"

Drake had to admit that he had been wondering the same thing.

| thirty-five |

Sammy struggled to keep up. He wasn't too used to these conditions, and he had to maintain a gap big enough to stay invisible. It was hard work, but all he had to do was focus on the big pay day lying ahead, and he found himself back on track.

His radar's alarm went off, and he instinctively slowed down, assuming he'd gotten too close to Jimmy and Drake. A glance at the screen, however, showed the blip to be behind him. It had been a while since any traffic showed up on his radar, and he marked it to have the hydro's DDU keep tabs on it. Just to be safe.

Five minutes later, the alarm went off again. The object had moved closer. Sammy thought he was doing a respectable speed, but the other vehicle was catching him quickly. It was still a decent distance behind him, so he decided to just monitor it for now.

Another five minutes passed before the alarm went off again. The vehicle was now entering visibility territory, and he looked at his rearview monitor to see if there was a visual yet. It was snowing, which made the visibility poor, and although he couldn't see it, he knew it was there.

When the alarm went off again, he didn't even bother to look at the screen or the rearview monitor. He knew the vehicle had to be close behind him. What he had to decide was to stop and let it pass, or keep going. He knew bandits roamed this area, and if he stopped, it might be the last thing he ever did. But the speed it was catching up meant they would be all over him in seconds anyway.

Sammy decided to ride it out and see what happened.

A second before the impact, multiple warnings and alarms went off, telling him about the imminent crash. He was driving at his limit, and the snow banks didn't allow any sudden maneuvers. He was bracing for the impact, waiting for it to happen. The screen filled with an update on all the systems, and in particular the damaged ones. It was mostly yellows and greens, with only one or two reds, which meant he could go on. But what was the point? They had him. They would keep bumping him until his hydro shut down or flipped over. So Sammy stopped, pulled over as much as he could, and got out to face them.

He expected the other hydro to slam into him when he stopped, but it stopped well short. Sammy immediately felt the cold cut through his clothes. He leaned back into his hydro and grabbed his jacket.

"Hello, friend," someone said right next to him, making him jump.

Sammy finished putting his jacket on whilst observing the three men that encircled him. They all looked the same to him—big, bearded, and smiling. None of them seemed to have any weapons on them. Two of them he didn't recognize. One he did.

"Sorry, man, but I needed a hydro, and you didn't seem to be using yours."

The man Sammy had shot in the back and left face down in the snow stepped closer to him, their faces almost touching. When he breathed, a cloud enveloped Sammy.

"Well, I need it now, so if it's okay with you, I'll just take it back."

"Sure, but maybe we can make a deal?"

The man stepped forward, his warm breath spilling out on Sammy. It reeked of beer and regurgitated white box meals.

"I don't think so. You left me in the snow, dickhead. Could've died too. Luckily, my friends saw me." The other two nodded in agreement.

"I am on the trail of a very lucrative bounty." Sammy stumbled backwards, and the man followed him.

"So what?"

"I am more than happy to negotiate the rental of your hydro." Sammy kept moving backwards, parting the two men behind him.

"At a very generous rate, of course." Sammy slowly made his way past them until all three were now in front of him.

"How generous?" the man asked.

"Let's just say—"

A crackle cut through the air as one of the other two men fell to the ground, blood flowing from his shoulder. Both men snapped their heads back to Sammy, who aimed his pulse gun at the man standing right in front of him.

"Don't worry, he'll be fine," Sammy said. "So how about you take your friends and go home, before I shoot everyone, okay?"

Sammy wished they would hurry. The cold had penetrated through all his clothing, and his feet were hurting from the freezing temperature. If they didn't move soon, he'd have to shoot them just to avoid frostbite.

"You are making a gigantic mistake. Either shoot us now, or give my hydro back." The men did not go or help their bleeding friend.

"Your call, buddy." Sammy lifted the pulse gun slightly to emphasize its presence. The cold and adrenaline was making his hand shake, and he hoped they couldn't see it.

Sammy had the feeling that more people were about to get shot.

The man stood his ground.

"I think Chuck is hurt, man," the man behind said.

"I'm not leaving without my hydro."

Sammy felt his hand tremble more.

"I'll make it easy for you. I count to three, then I shoot. Understand?"

No one moved.

"Fuck you."

"One ..."

"I ain't leaving."

"Two ..."

The man spat on the ground.

"Three."

A crackle and a thud.

"Jesus, let's just go!" The second man was lying on the ground, clutching his shoulder that now had the same wound to it as Chuck's.

Sammy's toes were burning from the cold. Snot kept running out of his nose, and his eyes were watery. The adrenaline made his heart race and head spin. He wanted nothing more than to get the fuck out of there, but he forced himself to hold his ground.

"Keep the fucking hydro, dead man."

The guy manhandled his friends back into their waiting hydro and left. It didn't take long for their lights to disappear in the falling snow, and Sammy jumped back into the hydro, setting the climate control to maximum heat and waiting for his body to stop shaking.

Warmth slowly crept back into his bones, but with the warmth didn't stop him from shaking.

The hunter was now the hunted.

∗∗∗

"The way I see it, you either tell me everything you know, or get ready to be replaced once we let it slip you talked."

Lt. Wells' heart was pumping. Confronting bad guys was a daily routine for her, but it got no easier. Knowing you could die any second, being on high alert, using every sense in your body. It was draining.

But it also made her feel alive.

She made a big show of taking a tactical team with her and positioning them at every entrance. Anyone who showed the slightest bit of attitude went to the ground. Hell, anyone who looked at them was a target. These weren't good people, and she had no issue treating them as such. She had the team ready and waited for Delgado to leave his warehouse before storming into the building.

"So, we already know it was Delgado who blew up those hydros, we're just tying up some loose ends and seeing how we want to proceed with the running of sector fifty-nine."

Wells looked on as Delgado's righthand man, simply known as Deon, sat behind his desk, seemingly unimpressed with all her bravado. You didn't become the second in charge of a notorious sector crime boss by scaring easily. She'd have to do much better than this.

Lt. Wells turned and walked out the door, onto the walkway that overlooked the warehouse. Crates and unmarked boxes filled the floor. The warehouse was almost filled to capacity. Business seemed to be flourishing. She leaned on the railing and turned her back toward Deon's office, taking in the scene below her.

"Quite the haul you have here. What is it? DDUs? Hydro parts? Don't tell me it's pulse weapons?" She turned to face him through the open door. "Must be worth a lot of credits."

Deon could just as well have been a mannequin. The man made no movements at all.

Besides their skill and weapons, the attribute Wells loved the most about the tactical units was their ability to follow orders. No questions.

"All ARPs off," she commanded.

As one, they all obliged and swiped their HICs to disengage any recordings of what was about to happen. No questions.

"This is your only chance," Wells said.

Deon took a deep breath, but didn't answer.

Wells calmly took a grenade from her hip, pulled the pin, and tossed it over her shoulder. Deon's eyes widened as he watched it tumble through the air before disappearing. A loud bang and a heat wave filled the office.

Now it was Wells' turn to be emotionless.

"I can toss grenades all day, or you can tell me what I need to hear before you allow your boss's building to burn to the ground."

"You just lost your job, little girl." A sheen of sweat formed on Deon's forehead.

Wells plucked another grenade and flipped it over her shoulder. Another bang and more heat followed.

"It's lieutenant." She could see a shift in his eyes now.

"I can assure you, I'm a much better ally than enemy, lieutenant."

"I have enough allies." Wells palmed another grenade.

"I don't—" Deon stopped as Wells grabbed the pin. "Wait! God damnit. Can you stop with this charade? I get it. You're the top dog. You are calling the shots. Okay. Just stop throwing fucking grenades."

Wells slowly hung the grenade back on her belt.

Deon looked angry and defeated. Just the way Wells wanted him to look.

"Okay, okay. Let me put out these fires and I'll tell you who you are really looking for."

| thirty-six |

The tiny roadside diner was a heaven sent to Drake. He was used to sitting in his Hydrostar for hours, but that was on beautiful, flat, wide highways. Driving the off-roader on the snowy roads took all his concentration, and he felt drained. So when the sign popped up on his screen that the last stop for hydrogen and food was coming up, he welcomed it.

The sign outside the eatery claimed it to be the last of its kind before reaching Wallen, another thousand kilometers north. There had been no mention on the bandit network containing their names or descriptions, and Drake felt confident that they were traveling in safety. Stopping now would only do them good.

"So, what are you going to do with Turner when we get him?" Jimmy asked through a mouthful of chewed up white box meal.

Drake wished he knew. He hadn't been thinking about it since they hit the road, but he knew he had to come up with some sort of plan soon.

"I'm not sure, Jimmy," he replied.

They both sat in silence for a while.

"You know what I reckon?" Jimmy asked.

Drake knew this would be brilliant or idiotic. There was no middle ground with Jimmy.

"What?"

"I think we catch him and give him to your girlfriend."

"She's not—"

"We claim the bounty, and forget about Lucy, Delgado, and Sammy. What are they gonna do, ya know?"

Drake wasn't sure which category this one fell into.

"If we hand him over and get the bounty, we'll have to pay Delgado, pay Sammy, and stab Lucy in the back. We'll come out with no credits and nothing to go back to."

"So what's your plan then?"

Drake took another bite of his meal, but the answer wasn't there.

The room was tiny, with only four tables and their chairs in it. An elderly woman sat behind a small counter, sleeping, not having much to do, apparently. The diner was self serve, with the white boxes stored next to a heating unit next to the sleeping lady. The opposite wall contained a DDU that displayed local businesses and attractions. Mostly based in Spatsel or Wallen.

Drake stared at the screen, zoning out, trying to not think. He knew he had some tough choices to make, but the fatigue and warmth of the diner made him want to shut down.

"Wow, same name as the list," Jimmy said.

Drake turned to face him.

"What was that?"

Jimmy pointed to the DDU on the wall.

"Just keep watching; it will pop up again," he said.

Drake watched as small business and attractions from Spatsel and Wallen tried to sell their goods. People inviting you to stay at their units. Homemade snow jackets. Hydro repairs. Boats for hire.

"There!" Jimmy yelled.

Drake looked at the ad on the screen.

Unique way to see the Wallen coast line.

See where the world ends!

Below it was a picture of a captain standing on a jetty with a bunch of moored boats behind him. Next to him was a ticket booth of sorts, with the name Major Swanson on it.

It took Drake much longer than it did Jimmy to remember the name from the list they'd received in Porterville.

"Shit—" Drake caught up.

"Funny, ya know? It's the same name as one guy on that list."

Drake felt relieved that he was still slightly ahead of Jimmy.

"No, that's it. It's the name of the boat! Mr. Turner must have used it to get across to Shangcorp territory."

"Ah." Jimmy slowly nodded.

"Eat up, buddy, we have a boat to catch."

***

The circles bounced around, avoiding each other, and Lt. Lily Wells doubted they would merge. She gave it a few more seconds and placed her finger on her HIC to swipe and disconnect. Five more seconds, she decided. The circles merged, and Lt. Wells quickly exhaled her breath that she only now realized she was holding.

"Hey," Drake said when the call connected.

He was sitting in an eatery somewhere, and Wells wished he would move around so she could try to get a clue where he was.

"Hi, Drake. Glad you answered."

"Sorry, I saw it was you and had to freshen up." He smiled.

"You should have taken longer, then." Wells had forgotten how easy it was to talk to him. "This is another official call, Drake."

"I figured. Sorry I haven't called back yet. I don't even have an excuse."

"That's okay, Drake, but we need to talk about you and Delgado and what happened."

Wells scanned the area behind Drake, but saw nothing to help her.

"Trying to figure out where we are, huh?"

Wells snickered. "Yes, sorry, I have to. You need to tell me what happened and where you are. Right now, it's just me asking, but it might not stay that way for too long."

Drake took a deep breath.

"We are south of a place called Wallen."

The name held no significance to her, so Wells noted it down to look up later. "Where the hell is that?" she asked.

"North. As far north as you can imagine. If you really wanted to, you can be here in a day or so. Or use some secret Penta flying machine and be here before we finish our meals."

"I could. Or you can tell me what's going on and save me the time."

"I guess."

"Drake, I'm serious. This, is serious."

"I know, and the trouble I might be in could also be serious. So, what's the deal?"

Lt. Wells took a moment to gather her thoughts.

"Hector Delgado is trying to expand his empire. His first step was to eliminate high-ranking members of neighboring sectors as a show of force. Basically, a 'join me or fight me' case. It's no secret that Penta tolerates him and even helps him from time to time, but he has gotten too ambitious for his own good. The hydro explosions tipped the scales."

"Okay, so shoot him."

"They kicked the idea around, but it would cause more trouble than good. Penta wants to make an example out of him, to warn others like him."

"You mean other crime lords who operate under Penta's approval?"

"Drake, I'm not here to defend Penta's policies. I'm here to make sure you don't go down for this."

"Oh, I thought you needed me to help bring Delgado down."

Wells took a second, then said, "Where did you pick the explosions up from?"

"Lily, I want to help you, I really do, but I would endanger someone else if I say anything."

"You mean Lucy Hughes?"

Drake's silence was all the confirmation she needed.

| thirty-seven |

"We have a problem," Sammy said the instant the call connected.

After his showdown in the snow, Sammy had risked every-thing and pushed harder than before to catch up to Drake and Something. Luckily for him, there weren't too many side roads or options, and he was quite confident that he was on the right track.

"I have problems of my own. Can you deal with it?"

Sammy looked at his telemetry. There was still no sign of Drake's hydro, but he knew it would pop up soon.

"Yes, I think. I don't know. A couple of bandits are after me. I scared them off for now, but they might be back."

"Are you still on the trail?"

Sammy glanced at the quiet DDU screen. "Yes, of course. I just wanted to keep you updated, like you said."

"And you have. Let me know if anything changes."

The connection went dead.

"Fuck," Sammy muttered.

He did not know what he expected out of the call, but a little support would have been nice.

Wind pushed more snow onto the road, and Sammy feared he would lose more time and distance from Drake. It was not the case.

A faint ping emanated from the DDU.

"Oh, hello boys." Sammy smiled as the ping grew louder.

***

"Yes, Lucy, but how—"

Drake shouldn't have been surprised that Lt. Wells already had all the bases covered, but hearing Lucy's name caught him by surprise.

"Drake, I'm good at my job. I am going to take Delgado down. And no matter what I do, your name will come up. I can't prevent that. The best would be for you to come back and cooperate so I can keep you safe."

If she already knew about Lucy Hughes, it would only be a matter of time before she found out that she'd contracted them to find Bob Turner, a man wanted by Penta. There was no likely scenario where Wells would not grab the opportunity to bring Bob Turner in as well.

"I don't think she knew what was in the parcels," Drake tried.

The look on Lt. Wells' face changed, and Drake feared the switch was about to be flipped.

"Drake, please do not underestimate me or patronize me." Her look emphasized her words.

Drake realized it wasn't Lucy he was trying to protect. He didn't want anyone else getting to Mr. Turner before him. He didn't know why, but he needed to get him first. Lt. Wells would find out the truth, but he needed to get into Shangcorp as soon as possible, and out of Penta's reach.

"I don't think I can help you, Lily. I'm sorry."

"Drake, do not do this. You are making a mistake," Lt. Wells pleaded.

"I hope not," Drake said, and disconnected.

***

Jimmy bit his bottom lip and raised his eyebrows.

"Dude, you are in so much—"

He didn't finish, and he didn't need to. Drake knew it.

"I need to get to Mr. Turner before anyone else, Jimmy. Okay?"

Jimmy nodded.

"Okay, let's get out of here. Time is not our friend anymore."

Drake and Jimmy walked by the sleeping lady and put their heavy jackets on before braving the cold outside. The wind was howling, and the cold found every bit of exposed skin as they shuffled as quick as they could to the hydro.

Drake had it up and running in record time, making sure the climate control was making the cabin as warm as it could. As the temperature increased, they both wrestled out of their thick jackets. Drake ran all the pre-checks, and Jimmy made sure the DDU was up to date and pointing them in the right direction.

Satisfied everything was in order and seeing the green line, Drake maneuvered out of the parking lot and got them back on track.

They drove in silence for a few minutes, the green line guiding Drake, and Jimmy immersed in his HIC.

"Uh oh," Jimmy said.

Drake wondered what celebrity gossip had Jimmy upset.

"What, buddy?"

Jimmy leaned forward and typed something into the hydro's DDU. A message thread appeared on the screen for Drake to see. He quickly engaged Autodrive and read the thread. He reread it and turned to Jimmy.

"Fucking Sammy."

"Why would they think we are with him, ya know?" Jimmy asked.

"I guess two groups of strangers arriving shortly after each other, both stealing hydros. I can see how they think we are connected. Also, knowing Sammy, he most likely told everyone in Spatsel we were working together."

Drake looked at the three images on the screen. They were fuzzy and low quality, but anyone who knew Drake, Jimmy, or Sammy Sanders would easily identify them. The thread contained their descriptions, their general travel direction, their affinity to steal hydros, and a bounty for the three apparent accomplices.

The bandits were about to come out and play.

| thirty-eight |

Lt. Lily Wells had a decision to make. She had already packed and was ready to go after Jimmy and Drake, but knew word would get out to Lucy Hughes that she had visited the warehouse of Hector Delgado and could be a flight risk. Wells didn't know how much truth was in Deon's story that Lucy was behind it all, but she couldn't neglect to follow up on such a lead. Everything about his story told her he was trying to buy time and send her on a wild goose chase. But if there was even the smallest truth in there ...

Wells struggled with her decision for a while longer, then made up her mind, got in her hydro, and drove as quick as she could.

She got to Lucy Hughes's house in minutes.

The place didn't look at all how Wells had imagined. It was in a rundown area, and fit in perfectly. It needed so much work, it would have been easier to demolish it than fix it.

Wells went up to the DDU mounted next to the door and announced herself.

A minute passed, and the door opened.

"Hi, is there a problem?" an ageless woman asked.

"I'm Lieutenant Wells from Penta security, and I'm looking for Lucy Hughes, whose last known address is this unit."

The woman smiled warmly at Wells.

"Oh, well, you've found the right place then. I'm Lucy Hughes."

Lt. Wells had a sudden urge to go throw some more grenades at Deon. This smelled like a distraction.

"I won't take up much of your time. I just have a few questions."

Lucy Hughes kept smiling her warm smile, and Wells' ARP showed no signs of increased blood pressure, heart rate, or body temperature for Lucy Hughes.

"Fire away," Lucy said, still standing in the doorway.

"Would you mind if we did this inside?"

Lt. Wells thought she saw a slight irritation in Lucy's expression, but she stepped aside and waved her in.

The inside of the house was better than the outside, but not by much. The hall was tiny, with a couple of doors leading it off. Lucy opened one, and they stepped into a small room. Lucy pointed to a well-worn in chair for Wells to sit in. Wells accepted and walked on the threadbare carpet to it, noticing the general state of the room and its furniture. It was all clean, looked after, but in need of replacement.

"So, what is this all about, then?" Lucy Hughes asked once Wells seemed settled.

"As I said before, I work for Penta Security and your name came up in a routine investigation." Wells stopped there and monitored Lucy's bio-telemetry. Everything showed her to be relaxed.

"A few days ago," Wells continued, "a couple of hydros got blown up near the fifty-nine and surrounding sectors."

Lucy Hughes was as calm as could be. Maybe a bit too calm.

"When we interrogated our prime suspect, they named you as a business partner."

Most people would show some sign of stress, being named in an investigation, but Lucy Hughes stayed as calm as the moment she opened the door.

"Our prime suspect, at the moment, is Hector Delgado." Bingo. A tiny spike in heart rate and a slight drop in blood pressure.

"Oh dear," Lucy said.

"Do you know this man, Hector Delgado?"

Lucy looked nervous for the first time.

"Yes, but lieutenant, I assure you, I do not know how I could be of any help."

"What is your relationship with Delgado?"

Lucy shifted in her chair and got up. Wells slipped her hand discreetly to her pulse pistol.

Lucy walked over to a small table that had two brown boxes on them and brought one over. She sat down again and placed the box on her lap, opening it.

Lt. Wells curled her fingers around the pulse pistol's grip.

"I'm afraid you got me, but you might be disappointed," Lucy said as she pulled a green apple from the box. "You see, I trade in fruit, small scale, and with no permits. Just enough to get by, really. Hector Delgado is one of my best customers. I have heard rumors of his, well, you know, escapades, but as you can see,"

Lucy waved at her humble surrounds, "I can't afford to be too choosy as to whom I deal with."

Lt. Lily Wells sat and stared at the gray-haired woman with the warm smile in front of her. Her gut, her most valuable asset, told her Lucy was hiding something, but all the telemetry said differently.

"Have you ever used the services of Benjamin Drake and Jimmy Something to deliver your fruit?"

"Oh yes, indeed. They were quite delightful, especially Drake." Lucy gave Wells a smile she didn't appreciate.

"You said were?"

"Yes, unfortunately they have gone off on some adventure, and informed me to look elsewhere for a delivery service. Pity. They were very reliable."

Lt. Wells knew she was wasting her time here. Everything Lucy Hughes told her fit what Drake had said, and her telemetry backed it up. She'd deal with Deon later.

Wells thanked Hughes for her help and showed herself out.

Back in her hydro, she saw a message on her DDU.

An intercepted bulletin, naming Drake, Something, and Sammy Sanders, awaited her. The bulletin was from some bandit network in the far north, claiming they were hijacking hydros. A bounty of three thousand credits was out on them.

"Idiots," Wells said as she programmed her DDU for Spatsel.

***

Hector Delgado surveyed the burned-out warehouse with a very nervous-looking Deon standing next to him. The damage was extensive, but not insurmountable. They clearly did this to send a message, and not to destroy him.

Delgado turned to Deon.

"I assume they used a blocker and disabled all our cameras?" Delgado asked.

"Yes, sir. Our ARPs too."

"And you are sure it's the same woman?"

"One hundred percent, sir. No doubt," Deon replied.

"I am curious, though. Why did she stop?"

Deon did not scare easily, but a sweat bead formed on his brow and trickled down his face.

"I told her Ms. Hughes was behind it all, sir, just like you told me."

Delgado nodded in approval.

"Good. Make sure this gets cleaned." Delgado marched off to his office.

Lieutenant Wells was really starting to irritate him.

| thirty-nine |

Wallen was only a few hours away, but with the bulletin out, Drake feared they might never reach it. The bounty out on them was pretty small, but out here, he guessed it was enough to get people excited. A quick bounty sounded just like the sort of thing a bandit would be interested in.

Drake had Jimmy monitor the radar and bandit network continuously. If they knew what was coming, they might stand a chance. He also had him send a message on the network to distance themselves from Sammy, but he doubted anyone would pay attention to it.

"How're things looking?" he asked Jimmy, who sat crouched over the off-roader's DDU.

"Nothing on the radar, but it seems Sammy roughed up some locals. Shot two of them. Bounty is now up to five thousand," Jimmy read from the screen.

"Five thousand? What the hell?" Drake said in disgust.

"I know, right?" Jimmy agreed.

"These bandits must be stupid or cheap. Five thousand?"

Jimmy just shook his head.

"I've received bigger fines for punching idiots in the face!" Drake couldn't believe how offended he was at the lowball bounty. "Anything else?"

Jimmy kept scrolling and mouthing words as he read.

"Nah, just lots of excited chatter about the credits. Seems people here think it's quite a lot, ya know," Jimmy said.

"Pfft."

"Most of the messages sound like single people and not groups or gangs, so I think we might be in for some minor scuffles and nothing too organized, ya know?"

Drake wondered how small these interactions would be. They were approaching Wallen at a good rate, which also meant entering more populated areas.

The chances of them getting jumped increased with every turn in the road.

***

Almost halfway to Wallen, and with only a few hours to go, the first bandit appeared. One solitary dipshit standing in the road in front of his snowcycle, pulse pistol drawn.

Drake stopped a hundred meters short of him, well out of his shooting range. The bandit was waving his arms around, but Drake didn't bother to find out what he was saying.

"Jimmy, switch on your thermal scanner and see if he brought friends."

Jimmy obliged, switched on the thermal scanner in his Augmented Retinal Projector, and swiveled his head as he scanned the area.

"It appears this is a solo act," Jimmy replied.

"Great," Drake said, and put the off-roader back into drive. "Hold on!"

The tires spun for a second, but quickly found grip and launched the hydro forward, straight toward the bandit and his snow-cycle. The man was jumping up and down, trying to get them to slow down, and with twenty meters to go, he gave up waving and fired at them. All the shots went wide. He jumped out of the way of the speeding hydro just in time to see it cut his snow-cycle in two.

Leaving the angry bandit behind, Drake looked over to Jimmy, who had his feet on the seat, arms curled around his legs, and face buried.

"All good, buddy. You can come out now." Drake laughed.

"Laugh all you want, but I'm not getting decapitated by some flying debris, ya know," Jimmy defended himself.

"Okay, run a systems check, make sure nothing got decapitated on the hydro, and let's keep going."

Like everything in life, nothing fazed Jimmy for too long, and he was already happily running all the checks needed to make sure they were still operational.

"All good, captain, full speed ahead!"

Drake got the hydro off-roader back up to speed.

"Okay, all eyes needed from here on. That was only the first taste. Next one might not be so easy," Drake said.

Jimmy nodded and got back to observing everything that might give them a heads up.

***

Lt. Wells ran the likely scenarios of the routes Drake would have taken to get to Spatsel, considering variables like the hydro they had and his knowledge of the roads being a hauler. A few places came up, and Wells had to go with her gut, like she always did.

She typed Porterville into the Ibex's DDU and waited for the green line to show the way.

According to her calculations, they most likely would have stopped in a town before heading to Spatsel. Porterville fit all her criteria. She didn't expect to learn too much going there, but felt it an important stop to make. Not only to walk in their shoes, but there was no need to exhaust herself either. She needed to stay sharp.

Drake was correct about her being able to get there in hours if she wanted to. Penta did indeed have flying things, as he called them. Penta called them Eagles. Tiny, two-seater, hydrogen-powered, tilt rotor planes that would get her there in hours. But the bureaucratic wheel turned slowly at Penta, and she would spend more time trying to get one booked out than just drive herself.

The green line sat waiting patiently on the road, and Lt. Wells started following it.

It had been months since she'd ventured outside of New Franco. Her recent work had kept her in the confines of the city, and she looked forward to having a change of scenery. The last time she'd left New Franco on a case was chasing Drake and Jimmy Something. Same as now. Seemed the only thing that got her out of New Franco where those two idiots.

Lt. Wells made herself as comfortable as she could in the small cabin of the Ibex and allowed the green line to pull her forward toward Porterville.

| forty |

Sammy saw the man a second before he jumped in front of the hydro. Something was burning behind him, and it seemed to him the man must have been in an accident. He was about to stop when he saw the pulse pistol, drawn and ready, in the man's hand. Sammy decided best to keep going and hit the guy at full speed, sending him flying through the air.

As he sped away, Sammy zoomed in on his rearview monitor in time to see the body hit the ground.

"Ouch," he said, as he slowed slightly for a sharp left-handed corner.

***

A single ping came over the DDU speaker, and Jimmy jumped into action. He enlarged the radar screen on the windshield in front of Drake and tagged the object so they could track it. Unlike the snow-cycle that was too small to register, this seemed to be a vehicle comparable to the one they were in. It seemed to be stationary, as its position stayed unchanged on the screen as they approached it. It was only a kilometer away and about to appear in their view.

Drake swiped the radar screen to the side to give him better visibility of the road.

"All eyes, Jimmy," Drake said, knowing Jimmy was all over it already.

The radar showed the vehicle to be straight ahead, but neither Drake nor Jimmy saw it.

"Anything?" Drake asked.

"No, but it has to be right there, ya know?" Jimmy sounded confused.

Snow was falling lightly and didn't help the visibility. Drake strained his eyes, listening to the increasing tempo of the radar ping, expecting a hydro or something to appear at any moment.

"We're right on top of it!" Jimmy shouted.

Drake had a look through the side windows, but couldn't see anything, so instead concentrated on the road, keeping up his speed, and trying to not get distracted.

"Jimmy, what the fuck? Talk to me!"

"It's supposed to be right here, ya know!" Jimmy yelled back, frantically scanning all the screens in front of him.

The ping's tempo slowed down, implying the object moving away from them, and suddenly it picked up again.

"Fuck, it's behind us!" Jimmy yelled, and zoomed in on the rearview monitor.

Now, clearly visible, was a hydro off-roader, much like their borrowed one, but in a white paint scheme, making it almost invisible against the snowy backdrop.

"Sneaky fuckers." Drake grinned, admiring their cunning.

"What do we do?" Jimmy asked next to him.

The hydro was matching them, turn for turn, keeping the distance between them constant.

"Make sure they are the only ones following us. Let's keep going for a while and see if they have any friends waiting up ahead," Drake ordered.

For the next three minutes, both hydros held their places, each one doing their best not to hit anything or roll their vehicles. It was a stalemate, but Drake knew something would have to give eventually.

"Jimmy, grab your pulse gun and start shooting. I can't shake them," Drake ordered.

"Huh?"

"Just fucking shoot them!" Drake yelled, almost sliding off the road, the hydro fishtailing for a few meters before Drake regained control again.

Jimmy got his pistol ready and lowered his window. A blast of cold air pushed him back inside.

"I don't know about—"

"Shoot!"

***

Jimmy stuck his head and one arm through the window, using his other arm to grab on and keep him steady. The icy wind felt like someone trying to scrape all the skin off his neck with a blunt knife. He aimed at the hydro behind them, but the smallest movement from Drake would send his arm flying about.

"Keep it steady!" Jimmy yelled back at Drake.

It seemed to have worked, and Jimmy found the hydro in his sights. A squeeze of the trigger, followed by an electric crackle, sent a pulse cartridge flying toward the off-roader behind them.

As Jimmy pulled the trigger, the hydro behind them tried to avoid the impact and slid sideways. The pulse cartridge made impact, and the hydro steadied itself again. A long gash was now visible on its side, but the damage seemed only cosmetic.

Jimmy's neck was on fire, and he did his best to pull his collar up. He achieved some success and focused on the hydro again. It fell back slightly after the first shot, but it had caught up to them again.

Jimmy acquired the vehicle in his sights and sent another pulse cartridge their way. This time it hit the windshield, and it exploded into thousands of fragments.

"Bullseye!" Jimmy hollered. Drake yelled something from inside the cabin as well, but the wind drowned him out.

The hydro fell back again, and Jimmy assumed it was over.

"I think we got 'em," Jimmy said as he slid back into his seat and closed the window.

"What happened?" Drake asked.

"Shot the windshield, and they gave up. Almost froze to death, ya know?"

Jimmy sat shivering next to Drake, waiting for approval, but Drake only had eyes for the road.

"Monitor the back and the radar. Make sure—"

A jolt went through the cabin, and both Jimmy and Drake flew forward.

Jimmy suspected they'd gotten rammed from behind and enlarged the rearview monitor to confirm.

On the screen, the off-roader with the gash on the side and missing windshield was clearly visible. So too were the two bandits occupying it. Both of them had goggles on and ice-crusted beards.

"These guys are tough, ya know," Jimmy said with some admiration.

The bandit in the passenger seat lifted his arm, revealing a large pulse rifle. They were close enough for Jimmy to see a big grin spread across the bandit's face.

"Stop! Now! Hit the brakes!" Jimmy yelled at Drake.

"What—"

Jimmy, with no time to explain himself, shot out both his legs, one kicking Drake's foot off the accelerator, the other stomping on the brakes.

The bandits, like Drake, had no time to react.

A violent shudder rippled through the hydro, and both Drake and Jimmy were thrown forward again. Drake bumped his head on the steering wheel, and blood starting flowing out of a cut above his eye. Jimmy hit his shoulder pretty hard, but didn't feel any damage. Unsurprisingly, all the hydro's safety devices had been disconnected.

Shaking off the energy from the impact, Jimmy jumped out of the off-roader and crawled toward the back of the vehicle, pulse gun drawn. The snow was turning red close to the rear wheel. As he approached it, he saw the body of the bandit, still grinning and gripping his rifle. Jimmy let him be, as no breath was billowing out of him.

The cabin of the bandit's hydro appeared empty, and Jimmy cautiously opened the passenger door, staying behind it and shielding himself from any unwanted projectiles. He counted to five and peaked over the door. The second bandit sat, holding the steering wheel, frozen in time—the big hole above him evidence of the pulse rifle going off on impact.

And decapitating him.

***

Jumping back into the cabin, Jimmy grabbed Drake by his jacket. "Decapitated! I told you it happens. It's a real thing, ya know?"

Drake was still lightheaded from the impact and did not know what Jimmy was going on about. Alarms and warnings were going off all over the place, and blood stained his hands.

"What happened?" he asked.

"I told you, the guy got decapitated!" Jimmy replied excitedly.

"Huh? No, what are you talking about?" Drake looked around. "Did we crash?"

Jimmy ignored him and instead focused on the DDU, closing the alarms one by one.

Drake's head was throbbing, and when he touched it, it was slick with blood.

A few alarms remained, and Jimmy muted them.

"What happened?" Drake asked again.

"I saw the guys behind us getting ready to shoot, knew we had no time to do anything, ya know, so I stomped on the brakes, and we crashed. They are both completely dead."

Drake recalled being chased by the bandits, but the crash was a blur.

"How bad is the damage?" he asked.

Jimmy scanned the screens once more.

"Not too bad. Tail lights are fucked, and the one wheel is flat, but we should be able to swap wheels with the other hydro.

Got some other minor issues, but we can work around them, ya know."

"Okay, let's get started then, buddy." Drake felt like a truck had hit him, which was funny, considering one did.

| forty-one |

"Motherfu …" Drake swallowed his words as he willed the pain away.

Hitting your knuckles when removing a stubborn nut sucked, but doing it in freezing temperatures made it ten times worse. Doing it three times in a minute was unbearable.

At last, he finished fitting the wheel to the hydro and went to see what Jimmy was up to.

"Anything worthwhile?" he asked as he peered into the cabin of the bandits' busted up hydro.

Jimmy was rummaging around, grabbing anything useful or needed for their own repairs. Drake tried not to look at the headless body in the front.

"Not really. Except for the rifle, ya know."

Jimmy leaned over the seats to the front, shoved the driver's body out of the cabin, and kept rummaging.

"Jeez, Jimmy. Show some respect."

Jimmy sat up.

"What do you mean?"

Drake shook his head and pointed to the boots still visible from the cabin.

"Him? You remember how they were trying to catch us and do who-knows-what to us, right?"

"Yes, but we killed him. His gone. The least we can do is to be respectful," Drake replied.

Jimmy stepped out of the cabin.

"No, Drake. This is life and death stuff, ya know. We will die out here if we get soft now. There are bad guys out to get us, and we are in their backyard. We need to be ruthless if we want to make it out of here."

Drake stared at Jimmy. The little guy who came into his life from another world and made himself at home. And now they were partners, if he liked it or not.

"I've never killed anyone before, Jimmy, that's all," Drake said.

"And you still haven't, ya know. I stopped the hydro. I caused the crash. It's on me, and I'm fine with the outcome, okay?"

Drake looked down at the little guy from another world that was now his partner.

"Thanks, Jimmy."

***

Lt. Wells' first stop in Porterville was the local security office. Except they called it the Department of Peace. Lt. Wells felt sick just looking at the name on the doors. She put on a brave face and entered the building.

Soft, calming music welcomed her into a pastel-colored space. There were no angles to be seen, only curves and spheres. Behind the contoured counter, a tall, bony woman tucked a gray curl of hair behind her ear and smiled at Wells.

"Welcome to the Porterville Department of Peace. My name is Star. How can we improve your day?"

Wells' white box lunch was fighting its way back up.

"Hi, Star," Wells replied in her softest tone. "I'm Lily Wells from New Franco. I was hoping to speak to someone about a case that I'm working."

"A case?" Star inquired.

Wells wanted nothing more than to punch Star in the face.

"Yes. As you can see, I'm a security officer." She waved her hands up and down in front of her, pointing out the obvious to Star. "Would I be able to talk to a fellow officer, perhaps?"

Star looked perplexed. "Oh, but you are. Not all law enforcers look the same, you know? Enforcers. Such an ugly, brutal word, don't you think?"

Star really didn't want to know what she was thinking.

"My apologies. I guess we live a harsher life in New Franco," Wells used more of her quickly depleting agreeable words.

Star nodded in agreement.

"Anyway, Star, I'm on the trail of two men, traveling north. I do not have a vehicle description, but I do have their names. I was hoping there was a way for you to see if they might have popped up in your system, or if I could look at your highway surveillance footage."

"I'll be more than happy to help you, Lily. Now, who do I contact at Penta to verify your position and clearance?"

Wells felt her muscle memory kick in as her fingers twitched, ready to grab her pulse pistol.

"Sure, of course. To be honest, though, you know how slow these archaic organizations move, and I would hate to lose the trail of these guys."

"Best give me those details quickly then!" Star quipped back.

So Wells did, and flopped down on a huge round soft chair, waiting for Star to cross all her Ts and dot all her infuriating Is.

***

Star turned out to be a very efficient worker. After about twenty minutes, she walked over to Wells, smiling.

"Here you go," she said as she swiped her HIC in Well's direction.

A faint vibration in her arm showed that she received a notification, and Wells looked down at her own HIC to see some files from the Porterville Department of Peace waiting for her. She quickly opened them up and scanned through them. As she did, Star narrated.

"It seems misters Drake and Something came through town and stayed the night at a private dwelling, did not venture anywhere else, and left in the morning. The details of the unit they rented the room from are in the notes. Then there is also this."

Star pointed to a surveillance video taken from across the road from where Drake and Jimmy stayed. Wells tapped it and watched as a man got out of a hydro, stretched, then relieved himself on the road, before getting back in and following Drake's hydro. She rewound the footage, paused it, and zoomed in on the face. It didn't ring a bell for her, so she sent it off to Penta for identification.

"Star, this is incredible work. Thank you so much, you've been a great help."

"No problem, Lily, and maybe next time you won't reach for your gun so quickly."

Lt. Lily Wells swallowed all the obscenities racing to escape her mouth and walked out of the Department of Peace as quickly as her legs could carry her.

| forty-two |

He had clearly been underestimating them.

The wreck was on the side of the road, most likely pushed there. Two bodies sat in the cabin. One held a head in its lap. Drake and Something were not playing around. An idea grew in the back of his mind, and nothing he could do would make it disappear. The idea kept growing, crawling further forward, entering his conscience, forcing him to acknowledge it.

He had clearly been underestimating them.

Sammy surveyed the damage one more time and made the call.

"We have a problem."

"Another one? Should I send someone to replace you? Someone who resolves problems, not tells me about them?"

Sammy didn't reply, but switched his ARPs point of view so the person on the other end could see what he was seeing. He walked over to the hydro, walked around it to get the complete picture, then stuck his head into the cabin. He made sure he spent an extra few seconds on the head lying in the decapitated body's lap.

"As I said," Sammy continued once he changed views again, "they have armed themselves and are getting serious. I don't think they are planning on capturing Turner alive."

"It seems we might have underestimated them, after all. Well, make sure you take precautions. Nothing changes."

The call ended.

Sammy took the scene in one more time, shook his head, and got back on the road.

***

Pushing the wreck off the road was hard work, and sitting back in their hydro, Drake felt the sweat running down his back. He wanted to bury the bodies, but Jimmy stopped him, rightly pointing out that they were getting close to freezing themselves and it would take them forever to dig into the frozen earth. So instead, they put the bodies back into the hydro, making it look as much as possible like an accident. It might fool the locals, but not any professional security force. Hopefully, none of them would come snooping around here.

Wallen was less than an hour away, and Drake was getting very nervous. He didn't know if they could withstand any more attacks. The hydro was barely hanging on. So was he. Jimmy looked fine, but Drake wasn't too sure.

"Hey, buddy. You really saved our asses back there. Thanks."

Jimmy was scanning the bandit network, rearview monitor, and radar.

"That? It's just what we do, ya know?" He kept searching and scanning.

"I know, but things are getting way more intense than I thought it would, and I guess, I mean, I am happy that I got you as a partner."

Jimmy kept searching and scanning, but a grin spread from ear to ear.

The road widened, and signs appeared on the windshield showing which turns to take for Wallen, distances to other places and some local attractions. Drake wondered if they might have overestimated the bandits' numbers and resolve. They were almost in Wallen, and no other bandits had shown up. Drake allowed himself to relax a bit. Once they got to Wallen, they could jump on the Major Swanson and make their way to Shangcorp mainland. Safety awaited around the next corner.

Also, a roadblock of four hydros blocking the entire road.

Drake brought the hydro to a stop, giving himself enough space to maneuver and get out of there if needed.

"Crap," Jimmy said. "I saw a message about a meetup to discuss the upcoming spring fair. I should have known it was a code or something."

"Don't beat yourself up. It's only clear now, because it makes sense. What else was in the thread?"

Jimmy found the thread and read it.

"Okay, so reading between the lines, I think this is the last attempt. No one else seemed interested in the bounty, except for this group. If we can get past them …"

Drake looked at the blockade up the road. The hydro would not take another beating. Ramming through them was out of the question. Drake looked back over his shoulder and saw the pulse rifle that Jimmy took off the bandits.

"Okay, buddy. Time to see how accurate your shooting is."

***

Sammy caught up to them in no time. With them crashing and moving the wreck, he made up all the time he'd previously lost. The road made a lazy u-turn, descending rapidly down to a bigger stretch of road. Drake's hydro sat at the end of the u-turn, and Sammy stopped at the start of the turn, high above them. From his vantage point, Sammy could also see the roadblock farther up the road.

Benjamin Drake got out of the hydro, followed by Jimmy Something, who jumped on top of the off-roader and kneeled down. Jimmy lifted a high-capacity pulse rifle up to his eye, and Drake started walking toward the bandits.

"You fucking idiots," Sammy said.

He couldn't risk the bandits killing or even injuring them. Drake and Jimmy were outnumbered had no chance in hell of getting out of there. Sammy knew he couldn't just charge in and lend a hand. He would have to be more subtle.

Sammy got an idea.

The road was quite narrow, so he opted to reverse back up the road instead of wasting time trying to turn around. Using the rearview monitor and keeping an eye on the side window, he pulled up parallel, but high above the bandits. A glance back down the road showed Drake still walking toward the bandits.

Sammy jumped out of the warm cabin and retrieved a pulse rifle of his own. A rock and fallen tree provided him with the perfect cover and a stable platform to shoot from. Looking through the rifle's scope, he counted seven bandits. It was tricky seeing into the hydros, but he felt confident they would all be standing outside, beating their chests, trying to scare the enemy.

Sammy swiveled his scope and found Drake. He was walking with his hands open and up in the air, demonstrating that he was not a threat. His mouth was moving constantly, but Sammy could not figure out what he was saying.

Sammy's index finger took up the slack on the trigger.

***

"I am unarmed, but my friend has my back. Please don't shoot. We have a deal for you."

Drake repeated the mantra every ten steps. He wasn't sure when they could hear him, so he kept talking as he approached them, arms in the air, glancing back at Jimmy occasionally. His feet were freezing, and the wind blew straight into his face, making his eyes watery.

"I am unarmed, but my friend has my back. Please don't shoot. We have a deal for you."

He was close enough now to make out every bandit's face. Four interchangeable bearded faces, one brave individual who went against the bearded trend, and two women. They seemed every bit as mean and hardened as the men. Drake glanced back at Jimmy before closing the gap some more.

"I am unarmed, but my friend has my back. Please don't shoot. We have a deal for you."

He knew he reached hearing distance as all seven rifles went up to meet his gaze. Seven black holes stared him straight in the eye. He stopped.

"What deal?" Drake couldn't make out who said it.

"Straight to the point. Okay. Um, well, as we see it, the bounty is what, five thousand credits?" Drake paused, but got no replies. "So, we will give each one of you a thousand credits to let us through."

No one moved or looked at each other. Drake expected them to discuss the offer, one he thought they would jump at, but they stood motionless.

"So, do we have a deal?"

"No. We can get more if we take you in and sell your hydro. So I think that's what we'll do." Drake pinpointed the voice, and the person most likely to be in charge.

"Okay, so let's discuss a better deal then."

"We are all about to get frostbite, so I think the time to talk is over. Tell your friend to stand down and walk over."

Drake always knew there were only ever going to be two outcomes. One, they would accept his offer and they would be on their way. Two, they wouldn't and they would have to shoot their way through. He didn't like option two.

"Two thousand each. Everyone walks away with something."

The man he thought to be the leader said something he couldn't hear, and a loud crackle resonated in the air. Drake fell to the ground, rolled to the side of the road, and looked over at Jimmy. He was still holding position on the hydro, that was now one tire lighter.

"Seems you're not going anywhere today," the leader said.

Drake swiped his HIC before standing up.

"No, it seems not," he replied.

***

Sammy watched Drake stop, chat, and then get shot at. Sammy wasn't sure if they meant the shot for Drake or Jimmy, but it ended up taking out the front tire of the hydro Jimmy was sitting atop. Drake did an elaborate tuck and roll to avoid it, and ended up on the side of the road.

Chicken shit.

Drake got up, and from his body language, it looked like he surrendered.

Sammy's finger was still tight on the trigger, ready to shoot in a second.

Drake's mouth moved, and from Sammy's left, a loud crackle erupted. Jimmy's gun. One bandit spun around and hit the ground.

It was on.

The bandits scrambled for cover. Drake hid in a ditch, and Sammy waited for Jimmy's next shot.

Sammy had a bandit in sight, and the moment he heard the unmistakable electric crackle of a pulse round leaving Jimmy's rifle, he squeezed the trigger. Only one shot rang out, as Sammy had a very good and very illegal suppressor fitted to his rifle. One shot rang out, but two bandits fell.

Sammy had to wait for Jimmy, as to not raise suspicion and blow his cover.

Jimmy jumped down from the hydro as the bandits fired back, destroying the hydro. Jimmy took a few potshots at them, and Sammy took the opportunity to take out two more bandits. Drake joined the fun and was blasting them from the side with a pulse pistol. He was as bad a shot as Sammy imagined him to be. Sammy helped him by doing something he couldn't—hitting what he aimed for.

One bandit left.

The last bandit fired blindly at Jimmy, too scared to show her head, but still pinning him down. Drake was doing his best to shoot from the side, but unless he moved out from his hiding spot, would never get close. So Sammy put everyone out of their misery and shot the bandit. Jimmy kept firing for a while and finally got the message from Drake that it was over.

Sammy looked at the carnage below him.

"You can thank me later, dickheads," he mumbled as he made his way back to his hydro.

***

"Stop! Stop! You got them! It's all over," Drake yelled at Jimmy on his ARP.

Silence fell over them, and Drake stood up. Pink snow was all around him, and he made his way back to Jimmy to check on him.

"You okay?"

Jimmy sat behind the hydro, panting, but seemingly intact.

"Wow! That was intense, ya know." Jimmy's eyes were enormous.

"You okay, buddy?" Drake asked again.

"Yes, yes, all good, partner. Few hairy moments there, ya know, but it seems we got them."

Drake had to admit that Jimmy's marksmanship had saved their backsides today.

"I really thought they would take the credits. Worse case, I thought a warning shot might scare them off, but this—"

"Nah, it pretty much went how I thought it would," Jimmy countered. "I knew we would have to shoot our way out, that's why I agreed to the plan, ya know."

"You did?"

"Hell yeah! These are bandits, partner, not disgruntled haulers, no offense."

Drake knew he had been naïve, thinking they would simply accept his offer and let them through.

"Well, it seems you saved the day, Jimmy. Again."

"All teamwork, partner." Jimmy blushed.

"Well, this team needs to find a working hydro so we can get out of this freezing cold," Drake said as he helped Jimmy stand back up.

| forty-three |

"Oh, did I miss a booking?" the man said upon opening the door.

"No, I'm Lieutenant Wells from New Franco. Would I be able to ask you a few questions?"

The man stood smiling, but didn't move. Footsteps grew louder, and another man, taller and skinnier than the first one, took a spot behind him.

"Fred, this is Lieutenant Wells all the way from New Franco," he introduced Wells.

"Hi, there," she said to the man behind.

"Oh, what did you say this was all about again?" the man blocking the door with his considerable girth asked.

"Just some routine questions regarding some people who we believe have traveled through Porterville and could be of help in a case we are working on."

"Oh, very exciting. Are you going door to door? You must be starving? Or would you prefer a drink?" the rotund man offered. "Fred, get the lieutenant something to drink."

"No, thank you very much." Wells stopped Fred from running away. "I'm fine."

"Oh, okay then. So how can we help?" the man asked, looking a bit offended.

"I never caught your name?" Wells said. She knew from the files she received from Star that it had to be Clive standing in front of her, already identifying Fred earlier, but didn't want to let on that she already knew more than she showed.

"Oh, my manners. Why didn't you tell me, Fred? I am Clive, dear," he said, extending a shovel of a hand.

Wells shook it. It was clammy. She forced herself not to wipe her hand on her pants.

"Nice to meet you, Clive. Now, as I was saying, I am looking for two men, and have reason to believe that they passed through Porterville, and might even have stayed here, at this address."

Clive looked at Fred, who nodded back at him.

"Oh, I think I know who you are talking about," Clive said. Wells waited for him to share this information, but it seemed Clive needed some encouragement.

"Now, I understand there is a lot at stake here for you, with customer privacy and such, so let me assure you, Penta Security holds nothing more sacred than privacy. Whatever you feel like divulging to me, stays with me." Wells hoped they believed the lie.

"Oh, I can't lie to that face! It was Benjamin Drake. *The* Benjamin Drake. The man who conquered Mars."

The man who conquered Mars? More like the idiot who almost got killed a few times whilst helping an actual criminal steal Mars.

"Yep, that's the one!" Wells forced the words through clenched teeth.

"Oh, and what a darling he was. So charming. And of course his little friend too, right Fred?"

Wells promised herself to punch Drake in his charming face next time she saw him.

"They are quite the pair, all right. So, they stayed the night then?"

"Oh, yes. Very good guests. Slept here one night and then left early the next morning. But I'm sure they'll come back again." Clive smiled at Fred.

"I'm sure they will. Do you know where they might have gone to once they left Porterville?"

Clive and Fred shared a look.

"Oh, okay Fred," Clive answered a mute Fred. "Are they in trouble?"

"No, not at all," Wells lied again. "But they are crucial in helping me arrest a very, *very* dangerous man." Wells emphasized the words as much as she could, playing on her observed tendency of Clive for the dramatic. He let out a gasp.

"Oh, then we better help, don't we, Fred?"

Clive told Wells about their friend, the note they found, and the names on it.

Paul Sullivan, Major Swanson, and Wallen.

Lt. Wells thanked the men for their time and hurried to her Ibex. This was way more than she expected. A general direction, or maybe a misheard name in a conversation was what she expected, but three clearly identified names? This information was priceless. Hopefully.

She entered the names into her Penta connected DDU and waited.

The wait was brief.

Wallen came up as a small town, up north, that gathered its fame from being the closest point to mainland Shangcorp.

Major Swanson had a few hits, but cross-referencing it to the other two names, the highest probable answer was a boat. Registered in Wallen and operating tours around the area. It could also transport hydros across to Shangcorp.

And the result that tied it all up was Paul Sullivan. His Penta records listed him as an ex-hauler, and a man with a violent history. His current job and location, Wells found, was operating a charter service on a boat called Major Swanson, in a small town called Wallen.

Even before finishing reading the reports, Lily Wells had already programmed the Ibex's DDU to take her to Wallen.

***

"I … have … never … been … so … cold … ya know," Jimmy said between bouts of clattering teeth.

The wind had picked up since the shootout, and both Jimmy and Drake struggled to get one of the hydros in a working condition. The off-roader they had been using was a wreck, as all the bandits focused their weapons on Jimmy. The bandits' hydros had less concentrated damage, being more spread out. Looking at the carnage, Drake wondered if it had been luck, more than skill, that Jimmy had hit any of them.

One of the hydros had less damage than the others, and they set to work, swapping out as much of the damaged parts as they could. Getting to Wallen was only part of the journey. They still needed a working hydro once they arrived in mainland Shangcorp.

The cold was making it a painfully slow process.

"I know," Drake replied. "Almost enough to make you miss the smoggy warmth of New Franco."

Jimmy jumped into the cabin of their newest loan hydro and started hacking the DDU.

"Give us a hand," Jimmy yelled, the wind blowing harder than ever.

Drake looked up to find Jimmy back out of the hydro, dragging a bandit toward it.

"What the hell are you doing?"

"It's fingerprint protected. If they are still warm enough, it will make the process so much quicker, ya know."

At least Jimmy didn't ask him to chop off a finger or a hand, so Drake went over to help before Jimmy thought of it.

"You sure this is the right bandit?" Drake asked, as Jimmy picked the biggest body to drag.

"No. Yes. Sort off. I mean, this fella stood right in front of this hydro, so, ya know."

Dragging the body was hard work. Drake stared at the man's wrist, wondering how easy it would saw through.

"That should do it." Jimmy saved him from further contemplating butchering the man.

Jimmy pulled the dead bandit's glove off and pressed it against the sensor. A red message appeared. Drake couldn't make it out, but red never meant yes. Jimmy tried again.

"I think it's gone too cold," he surmised.

Taking the man's hand, Jimmy lifted his shirt and jacket, pressed the cold dead hand under his armpit, and dropped his arm, squeezing the hand between his arm and ribs.

"Let's give it a minute, ya know," Jimmy said casually.

Drake looked on as Jimmy sat in the cabin, door open, a dead body propped up against the wheel, arm stretched out and disappearing under Jimmy's clothing.

Jimmy pulled the hand out, tried again, and a green light illuminated the cabin.

"Here we go," Jimmy said as he unceremoniously dropped the dead hand back to its owner.

Drake was glad he didn't have to go through this process with more bodies. Dragging them through the snow, piling them up, as Jimmy used his body to warm them up. Very glad.

It took them another ten minutes to each finish their tasks before they collected all their gear from the old hydro and packed it in the newest one.

"Okay, buddy, hopefully that was it," Drake said, as they pulled away, following the green line to Wallen

High above them, another hydro slowly pulled away as well.

| forty-four |

The drive to Wallen was short and uneventful. The radar kept blipping and showing things popping in and out, but nothing ever materialized. Closer to Wallen, they came across several hydros, all going about their business, no one giving them a second glance.

Wallen was much bigger than Drake imagined. It was still tiny, but it had a major street, with many businesses along it, and housing units spreading out from the center.

"Looks like we made it, buddy," Drake said as they pulled into the main street.

With all the shooting and corpse warming, they arrived much later than planned, and Drake doubted anything but the bar would be open. A thought shared by Jimmy.

"Could really go a beer, ya know?" he said, as if reading Drake's mind.

Years on the road as a hauler had made bars almost a second home to Drake. Whenever he stopped, it was usually at a bar. Credits that could have been saved or spent on upgrades for the Hydrostar usually ended up flowing down his throat. He was as home on the road as he was in one of these dives.

Jimmy, either getting used to Drake's habits, or just sharing the same vices, had already found a suitable drinking hole, and had the DDU guide them toward it.

The size of the town struck Drake again as they drove down the main street. The signs on the buildings and business all had something in common. Most of them had the word gold in them. For the first time, Drake noticed that the people walking on the sidewalks, bracing themselves against the cold, were, in fact, huge. Moon miner huge.

Drake had Jimmy search on his HIC, which confirmed that gold mining was indeed the biggest business around here. It seemed, from Jimmy's quick search, that it was hard, unforgiving work, and usually done by Moon miners who'd had enough of life on the Moon. Moon miners got favored over robotics, as the cold played havoc on the robots, whereas the Moon miners were used to the conditions.

Which also explained the lack of bandits close to town. No one in their right mind would ever go up against a Moon miner. And if they did, it would be the last thing they ever did. Drake recalled the times Mr. Turner would merely have to get out of his chair to intimidate any foolish hauler into submission.

"Here we go!" Jimmy announced as the green line ended in front of an old but well-kept building.

***

The warmth on the inside immediately lifted their spirits. Being in the snow most of the day had drained their energy, and morale was getting low, but walking into the bar, everything felt better. Drake looked over at Jimmy, who seemed to feel the same.

No one looked up or showed any interest in them as they walked in. Huge Moon miner bodies sat huddled together, drinking and laughing. Scattered amongst the behemoths were a couple of normal sized humans, which helped Drake and Jimmy blend in.

Drake went up to the bar to get scanned and buy beer for him and Jimmy, whilst Jimmy found them a table to sit at.

The bartender seemed to be sized between a miner and a normal person. Small for a miner, pretty big for a human.

"Hey, buddy, two beers please," Drake said, and lifted his arm to be scanned—a formality he had to go through every time he went into a bar. No one wanted trouble, and serving people with outstanding warrants was some sort of offense, he had been told.

Drake waited for the barkeep to finish and start pouring the beer.

Only he didn't.

"Seems you are a person of interest to Penta," the barkeep said, looking at his scanner.

"I mean, I was, but I don't think I am anymore," Drake said.

After the Zuma incident, Penta had cleared both Drake and Jimmy of any criminal wrongdoings. There was no reason for them to be persons of interest. Unless—

"Lily," Drake said to the bartender.

"Huh?"

"Never mind. I'll be back." Drake left and found Jimmy at a table.

"Seems the lovely lieutenant has marked us as persons of interest," Drake said.

Jimmy leaned to the side to have a better look at the bartender.

"The barkeep is a lieutenant?" Jimmy asked.

"No, fucksakes Jimmy, Lieutenant Wells. Lily. She must have named us in her investigation of Delgado, and now we are on Penta's shit list. Again."

Jimmy nodded. "Yeah, that makes more sense."

The bartender was serving other patrons, but kept an eye on them.

"I think we might overstay our welcome here soon," Drake said.

The moment the bartender scanned Drake's HIC, a notification went to Penta HQ, informing them of Drake's whereabouts. As soon as someone there saw it, they would verify it and inform Lt. Wells. In a matter of minutes, she would have a lock on them.

It was time for another call.

***

Under different circumstances, the scenery would be breathtaking. Snow-covered mountains, gigantic trees, and clear blue skies. But driving at breakneck speeds, Lily Wells barely had time to take it in. Two minutes ago, a message came through. Drake's HIC got scanned in Wallen. She had an urgent flag on both Drake and Jimmy's names, and the notification came through almost as soon as his HIC got scanned. She was glad, but not surprised, to see they were in Wallen.

What surprised her slightly was the location the notification came from. A bar. If they were having drinks, it meant they were staying put for the night. Which meant they wouldn't cross to

Shangcorp till morning. This gave her enough time to catch up to them. She pressed the accelerator even harder.

Three dots jumped into her field of view. She slowed down, switched Autodrive on, and looked at the caller ID on her HIC. She swiped to answer.

"Hey." Drake smiled at her.

Some of her anger dissipated immediately. She wished it didn't.

"Stay where you are. Do you hear me? Do not sneak out of Wallen or try to outrun me, Drake. I swear, if you as much—"

"Okay, okay. We'll stay," Drake replied.

"I'm serious, Drake." She felt more anger slip away.

"On one condition."

"This is not really a negotiation," Wells said, puzzled. What ace did he have up his sleeve?

"Clear our statuses, so we can at least have a drink while we wait for you."

Wells ended the call.

***

"You really think it'll work?" Jimmy asked as Drake finished the call.

"I don't see any other option, buddy. She knows where we are, and I'm sure she'll be here soon. There is no way she'll let us leave and enter into Shangcorp territory."

Drake stood up and went back to the barkeeper.

"I think this will work now," he said, holding up his HIC.

"Doubt it. Unless you know some people in high places."

The bartender scanned his HIC again.

"Huh," he said, and walked toward the unmarked beer tap. He took two glasses, filled them, and brought them back to Drake. "First one's on me."

Smiling, Drake grabbed them and headed back to Jimmy.

"So far, so good." He grinned.

| forty-five |

Sammy arrived in Wallen, and being a hauler himself, knew Drake would seek out a bar first before doing anything else. He didn't have to drive too far before he saw a building that appeared to be a bar. Sammy slowed down and made a visual confirmation of Drake's newest stolen hydro sitting in the parking lot. Unlike those two idiots, Sammy planned on going straight to the housing unit he rented a room in. It has been days since he'd slept in a proper bed, and Sammy was dying to stretch out and fall asleep. He was cold, hungry, and tired. This entire trip has been nothing but a pain in the ass. When he came up with the idea to partner up with Drake to catch Turner, he thought it would be a breeze. Instead, he'd gotten stabbed in the back by Drake, forced into a loan he didn't want, and ended up working with someone who he knew best not to disappoint.

The small block of units appeared on his right, and Sammy parked in front of it. He was fairly sure the two idiots wouldn't be able to link this hydro to him. He needed to leave it where he could access it quickly and get out as fast as possible if needed.

Sammy scanned himself into the unit and was grateful there was no one to talk to. He picked this unit not only for its location but also because it was self-service.

The unit was tiny, but more importantly, it was clean and warm. The cooling unit contained white box meals, and the bed looked clean and soft. It had everything he needed.

Sammy fell down on the bed and into a deep sleep.

***

It was late when Lt. Wells parked in front of the bar, but judging by the hydros filling all the spaces, people were still far away from calling it a day. She grabbed the door handle of the Ibex and froze.

It had been months since she'd walked out of the hospital room, leaving Drake behind. Months of her putting him behind her and getting her career back on track. She'd succeeded in both areas. Until tonight. Walking into that bar would put Benjamin Drake squarely back into her life. She couldn't deny it. Talking to him via her ARP was already a struggle, but seeing him in the flesh was going to be even harder. All the hard work of the last few months, putting him behind her, was about to be undone. She knew it.

She put her weight on the door, but hesitated. She took a deep breath, pushed the door open, and climbed out of the Ibex.

The icy wind stung her face and made her eyes and nose watery. She pulled her jacket tighter around herself and walked toward the entrance.

***

Drake watched Lily Wells enter the building, stomping her feet on the ground to remove the snow and ice from it. Her nose and cheeks were red from the cold, and she was still hugging herself, despite the heat inside the building. She seemed all business, as she went straight to the barkeeper, showed him her credentials, and immediately asked him questions. Wallen was not a Penta territory, but part of the vast and sparsely populated Maplon territory. Maplon relied heavily on trade and goods from Penta, and gave Penta Security forces almost free rein in their territories. Which meant Lt. Wells had all the authority she could dream of.

The bartender knew this, and didn't hesitate to point to Drake and Jimmy as she was talking. Lt. Wells turned her head to face the way the barkeeper was pointing and looked straight at Drake.

He thought he saw a small smile, but put it down to wishful thinking.

She said something to the bartender and walked over to their table.

"Jimmy. Drake." She sounded nervous to Drake.

"Hey, lieutenant!" Jimmy replied.

Drake got up, unsure of himself, and awkwardly lifting his hand. Either as a handshake or maybe a hug? He felt so damn awkward, suddenly. Wells stepped forward, grabbed a chair, and sat down. That settled it.

Drake sat back down in his chair.

"Been a while," he stumbled over the words.

He had forgotten how much he liked her face.

"You need to come back with me. Tonight." She brought him back to focus.

"Hang on, we are actually on a job here," Drake protested.

"Yeah," Jimmy softly agreed.

"Hector Delgado is on the verge of taking over several neighboring sectors. An inner city war is about to erupt. Tensions are already at a breaking point over the occupation of Mars. Penta can't have two wars to focus on."

Drake had seen this look in her eyes before.

"Lily, I get it, but why do you need me back in New Franco? I'll go on record right now, telling you everything I know. Everything we did."

The look stayed the same.

"That's not enough. Penta wants to do this one by the books. They want it in the news. They are going to prosecute him. It's a power thing. They need to flex their muscle, but can't do it by force."

"That doesn't sound very Penta-like?" Drake replied.

"Something is coming, and they need the public's support. They can't just go in and shoot civilians, even if it is a crime lord."

"Something big involving Mars?"

"You know I can't say, Drake."

That was as good as a yes.

"Okay, so you need me—us—to go with you and testify against Delgado in a public, drawn-out court case?"

The look in Wells' eyes changed.

"Yes. You're not going to do this, are you?"

Drake remembered he had a beer and took a sip.

"No. I can't. We are on the verge of catching up to Mr. Turner. A court case like that would take months. And besides, I'm broke, Lily. I really need this."

"We'll pay for your accommodation and—"

"I can't. I'm sorry. I need to do this."

Wells sat still, staring at him with eyes that searched for a solution.

"I don't think you grasp how important this is. I don't want to arrest you, Drake, but I will if I have to."

He believed her. He knew her job was the most important thing in her life.

"It's late. We have a double room. Can we please wait till the morning before we head back?" Drake crumbled.

"Huh?" Jimmy stammered next to him.

"Sure. We're all tired. Let's leave in the morning." Wells smiled at him.

"Okay, but promise me you won't disappear on me again, once it's over."

"Let's discuss it on the road," she replied.

Drake wished she'd answered differently.

***

Drake opened the door of the unit Jimmy had organized for them at the bar and let Jimmy and Lt. Wells go in first. It was a decent size, with a living and eating room, two bedrooms, and a separate bathroom.

"You grab that room. Jimmy and I will share this one," Drake said.

"Thanks, Drake," Lily replied. He liked how she didn't pretend to protest and just went with the plan. No fuss. Just get on with it.

"It's really nice seeing you again, Lily."

"Drake, we have so much to talk about, I get it, but until this thing is over—"

"Like you said, we can chat once we are on the road."

Wells looked relaxed. Mission accomplished. She came to find them and take them back to New Franco, and so far, everything was going to plan.

Until an electric crackle filled the room and a pulse cartridge knocked her out.

"That should do it," Jimmy said, pulse pistol hanging by his side.

Wells fell straight forward into Drake's arms.

Drake held on tight, knowing this might be the last time he got to do so.

| forty-six |

Jimmy barely slept at all, checking in on Lt. Wells continually. He worked out the pulse shock to be enough for eight hours, which was getting close to the maximum safe amount of joules. He wasn't too worried about her waking up, but knocking someone out with a pulse cartridge, even one set at a non-lethal amount, was always a risk. Sending an electrical charge through someone's body that was high enough to knock them out for hours had side effects. Jimmy was just checking in, making sure she didn't have any, and monitored her vitals.

A noise in the unit told him Drake was awake. Jimmy listened to Drake's wake up ritual, one he had gotten used to while sharing the unit in New Franco. First there was the big stretch, kicking all the covers off him, accompanied by a loud yawn. Then a minute or two of silence, as Drake apparently took stock of all his life's decisions, before he jumped up and made for the toilet, finally forced out of bed only by a full bladder. This could take a while. When he emerged, it was time to be fed.

"Shhh!" Jimmy scolded Drake, as he finally came into the room.

"Sorry. Have you been up all night?"

"No. Just came in to see if she escaped, ya know?"

"Bullshit," Drake snapped back. "You look like shit. Did you sleep at all?"

"Yes, a bit. I could have killed her, ya know?"

Jimmy hated Drake's plan to knock out Lt. Wells, but agreed there was no other option. She'd lifted the persons-of-interest bulletin on them, which meant they could cross over to Shang-corp. If she was still conscious, she would put it back in place the moment they made a run for it.

Still. He hated putting her in harm's way. Although she worked for Penta, she had never done him wrong. Which put her on a very short list of people he trusted.

"You okay, buddy?" Drake asked.

"Yeah, always. You know me!" Jimmy smiled and jumped up. His stomach was hurting like a sonofabitch. "Let's go get us a bounty!"

***

Drake knew Jimmy was lying. Whenever something bothered him, he got stomach cramps so bad, he couldn't walk up straight. Like he was now. Drake also knew pushing him to talk was pointless, and that he would suddenly blurt it out when Drake least expected it. For now, he just had to be gentle with him.

"You hungry, or do you think we should get a head start?" Drake asked as they got in the hydro, leaving a sleeping Lt. Wells behind.

"Let's find this Paul guy and then see," Jimmy replied.

Which meant his stomach was hurting too much to eat. It was clear to Drake it was about Lt. Wells. Finding him sitting there this morning, looking like he had no sleep. He seemed so keen on the plan, but obviously it tore him up, having to shoot her.

"My thoughts exactly, partner." Drake slapped him on the thigh. "Let's find this boat."

Jimmy searched for the docking location of the Major Swanson and entered the details into the DDU. Drake ran the startup procedure, and when the green line appeared, he was ready to go.

The drive was short, and within a few minutes, they stopped at the small harbor. A few boats sat bobbing in the water, with people scattering around on them. Drake and Jimmy got out and walked to the jetty that ran between all the boats.

"Wow, it's so big, ya know?" Jimmy said.

Jimmy's eyes were shining, a silly, little smile frozen on his face, his whole body taking in the scene in front of him. Clearly, for the first time.

"First time seeing the ocean?"

"It just goes on forever," Jimmy replied.

Drake looked at the vast expanse of water lying beyond the boats. Jimmy was correct. It looked endless.

Drake patiently waited for Jimmy to take it all in. The smile never faded, but eventually, he turned to Drake.

"Thanks."

"Okay, let's find this boat." Drake slapped Jimmy on the back and made for the jetty.

All the boats had their names on them, and one or two had a little booth next to them. They kept walking until they found the one offering to *See where the world ends*.

The small booth appeared closed, and behind it was the Major Swanson itself. The boat was far newer and sleeker than Drake imagined. The vibe of the town and people made Drake think the boat itself would be old and quaint. He half expected a wooden boat with peeling paint. Like most of the boats in the harbor. But the Major Swanson was a sleek, black modern vessel. It looked like it could double as a space shuttle, too. The way they moored it made it difficult to see the back end, but Drake could see a big loading area for cargo, big enough for a hydro.

"She is quite a looker, hey?" A voice startled Drake.

The man from the advertisement they saw in the diner stood next to Drake. Like half the population in Wallen, he had the look and built of a Moon miner. He stuck out an enormous hand that engulfed Drake's.

"Paul. Paul Sullivan." He introduced himself by crushing the bones in Drake's hand.

"Benjamin Drake, and this here is my partner, Jimmy Something."

Jimmy just waved, keeping his distance from Sullivan's bone crushing grip.

"Not the same Benjamin Drake and Jimmy Something that helped Santo take over Mars, is it?" Drake tried to pull his hand free, but it was stuck in a vice.

"Yes, it's us, but no, we didn't help him." Drake had gotten used to people's assumption that they had something more to do with it than they did.

Paul Sullivan gave Drake a dubious look.

"Anyway, something tells me you're not here for a sightseeing tour?" Sullivan said.

"No, and looking at the Major Swanson, I don't think that's all you offer," Drake replied.

Sullivan crossed his arms and regarded Drake.

"I think you are mistaken, son. She might be overkill, but that's all she does. Taking people around the bay and showing them the sights."

Palms needed to be greased for this conversation to progress.

"How much to get us to mainland Shangcorp?" Drake asked, straight to the point.

"Now, as you know, things are a little tense between Penta and Shangcorp, with all that Mars business that you had nothing to do with."

"Okay, we had a small part, I guess, but Penta cleared us of any wrongdoing. And we know things are tense, that's why we came specifically to you."

Drake tried to get a feeling for which way Sullivan was leaning, but the man had the emotive range of a rock.

"Specifically me?"

"Yes. A friend gave us your name."

The standoff continued. Drake could hear people on the other boats scuffling about, readying their boats for the day. Water slapped against the legs of the jetty. Time itself stood still.

"And who might this friend be?"

Drake knew the next sentence would either make or break the deal.

"Bob Turner."

Finally, Sullivan cracked a smile.

"And why on Earth would I help you after what you did to Bobby?"

Bobby?

"We did?" Drake snapped at Sullivan. "He is the one who used us and then disappeared."

"I heard there is a nice bounty out on him." Sullivan ignored Drake's outburst.

"Yes, but we're not after that, in case you were wondering."

Sullivan looked over Drake's shoulder. Drake turned around to see people, presumably tourists, walking toward them.

"Seems I have some legitimate customers coming," Sullivan said.

"Listen. I gather you worked with Mr. Turner on the Moon. And I presume he used your friendship as leverage to get him to Shangcorp. We are trying to help him. Penta is hot on our tail, and if we can cross now, we can beat them to him. He needs us." Half-truths with a sprinkle of lies.

The tourists were taking their time reading the other booth's information, trying to make the right decision and not blow out their holiday budget. Their next stop would be Sullivan's booth.

"Maybe I helped him. Maybe I had an old debt to be paid. Doesn't mean I owe you shit."

Drake heard the tourists walking up behind him.

"I lied. We are after the bounty, and the clock is ticking. Name your price and let's get this boat going."

Working for Turner all these years had taught Drake a thing or two about the types of people who became Moon miners. One of them was their low tolerance for bullshit.

The smallest of grins on Sullivan's face told him he was correct.

"Twenty thousand, right now, and we will be in Shangcorp in thirty minutes."

Bingo.

Except for the credits.

"Done. Do whatever you need to do to get a boat ready, and I'll get the credits," Drake said.

***

The dots merged, and Drake almost hung up.

"Well, well, well. I did not expect to hear from you so soon."

"I need twenty thousand credits—right now."

"I'm not sure you are in a position to make lofty demands, Drake."

Drake felt his throat tighten, trapping the air in his lungs and preventing fresh air from coming in. He deserved no less.

"I can help you with your Penta problem," Drake forced the words out.

Hector Delgado sat up. "I wouldn't call it a problem yet, but you've got my attention, Drake."

"Lieutenant Wells is here, in the same town as us. We are her only hope to get to you. So if you get us the twenty thousand credits, we can get over to Shangcorp and she'd be out of luck. But it needs to happen now!"

Delgado's upper lip twitched as he mulled it over.

"I usually kill people who disrespect me like that, Drake. Or," Delgado picked something out of his teeth, "I promote them. Consider this loan a promotion."

The call ended.

Jimmy's HIC buzzed.

"We've got it!" Jimmy said.

Drake turned to Sullivan, who waved them onto the boat. "Welcome aboard!"

| forty-seven |

Lt. Lily Wells woke up, her entire body hurting. She sat up slowly, taking in her surroundings, but nothing made sense. She did not know where she was or why she was there.

Her Human Interface Console made her arm vibrate every few seconds, telling her she had unread messages waiting for attention. Her mind was a blank, so she opted to read the messages. Maybe they could help.

There were a ton of them, mostly from Drake. One, marked as urgent, stood out, so she read it first.

Lily,

I'm sorry. More than I can explain here, but believe me, I had no option.

I had Jimmy shock you, to knock you out, so we could leave for Shangcorp.

Sorry.

I need to get to Turner before anyone else does. I can't explain it, but I have to.

I have sent you all the ARP footage, messages, and everything else I have on dealing with Delgado.

It's a lot. We recorded every transaction. I hope it's good enough.

I'm sorry.

Drake

The drive to Wallen, all the snow, arriving late at night, the cold, the bar. Drake.

Everything came flooding back to her, up to when they'd left the bar. That must have been when Jimmy shocked her. Little shit.

Wells glanced at the other files Drake sent and found them to be just like he said.

She forwarded them all, except for the note, to Penta HQ for processing. It would only be a matter of time now before she would get the go-ahead to arrest Delgado.

Till then, she would keep chasing Drake.

***

None of the other boats looked remotely as fast or capable as the sleek black one, but Sammy Sanders knew he could not be too picky. He watched as Drake and Jimmy negotiated a deal with a big man, presumably the captain of the black vessel. He was too far away to hear anything, but eventually it looked like they came to an arrangement. Jimmy left Drake with the captain and walked back in the stolen hydro's direction. The captain and Drake boarded the black boat, and soon water bubbled behind it. Slowly, it turned around in the small harbor and puttered away. Sammy followed its path. It did a lazy turnabout and came back to a smaller but sturdier loading dock.

Jimmy drove the hydro to meet them at the new dock. After some maneuvering from the boat, Jimmy drove the hydro onto the back of the boat. Sammy didn't think it would fit, but clearly the captain had done it before, as he guided Jimmy onto the cargo area. Jimmy jumped out, Drake and the Captain secured the load, and minutes after boarding it, the black boat left the harbor.

Sammy stayed put and waited for it to be out of sight before he ventured down to the dock.

A bunch of tourists were taking up most of the space on the dock, indecisively moving between the three charters still left. Sammy pushed his way through them, causing them to hurl abuse at him, trying their best to hurt him with their words. He made for the one boat that looked to have a loading area big enough to carry a hydro.

The sign on the booth next to it proclaimed it to be the oldest vessel still operating in Wallen, dating back to the days of the first gold rush. Sammy believed every word. Unlike the super sleek, modern vessel Drake and Jimmy had boarded, this thing looked like it came from a different century. Which it did. Like any antique, the drivetrain had to be replaced by a cleaner one, and a hydrogen motor sat cleverly disguised in the back. But even with a new power unit, Sammy doubted it would keep up with the other boat. Still, he had no other options available.

A man, presumably the captain, stood watching him from the deck.

"You coming aboard, friend?"

Sammy smiled at him and took him up on his offer.

"Sammy Sanders," he said, hand outstretched.

The captain shook it. "Welcome aboard, Sammy Sanders. Looking at exploring our beautiful coast line?"

Sammy looked around and saw none of this beauty the old man referred to. All he saw was water.

"I wish I could. But unfortunately, this is strictly a business deal. You see, my partners left for Shangcorp earlier, but I'm afraid they left some samples behind, and I need to get it to them pronto!"

The captain's hands busied themselves with a rope as Sammy spoke, and the captain seemed more interested in the task at hand than Sammy's story.

"Seems like a strange spot to cross over to Shangcorp," the captain said, looking at his hands working the rope.

"Exploring new markets and such."

The captain stopped with the rope and looked Sammy in the eye. "I'm sorry, sir, but I don't think I'll be heading out that far today. Good luck finding your partners." The captain turned around and found more work to do.

Sammy, defeated, stepped back onto the jetty. If he lost contact with Drake and Jimmy, he would not be there when they found Turner, and would have no chance to claim the bounty. Which meant he'd have to repay Delgado. Something he couldn't do. Being in Delgado's debt was not a place he wanted to be.

His hand found the coldness of his pulse pistol.

"Excuse me! Lt. Wells from Penta Security. Can I have a word?" The voice startled him.

Turning around, fearing the worse, Sammy let go of his pistol and lifted his hands in surrender. He quickly dropped them when he saw a Penta officer boarding the boat, oblivious to his existence.

Sammy scurried to get some cover, as close to the boat as he could, huddled down, and eavesdropped on the conversation.

***

"Hi, I'm Lieutenant Wells from Penta Security. I need transport for myself and my vehicle to Shangcorp mainland. We'll pay you your current commercial rate, as well as a citizen's reward, for helping in an investigation."

Wells walked right up to the man she assumed was the captain, invaded his personal space, and made sure she gave him no options. This was an order, not a request. HQ hated paying citizens rewards, but she would worry about that later. Now she needed a boat, and this was the only one around that satisfied her criteria.

"We need to leave ASAP, as I am chasing a suspect. Where do you load cargo from?" She overwhelmed the captain and did not give him a chance to object.

"Over there." He pointed to the smaller docking bay. "But—"

Wells saw the dock and was already on her way to get the Ibex.

When she arrived at the smaller dock, the boat was already waiting. She stayed in the Ibex, and the captain guided her on. Once aboard, she gave him orders to go, and she got busy on the Ibex's DDU.

Once she felt no one had eyes on her, she allowed herself to relax. Her mind was still playing catch up after the shock, and she needed some time to recalibrate.

Looking out at the water and the snow-covered mountains behind them, Lieutenant Lily Wells breathed.

| forty-eight |

Jimmy had experienced nothing like this before. The first part of their journey on the water was calm and peaceful. He loved how the boat gently pushed the water in front of it, making a tiny wave. For a moment, Jimmy Something felt peace.

He decided the ocean was his most favorite thing in the world.

Then the captain increased the speed, the waves came, and he vomited everywhere. Everything in his body tried to come out. He was hanging over the side of the boat, Drake anchoring him, slowly dying. He tried to ask Drake to just let go of him and let it be over. This was inhumane. It was torture. He could feel the nausea stretch all the way to his toes and back to the tip of his skull. There was no place to hide. The cold, watery abyss was his only salvation. If only Drake would let go.

"Shangcorp mainland, gentleman," the captain's voice announced.

Jimmy struggled to his knees and looked over the railing. It looked exactly like Wallen.

"You sure we didn't go in a circle?" Jimmy asked Drake.

"Can't say for sure, but while you were studying the water, I kept an eye on the captain. I think we are here, buddy."

Jimmy slowly got up, head spinning, legs wobbly, and made for the short jetty.

"Thank you," he mumbled as he walked past the captain, onto the jetty, and fell to the ground.

***

"He's certainly not cut out for the sea," the captain said, as Jimmy shuffled past him.

"First time even seeing the ocean," Drake replied.

"We'll I'll be damned." The captain shook his head.

The jetty looked rundown, and there were no buildings in sight. An overgrown trail led up a hill and disappeared.

"This is the place I dropped Bobby off. Figured it would be where you wanted to go too."

"Thank you."

The captain didn't move. "You know, he is a good man. Flawed, for sure, and a temper like no man I know, but a good man. I hope I didn't make a mistake." The giant man stared into Drake's soul.

"Me too," Drake said.

The captain turned and unhooked the hydro. Drake helped, then jumped in and drove it off onto the shaky jetty. He stopped next to a shivering Jimmy and opened the passenger door. The noise of the boat's engines grew louder, and he watched it pull away.

"You ready to move again?" Drake asked through the open door.

Jimmy grumbled, got on all fours, and crawled over to the hydro. He pulled himself in and fell into the seat.

Drake had to stop himself from laughing. Jimmy had been through a lot the last day and didn't need to be ridiculed right now. Later, but not now.

With no green line guiding the way, Drake took the overgrown trail and drove to the top of the hill. It met up with a bigger, but still pretty rough, dirt road. Drake let Jimmy be and jumped on the hydro's DDU, trying to locate their position.

He suspected there to be some border control along the way, close to the coast, monitoring traffic. Looking at the map on the DDU, the area looked sparsely populated with only a handful of small towns and villages. The biggest hurdle they faced was not being able to register their arrival. With Penta and Shangcorp on the verge of war over Mars, travel between the two corporations had been restricted. Getting in and out was close to impossible. By not registering their arrival, they could move around freely, but could not use their HICs, which meant no way to pay for things or to identify themselves with. From here on, they had to stay off the grid and out of trouble. Easy.

Jimmy moaned as Drake started driving again, motion now his mortal enemy.

"You okay, buddy?" Drake asked, but received only a grunt in return.

Wallen was only a few kilometers across the ocean, but he felt like he had traveled thousands of kilometers. Once they left the ocean behind, the entire landscape changed. Endless grassy hills replaced all the mountains and forests. There were no trees, mountains, or any discernible features. Just a vast green landscape stretched out from horizon to horizon. An icy wind moved the grass around and tugged at the hydro.

The hydro bounced around on the dirt road, and Jimmy moaned every time it hit a bump. As the drive continued, Drake notice the moaning slowing down, until loud snoring replaced it.

Drake made himself comfortable and settled in for a long haul.

***

The ocean was rough, and waves crashed over the sides of the boat, drenching Sammy. He barely had enough time to jump on board the boat before it left, and finding a good hiding spot was now his primary aim. Crawling on his belly, he moved toward the only thing he could see that might offer him some protection and shelter. An old tarp that was partly covering a gigantic container was flapping in the wind. If he untied it completely, he could hide underneath it. The wind was picking up, and rain was falling now too, and Sammy hoped the captain's priority would be to steer the boat, not fix a tarp.

With salt penetrating his eyes and mouth, he crept to the tarp, staying as low as he could. The windows of the bridge were too high for him to see into, and he hoped nobody inside could see him. The knots used on the tarp looked intricate, and tugging on them proved pointless. One end of the rope protruded through the knot, and Sammy yanked it out of frustration. The whole knot disintegrated before his eyes. He crawled to the other side and pulled on the same protruding pieces. On the last piece, he held on to the tarp as well, making sure the winds didn't carry it out to sea.

Moments later, Sammy sat, wet and shaking under the tarp, plotting his next move.

| forty-nine |

"The closest port where we can unload your hydro will be at Ulon. But..."

Wells held onto the cabinet next to her. Her head was spinning from the rough seas, and she had a mild case of nausea that kept getting worse. All she wanted was to get off the boat, wherever that might be.

"But?" she prompted the captain.

"But I'm not so sure they'll be too happy to see a Penta officer."

Lt. Wells hadn't had time to think of all the logistics involved before jumping on a boat to a Shangcorp territory. With the impending war coming, getting into Shangcorp would be hard, if not impossible. Being a Penta officer made it even harder.

Unlike most of the people she saw in Wallen, the captain was quite small for a man in Wallen. Lily Wells was quite tall and muscular for a woman.

"Give me your clothes," she demanded from the captain.

"Excuse me?"

"Sorry, I didn't mean to be so blunt. If we swapped clothes, it would really help me blend in better."

The captain sized her up.

"And I'll get reimbursed, I assume?"

"Yes, of course!"

"I keep some spare clothes down in the cabin. You can get dressed there."

Wells thanked him and went down into the cabin below.

A small room with two beds, some cabinets, and a little table made up most of the cabin. Another smaller room contained a shower and toilet. Wells opened a cabinet and found some pants, a shirt, and a warm jacket. She undressed and swapped over to the captain's clothes, keeping her own boots. She folded her clothes in a neat pile and left it on the bed. An old, glass mirror surprised her when she turned around and made her jump. Staring back at her was an exact copy of the sea captain from the neck down. She went back to the cabinet and found a woolly hat. She turned back to the mirror and put the hat on.

The transformation was complete.

***

Entering the bridge, the captain burst out laughing.

"That bad, huh?"

"No, it's fine." He kept laughing.

Wells ignored him and went over to the boat's DDU that blended in with the wood cabinet to make it seem more period correct. They were halfway to Ulon, and it showed the time left to be less than an hour.

"How far do you think you'll get before they find out you're Penta?"

Wells was less worried about how long it would take than the repercussions. She had no authority to cross into Shangcorp, and if caught, Penta would distance themselves and leave her to rot. The tension between the two corporations meant they could not risk having a rogue operator out there. Shangcorp would see her as a spy and treat her as such, if caught. Penta would concoct some story of her going off the rails and chasing Drake out of a personal vendetta. From here on in, she'd have to be a shadow.

"Why are you doing this? It seems you have a lot to lose," the captain observed.

"Because someone I care about is in way over their heads, and I need to get them out of here before it's too late."

Hearing the words come out of her mouth, she realized she hadn't acknowledged it to herself until now. She had all the data she needed to get Delgado. Going after Drake had no importance to her case anymore.

She was not trying to catch him.

She was trying to rescue him.

***

Ulon appeared to be about the same size as Wallen, but devoid of all its color. Every building was concrete and gray. The captain steered the boat into the harbor and found a spot to moor. He switched the engine off and signed the waivers on the screen, acknowledging their entry into Shangcorp.

"Why did you do that?" Wells asked, feeling betrayed.

Her hand went to her hip, finding her pistol. Her eyes darted around, surveying the dock. Any moment now, Shangcorp Security would descend upon them.

"Relax. Believe me, no one is coming." The captain walked out of the bridge, onto the deck.

Wells kept her hand on her gun and her senses on high alert as she followed him out.

"Why? Why is no one coming?" She surveyed the deck and the dock, but also kept an eye on the captain.

He walked to a big container that was secured to the deck next to her Ibex. Taking some tool out of his pocket, he opened the door of the container. Wells stepped forward to have a better look.

White box meals. Hundreds, if not thousands, of them.

The captain smiled at her.

"These aren't exactly legal, so I couldn't have said anything before. Needless to say, I have a few contacts here in Ulon. So trust me, no one is coming for you." He turned and walked back to the bridge.

Wells ran to catch up.

"So you're a smuggler?" Wells asked when she caught up.

"I guess you could say that." The captain sat down on a stool. "The people in Ulon are starving. I saw an opportunity and grabbed it. They get to eat, and I make some money. I don't overcharge them, and they know it, so I have made a few friends and connections."

"What you're doing is still illegal. Selling supplies to a foreign territory that we are about to go to war with—" Wells stopped herself from lecturing the captain.

The eyes that looked back at her had no malice in them. This was not an evil man. Wells' world revolved around black and white. Gray areas did not exist in her job, yet lately she kept finding herself in these gray waters.

It made her very uncomfortable.

"Sorry," Wells said.

"I will introduce you to my contact in Ulon, but I can make no guarantees."

"Thank you," Wells said, lost for any better words.

| fifty |

As the boat slowed down, Sammy jumped over the side, onto the jetty, and scrambled for cover. He made sure that he had a good vantage of the boat. The captain emerged from the bridge, followed by another version of himself. It took Sammy a second to realize it was the lieutenant dressed up as the sea captain. They looked at something in a container, then went back into the bridge. Sammy waited patiently, and eventually they came out again. The two captains disembarked from the boat and followed a path that led to a flight of stairs. Sammy had to break cover to see where they were going next. Once he was in a concealed spot again, he saw them talk to a man standing next to a beat-up hydro. The captains came back down the stairs, boarded the boat, and got busy unloading the small hydro. It took them several minutes, and once done, they shared a hug. Sammy watched as the hydro made its way to meet up with the man at the top of the stairs again. Once he saw the other hydro approaching, he got in his, started it up, and lead them away.

"Fuck," Sammy spat out.

His plan was to stick to the lieutenant and let her do the hard work of catching up with those two idiots. But now he found himself stranded.

Water bubbled, and he saw the old boat pull out of the harbor.

Sammy Sanders had no choice now but to keep moving and play catch up.

***

"Are you sure about this?" Drake asked.

Drake and Jimmy sat on the roof of the hydro, observing the township at the bottom of the hill. It seemed quite small, with only a few hydros coming and going in the hour they sat there. Jimmy was shaking in the cold, but he seemed to be over his need to vomit consistently.

"We can't use credits here, ya know. The moment we get scanned, the local security will be all over us," Jimmy replied with clattering teeth.

"But what if we need it later on?"

"Then we'll burn that bridge when we get to it."

"I don't think that's how it goes," Drake said. "I guess you're right, though."

"About the bridge?"

"No, Jimmy, about worrying about it later. Let's get down there and see what happens."

The road was still unsealed, and Jimmy didn't look too happy bouncing around again. Luckily for everyone, it was a short drive. Drake parked the hydro in front of what seemed to be the only shop in the village. The people walking around were quite small and had weathered, tanned skin. The wind seemed to be ever blowing, resulting in furrowed faces, forever squinting.

The small shop was warm and welcoming, cluttered from floor to ceiling with many goods. This was the place to get anything and everything you needed.

"Welcome, stranger, how can we help?" Drake had to ask the stranger to repeat himself as he switched his ARP to translation mode.

"Hi there. I'm Drake, and this is my friend, Jimmy. We are travelers, and hoping to trade with you for some goods."

Jimmy stepped around Drake and revealed the big pulse rifle they'd gained from the bandits.

The shopkeepers' eyes lit up.

"Mmm, and what did you have in mind to trade for?"

Drake looked at Jimmy, who nodded.

"Powdered white box meals."

The shopkeeper looked surprised.

"White box meals for the gun?"

"Powdered meals, yes."

The shopkeeper did some mental arithmetic. "I can give you fifty meals."

Drake knew he was low balling him, but at least they were negotiating.

"Hundred and twenty," Drake went high.

The shopkeeper seemed to take this seriously and gave his next offer considerable thought.

"Sixty."

"Hundred."

"Seventy."

"Ninety."

"Seventy-five."

The number Drake had been waiting on. He shook the man's hand.

"Seventy-five."

The shopkeeper disappeared into the back and came out with a sealed box of dehydrated white box meals. He placed it on the counter in front of Drake and cut it open.

"One, two, three ..." he counted out, till he got to twenty-five. He resealed the box and gave it to Drake. "Box of hundred, less the twenty-five," he explained.

Drake took the box, and Jimmy handed over the gun, completing the deal.

***

Jimmy knew the look of starvation. He had seen it many times. Especially in reflections when he was younger. The faces he had seen since crossing the ocean all had the look. He knew what they needed. Knew what they could use as currency. When people were hungry, they'd do anything for food.

He sure had.

"Not sure how far this will get us, but at least we have something, right?" Drake said.

Bartering your way through a foreign territory was not an exact science, but Jimmy had faith in the amount of meals they had.

"We have the next best thing to credits, ya know," he said with confidence.

He knew it was even better than credits, especially here in the far out regions. When they sat on the roof of the hydro, observing the village, he saw almost no one reaching for a HIC or swiping their arms. Human Interface Consoles were part of life in New Franco, but here it was a luxury, an item not needed for survival. Even if they wanted to pay these people with credits, they wouldn't be able to transfer it to them. The shopkeeper had one, and Jimmy figured he ran the town. Everyone else seemed to be only concerned with surviving.

Which meant food, and that they had.

"Okay, partner, where to first?" Jimmy asked Drake, ready to input their destination into the hydro's DDU.

The village and the surrounding villages were so remote that no roads showed up on the DDU map, only trails. Jimmy hoped they were big enough to fit the big off-roader. He sat, patiently watching Drake as he plotted their next move.

An alarm pulled his attention back to the DDU's screen. A warning flashed in red. A serious warning.

"Drake..."

***

Having no roads or infrastructure to travel on was way out of Drake's comfort zone. He used to live on the road, but that meant well-maintained roads, hydro stations, and places to eat. And importantly, places to drink. He could stay away from home for weeks, knowing everything he needed would be on his journey.

But now, he knew nothing of what lay ahead. The map on the screen only showed green, with a few tiny, squiggly lines drawn between tiny dots of towns. This place was barren, almost void of life. It offered him none of the things he needed.

"Okay, partner, where to first?" Jimmy asked.

He did not know, but didn't want Jimmy to know he felt lost and untethered. He picked the next town as their destination, and then he would pick the next one again, and again, until they finally came to civilization.

"Drake ..." Jimmy said.

Drake realized an alarm was going off.

"Some issue?" he asked.

"Um, yeah. We're almost out of hydrogen."

Drake's finger nervously tried to find the crack in the steering wheel, but his muscle memory didn't know they were in a different hydro.

"Dammit, Jimmy. Fuck, that's not good."

"I'm sorry."

"No, it's not your fault. Obviously. I just don't think anyone here has hydrogen."

Why didn't Jimmy tell him to refill before they left Wallen? Drake could strangle him right now, but yelling and screaming would not make hydrogen magically appear.

"Time to use those barter meals of ours and see if we can get out of this mess," Drake said as calmly as he could, his thumb still searching for the crack.

| fifty-one |

Hector Delgado woke up with a pulse rifle in his face. It wasn't the first time it had happened, so it didn't faze him too much. Usually, the person holding the gun ended up dying, not him. He sat up, brushing the gun aside, and took in the room.

It was full.

Penta Security officers filled the room from wall to wall, everyone pointing a pulse weapon at him. Deon was kneeling, hands tied behind his back, staring at him expressionlessly. No one was saying a word or yelling orders, so Delgado sat and waited.

Word must have gotten out that he was awake, as bodies shuffled to the side to part way for someone important to walk in. Someone to come and claim their prize.

The head of Hector Delgado.

A woman dressed in the Penta Security uniform walked up and took a place in front of him. Nothing about her stood out to Delgado. She struck him as boring and insignificant. He didn't acknowledge her, instead fixing his gaze toward Deon. Dean gave him a slight shake of the head. He'd kept his mouth shut. Good boy.

The bodies shuffled back into place, securing the room and trapping the big, dangerous man.

"Hector Delgado, you are now in custody of Penta Incorporated Security Forces on suspicion of terrorism. We have now revoked all your rights as a citizen of Penta Corporations."

The woman nodded, and two officers grabbed him and lifted him to his feet. It seemed this woman had more power than he assumed.

"Surely, we can work this out, without all this." Hector did a swoop of the room with his head.

"Take him away," the woman ordered.

The sea of bodies parted again, and the officers ushered him out of the room.

"Deon, call her," Delgado said, as he passed his right-hand man.

***

The driver in front knew these roads like the back of his hand. He was driving at an incredible speed, and Lt. Wells had to put all her extensive training to the test. She loved it. For a second, she almost forgot what her goal was and instead immersed herself in the race. She knew it wasn't an actual race, but the adrenaline was pumping and she pushed even harder. Some parts of her job were borderline addictive. The chase, the hunt, the endorphins. She wasn't sure if she could cope without them. Even on her days off, she had to blow off some steam, chase that rush, spending hours in the gym or shooting range.

The hydro in front of her made a sharp turn, and she followed suit. The more she pushed, the faster he went, getting closer to his limits. His hydro started sliding in corners, and fishtailing out of them. Wells knew she'd have to slow down a bit to avoid him or both of them crashing. Her competitive side, however, wouldn't allow it. She inched even closer to him, almost touching his bumper. Her reactions to his needed to be within a fraction of a second. And it was.

Then the finish line approached.

A small village, dissected by the road. The driver in front knew his stuff and pumped the brakes twice to warn her to slow down. Wells' heart was racing. She could do this all day.

The hydro pulled over, and she stopped next to it. The driver opened his window.

"Where did you learn to drive like that! It was incredible!"

Wells just smiled. He was right. It was.

"If you're going to hang around for a while, we actually have races on the weekend."

"Maybe next time. But first I have some business to take care of."

The driver looked dejected.

"Sure. Would be great to have some actual competition. Okay, let's go." He jumped out of his hydro, and Wells followed him.

The driver took her into a small building, built from materials blown here by the wind, it seemed. None of the walls or panels making up the walls matched—some were rusty and others painted. Wells hoped it wouldn't cave in on them.

Inside the death trap, it was warm, but too dark for Wells' liking, preferring to see her environment and would-be threats. She switched her ARP on and set it on low light conditions, not full night mode. The interior became brighter, and all the shadows disappeared, revealing a room with a counter and a workbench behind it. First impressions were some kind of workshop. On the side walls, junk cluttered the shelves. Wells had seen many chop shops before, and this one, albeit much smaller than a regular one, had all the trademarks.

A sound from a back room announced the shop's owner's presence. Footsteps followed, and a figure emerged from the back.

A small, leathery, gray-haired woman.

"What do you want?" she snapped at them.

"Hi, Nanna, this is my friend Lily," the driver replied.

Nanna? Wells' face asked the driver.

He clearly understood her expression. "Lily, this is my grandmother, Anna. But everyone calls her Nanna."

Nanna glared at Wells through dirty goggles. She seemed like a sweetheart.

"Hi, I'm Lily," Wells said.

"I know. He already told me. What do you want?"

Wells reminded herself to keep smiling and not slap the old witch.

"I was told that you might help me with some items I require."

Nanna tilted her head. "Who told you?"

Wells, smiling, lifted her HIC and swiped a message from the sea captain to Nanna's HIC. Wells saw Nanna's HIC light up as the message went through, but Nanna kept her gaze on her. Wells looked at Nanna's grandson for some backup, but he clearly knew to not rush her. All she got from him was a weak smile.

Finally, Nanna tore her eyes away from Wells and read the message on her HIC.

Still reading, she walked over to a shelf and grabbed something from the junk shelves. She returned it to the counter in front of Wells.

"It's old and stinks, but it works and can run on external batteries."

Wells looked at the antique Human Interface Console lying on the counter. The top layer of skin was missing, but dried skin on its edges told her that this had to be done on the black market. This extraction involved no professionals. She refused to think who it belonged to or how it ended up here. She'd busted many illegal HIC operations before, but this was her first time buying from one. She picked it up and placed it on top of hers. She shuddered, feeling the dead skin touching hers. She swiped it, and it came to life.

She now had a working Shangcorp issued HIC.

***

"Your grandma seems nice," Wells said, back at the hydros.

"She can be."

"Thank you for your help. I wish I could pay you, but I can't risk connecting you to me."

"No need. As long as you promise to race me again one day."

Wells liked the young man. "I promise."

The young driver wished her luck, got in his hydro, and left, wheels spinning, going the only speed he knew.

Wells got back in the Ibex and set up her new HIC. Nanna, or the black market dealers, had already formatted it and there was no information on it. A clean slate. She used her actual name to ensure she didn't get it wrong somewhere and transferred a small amount of her personal credits over to it. Once done, she secured it to her arm, covering her Penta issued one. It looked dodgy as hell, but it would allow her to move around freely, buying essentials like food and hydrogen. If a Shangcorp official scanned it, it would pass, as long as they looked past the bad installation.

Luckily, Shangcorp was the land built on bribes.

The map on the Data Display Unit awaited her input. It was a sea of green, with thin lines connecting small dots. She zoomed out, found the first sizeable town, and dropped a marker on it. She would not find Drake and Jimmy out here in the wild, where kids raced each other on the public roads and wind provided people with their building materials.

No, she needed to go where Drake would go. He was a city boy and needed to be in a city to thrive. That's where he would go.

So that's where she would go.

| fifty-two |

The apple exploded into juicy fragments, staining the wall and littering the floor. Pieces of apple, once stuck to the wall, lost their battle with gravity and joined the rest of the residue on the floor.

"That narcissistic prick!"

Another beautiful ripe apple met its fate against the wall.

"Why couldn't he stick to the plan and use one at a time? No, no, no. He had to use them all in one day and attract even more attention to himself."

Another ill-fated apple flew past Deon's head and smashed into pieces. He didn't flinch. Not only because he'd had worse things than fresh fruit thrown at his head before, but also because he wasn't even in the same room. In fact, the only person who could see him was Lucy Hughes, on her Augmented Retinal Projector. All the apples she threw was at an image only she could see.

But it made her feel better.

If only for a moment.

"What's the plan?" Deon asked her in his emotionless, monotone voice.

What was the plan? It used to be, manipulate Hector Delgado and run most of New Franco's crime scene from behind very safe doors. And for a few years, it worked out so well.

Then he forgot who his financial backer was, and his ambition outgrew his expanding waist. Week by week, month by month, she watched him drifting further and further away from her control, gaining confidence and getting big ideas.

Ideas that didn't include her.

It did not upset her that Penta had him. She was going to sacrifice him to Penta as a trade to keep Bob anyway. She was angry that it didn't happen on her terms and under her control. She hated not having control over every aspect of her life.

Over everyone in her life.

"The plan, Deon, is for you to show everyone in sector fifty-nine that everything is under control. You tell them that Hector will be back shortly, and until then, they answer to you. Understand?"

Deon nodded, and Lucy ended the call.

She looked at the apple she was clutching and spared its life.

***

According to the telemetry on the screen, they would make it to the next town, but not much farther. Which put a lot of pressure on the tiny village to have a ready supply of hydrogen. Drake had seen some hydros around, and they had to get their fuel from somewhere. Hopefully, for them, that somewhere was close by.

The villages were quite close to each other when traveling by hydro. People still traveled by horse when the villages started, so they must have felt far away from each other. Back then, it would have taken a day to travel between two settlements. Only a few hours after leaving the first village, the second one came up on the screen.

The speed Drake was going also made it go quicker than normal.

"Wow, I didn't even get time to puke, ya know?" Jimmy said, white knuckles holding onto the door rail.

"Sorry, buddy, but night's falling, and we need to get hydrogen before we get stranded here. Wherever here is."

Drake slowed down as they entered the tiny village. It looked the same size and layout as the previous, and his hopes of finding hydrogen waned.

"See if you can't spot a shop or someplace that sells, I don't know, anything. Okay?"

"Okay, but there doesn't seem to be any shops around, ya know?"

Jimmy was right. The few buildings that made up this village looked all like housing units. None of them seemed big enough or had any signs that marked them as a commercial property.

"Anything?" Drake asked.

"Nah. Has to be something though, right? I mean, where does that guy buy his from, ya know?" Jimmy asked.

Drake looked over at Jimmy, who pointed out his window.

A Hydrocomet loomed behind a small dwelling, looking comically out of place.

"Jimmy! Yes!" Drake couldn't believe how exited he was, seeing the big truck.

"Yeah!" Jimmy replied with gusto in his voice, but confusion on his face.

"Let's find that hauler. Doubt that I'll know them, but we have a chance here at least."

Drake grabbed the door handle, ready to get out, but Jimmy pulled him back.

"Or," Jimmy started, "we can *borrow* the Hydrocomet."

A thought that never crossed Drake's mind.

"No, Jimmy, I mean—"

It would be the easiest way. Draining hydrogen out of a vehicle was slow and potentially lethal. And if the hauler was like most haulers Drake knew, he would rather shoot him in the face than help him out. They were a brotherhood, but you had to know your brother.

"I'll hack it in no time, ya know. Easy-peasy, elbow greasy."

Drake imagined being behind the wheel of a truck again, albeit a more modern version of his beloved Hydrostar. He could already feel the sensation of it gliding along the road, soaking up all the bumps that rocked normal hydros. Looking out from his high perch, taking in the landscapes.

Feeling free.

"So, what do you say?"

"Can you run a scan on it first? See if it belongs to an individual or a company?"

"Sure, but it makes no difference if I can hack it or not, ya know," Jimmy replied.

"It makes a difference to me, okay?"

Jimmy rolled his eyes and got to work on his HIC. The Hydrocomet's registered identification number was visible from their position, and Jimmy used it to access the Shangcorp registered vehicle database.

"Company. Called—" Jimmy burst out laughing. Drake couldn't see his arm and had to wait for him to calm down. "Ace Haul!" He started again.

"Acehaul?" Drake chuckled.

"Yup, poor guy works for an *acehole.*"

It took them another two minutes before they could talk again.

"And the hauler? Any data on them?"

Jimmy searched further. "Nicholas Wei Brown the third," Jimmy read out the name.

"Must be the fanciest hauler I've ever heard of," Drake replied.

"According to his record, he is anything but, ya know. Multiple drunk-and-disorderly, aggravated assaults, drunk driving, public urination. Sounds fancy, but just a hauler like you, ya know?"

Drake couldn't even fake to be insulted. The list Jimmy read was a copy of his and almost any other haulers' record. Nicholas Wei Brown the third, fancy by name, hauler by actions.

"And, it seems he has only been working for the aceholes for a month. Previous two companies fired him, on suspicion of theft. No details given."

Okay, so maybe slightly worse than himself.

"Let's do it," Drake said.

Jimmy's eyes sparkled.

It was his time to shine.

| fifty-three |

Sammy Sanders had never felt so lost and alone in his life. Sitting on the jetty, he had no plans, no resources, or any contacts to help him out. Back in New Franco, he could get anything he wanted whenever he wanted. Multiple people owed him favors and would do his bidding for him.

But out here, he was a no one with nothing to help him.

The sun was getting lower, reflecting brightly on the water. It took Sammy a second to see the three circles dancing around in the glare.

"Sorry, I was going to call—"

"Where are you?"

"I'm in Ulon, on the coast of—"

"I know it. Go to the harbormaster's office. I'll transfer credits to him, and he'll set you up with a hydro. Do you need a pulse gun?"

"No, I still have—"

"Good. Go now. And Sammy?"

"Yes?"

"Do not fucking fail me."

Without hesitation, Sammy jumped up and ran to the harbormaster's office.

***

Lily Wells had a tough decision to make. Night had fallen, and she was stuck in a small village in the middle of nowhere. She knew Drake and Jimmy had to be close, but didn't know how far ahead or behind they were. She was tired, cold, and in a strange territory. Penta had also been calling all day, trying to get a hold of her. Luckily, the information Drake had given her was enough for them to proceed in capturing Delgado without her there. Everyone knew she did things her own way. It might land her in trouble occasionally, but her results gave her a freedom others didn't have. She would have another few days before they sent for her.

The village was only a few living units, and Lt. Wells couldn't see anywhere offering lodging. The Ibex, although small, contained a heating unit and a portable tent, more for emergencies than anything else.

Wells drove away from the village, toward a small hill, and parked the Ibex next to an outcrop in the rock. It would not provide much shelter, but would help keep the icy wind at bay. She set up the small tent and emergency bedding and got inside. It was freezing. The blanket, plugged into the Ibex, began warming up, and shortly after, she felt the warmth penetrate her body. It made her feel better.

And worse.

Lily Wells cried. She didn't try to figure out why, she just let it happen. All the stress, the frustrations, the loneliness. Chasing a man she should have nothing to do with. It was none of these things, and all of them together. She always had control of everything in her life, especially her emotions, but tonight, lying alone in the middle of a barren landscape, freezing cold, she had no resistance.

There was no need to go after Drake anymore. His only use was his knowledge to get to Delgado. He gave her that. He made sure she had everything she needed to do her job. But she couldn't stop chasing him. She had to catch him. She had to find him. She felt angry at herself for allowing this. For going against everything she stood for. The only person who mattered to her was herself. She was all she had. So why was she trying to save this man from getting himself killed in this foreign territory?

He was in way over his head. She saw how he operated with Zuma, making shit up as he went, relying on luck rather than skill or knowledge. The man was an idiot whose luck was about to run out at any minute. Running around Shangcorp, with Jimmy in tow, was a recipe for disaster.

If she had the chance to save him, an opportunity to prevent his death or capture, and she didn't take it, it would haunt her forever. She couldn't deny it anymore. His life mattered to her.

Wells felt better, having cleared her mind and purging her emotions. Admitting to herself why she was in this foreign place. Finding her purpose.

She had to save Benjamin Drake.

***

The harbormaster had everything Sammy needed. A hydro, food, and some fresh clothes. He said little, just gave Sammy the codes to operate the hydro and a box with the supplies. It was getting late, so the harbormaster allowed him to stay in a room at the back of the office. It was warm and dry, and that's all Sammy wanted.

The floor was his bed, but he fell asleep in seconds.

The next morning, Sammy woke up refreshed and ready for action.

He now had two parties to deal with. The lieutenant and the idiots. The plan was to track and follow them to Turner, and then bring him back to New Franco. Now there was also the lieutenant to worry about. He didn't know how much farther ahead of him she was, but knew he had to beat her to them, or eliminate her.

Either was fine by him.

Sammy packed his things into the hydro and noticed a young man observing him the entire time. The kid just stood at his hydro, watching his every move. He lifted a hand in greeting, but got nothing back.

"Well fuck you too," Sammy mumbled as he got in his hydro and sped off.

✱

Lily Wells woke up at her normal early hour and organized herself for the day. She ate a white box meal, ran diagnostics on the hydro, and broke up camp. She studied the map and set her new destination. The sun poked over the horizon, bathing the landscape in color and showing her the vastness of this strange land.

She was about to drive off when three circles danced in front of her. She looked at her HIC, but it showed no caller name. Confused for a second, Wells remembered the old, stinky HIC she'd acquired the previous day. She'd taken it off before bed last night and placed it in her carry bag. Rummaging through it now, she found it, and swiped without looking at the name.

"Hey, lieutenant. I didn't know if you would answer."

It was the young driver she raced and who helped her obtain the smelly HIC.

"Hey," she replied, realizing she never even asked his name.

"So, it might be nothing, or maybe it is, I dunno, but I saw this guy at the harbor, and he's not from here. Usually that means nothing, but something felt wrong about him."

Wells watched the young man fumble on his outdated HIC.

"There, I've sent you an image I got of him. It's not great, but maybe you can use it. Like I said, it's most likely nothing."

"Thanks so much. It seems I owe you two races now?"

His smile made Wells' heart ache. War was coming. She would most likely never see him again, yet the thought of her racing with him and his friends gave him hope.

Wells prayed she would not have to break her promise.

They said their goodbyes, and Wells opened the file.

It was a grainy, out-of-focus image of a man climbing into a hydro, his face barely recognizable.

Barely, but not impossible. Wells swiped the file to the Ibex's DDU and used some Penta software to enhance the image, which also simultaneously ran an identification program.

It only took a minute.

It was the same face that Star had showed her in Porterville.

A note on the image stated this man to be part of an investigation. She clicked on the note, and it showed the footage she received from Star. The faces matched, and therefore automatically lodged as part of her investigation. A positive ID also came through.

Sammy Sanders.

A small-time crook and hauler. His record read like most haulers, but something stood out to Wells. He'd done an extensive amount of work for Bob Turner. Which meant he knew Drake.

You didn't need to be a top-notch security officer like Wells to make the connection that he was after Turner's bounty.

The only question was, what would he do to get it?

| fifty-four |

Drake could not have slept any better.

He would never admit it to anyone, even himself, but the Hydrocomet blew the Hydrostar out of the water, comfort-wise. The twin bunks, the small kitchenette, and even the bathroom were bigger than the ones in the Hydrostar. Unlike in the Hydrostar, his head and feet did not touch the walls when sleeping. Nor did his knees hit the wall when taking a dump. But he could never admit to it.

"Wow, what a nice truck, ya know?" Jimmy announced from the top bunk.

"It's no Hydrostar, but it's okay, I guess," Drake lied.

"Pfft. You and your Hydrostars. We are going to need a long chat when we're done here about what truck we're buying, okay?" Jimmy sounded very serious.

"Okay, partner. We'll cross that bridge when we get to it."

Everyone was in a good mood this morning. Last night went off without a hitch. Nicholas Wei Brown III was not in the truck, and must have been sleeping in one of the housing units next to the Hydrocomet. One less thing to worry about. As Jimmy set to work on the truck's DDU, Drake got to work on the hydro. It was close to running out of fuel, but he also deflated all the tires and cut the air hose, so whoever jumped in it could not use the onboard tire inflator. If Nick chased them, it would not be in this hydro. He would most likely find another one, but Drake planned on being far, far away by then.

Jimmy had the truck hacked in minutes, and Drake jumped into the driver's seat. He made sure he knew exactly which direction to travel in, before flooring the accelerator and high-tailing it out of there. He kept the speed high, Jimmy monitoring the radar and rearview monitor, but after an hour, it was clear no one was chasing them.

They'd found a spot to park and made themselves at home for the night.

"So, if we drive all day, we'll be in Cathapore by night, ya know?" Jimmy said, jumping down from his bunk.

Drake knew they were close, but hadn't looked at the numbers last night.

"Oh," he replied.

"So, I say, let's get some food in us and hit the road."

Drake took a deep breath. The next twenty-four hours were going to be crucial. Two strangers seen traveling in remote Shangcorp would surely attract some attention. Chances were, someone could already have spread the word about their presence here. If Mr. Turner was indeed in Cathapore and he heard these rumors, he might disappear forever. They had to get there fast, but also stealthily.

After a couple of white box meals, Drake and Jimmy set themselves up for the last leg of their journey. Drake ran all the system checks, and Jimmy made himself comfortable for a long day of napping and playing on his HIC.

"Huh," Drake muttered, as he pressed the start button.

"You forgot how to start it?" Jimmy asked.

"Um, no, it's just ..." Drake scanned the telemetry, but saw nothing wrong.

He pressed the start button again, but nothing happened.

"Oh, shit!" Jimmy yelled.

"What?"

"It's locked. Look at the numbers on the screen. Everything is static. Dickhead the turd must have called it in, ya know."

Security forces would already be on their way, and depending on when the notification went through and where they were located, could be on top of them any minute. It was time to ditch the truck and run.

"Grab your stuff. We need to move!" Drake unbuckled and jumped into the rear cabin, grabbing things as he went.

Jimmy followed his lead.

Bags packed, Drake swiped the small DDU next to the door to exit. Nothing happened.

"Shit. We're locked in."

"Um, just shoot out the windows!" Jimmy suggested, pulse pistol already drawn.

"No good, buddy, they're bulletproof."

Drake moved Jimmy aside and went into the bathroom.

"Good idea. We should go before we leave," Jimmy said.

Drake kneeled down in the small shower, took the drain out, and removed a panel from the floor. He grabbed a small lever, turned it, and the doors swung open.

"Emergency exit. Guess they didn't figure on a hauler stealing a truck."

Drake and Jimmy exited the Hydrocomet and ran a few meters. The landscape was barren, and they tried to spot the incoming forces.

"Anything?" Drake asked Jimmy.

"Nah, nothing," Jimmy replied.

"We can't stand here all day waiting for them."

"Wait. There! Yes, look, over there!" Jimmy yelled.

Drake followed Jimmy's finger and looked in the direction he pointed. The land was open, with small, undulating hills, and they could see for kilometers. Drake strained his eyes, but could not make out the source of Jimmy's excitement. He switched his ARP on and zoomed in as much as the ARP allowed, which wasn't much. But it was enough for him to spot a small dust cloud drifting in their direction.

"Looks like a small hydro, ya know?" Jimmy said.

Drake observed it a while longer. He wanted to make sure it had no insignias or logos on it. The closer it came, the clearer it was. It was an old junker. A tiny rust bucket barely plodding along.

"We need to get to that road, Jimmy. We need to haul ass. Let's go!" Drake slapped Jimmy on the back and set off running.

"Ah, man," Jimmy muttered as he followed Drake, "not running again."

***

It was going to be close.

The old hydro was taking its time, allowing Jimmy to catch up. Drake was already standing in the middle of the narrow dirt road, ready to stop the hydro. Jimmy was still running toward him, stopping every ten seconds to catch his breath, before setting off at a blistering pace again. Drake was a spectator in the world's slowest race. He hoped Jimmy would win, but the smart money was on the hydro.

Jimmy was still shuffling and puffing his way toward Drake, and the hydro was now close enough for Drake to wave his arms around in the hope it would slow down and stop.

"Hurry, Jimmy!" Drake yelled, fearing they might lose their opportunity to catch a ride.

Drake could now see the driver's face and intensified flailing his arms.

A dust cloud went up in the air as the driver hit the brakes, bringing the hydro to a standstill. Drake waited for the dust to settle, as to not startle the driver, and give Jimmy time to catch up.

"Okay … just … give … me …" Jimmy breathed next to him, before falling on his back in the dirt.

"Seriously?" Drake looked down at him. Jimmy just stayed there.

"Is your friend okay?" a voice came from the hydro.

Drake refocused on the hydro and the driver leaning out the window. Like the hydro, its driver had seen many miles.

"Thank you so much for stopping. Our hydro broke down, and we're trying to get to the nearest town." Drake stuck to the truth as close as possible.

"I see. I know most people around here, but you two—"

Drake smiled and shot Jimmy a look. The look meant, *get your pulse gun ready.* But Drake could only imagine what Jimmy would think it meant.

"No, we are not. We are trying to find a friend that went missing. To be honest, we are really worried about him, and completely out of our depth." That one was almost all true.

The man looked suspiciously at Drake.

"Is he in trouble? Your missing friend."

"We don't know, but he might be if we don't find him."

The man sat, studying him.

"I don't know. Something seems off. Where is your broken hydro?"

Drake shot Jimmy another look.

"We can pay for your services," Drake said, remembering the stack of powdered white box meals they had.

"So you lied?"

"No, we are trying to find a friend. I'm just offering to compensate you for the service of transporting us."

They were wasting precious time. The local security force could descend upon them at any second.

"Please," Drake tried for the last time. Next time it would be Jimmy's pulse gun doing the talking.

"How much?"

Drake heard Jimmy rise behind him, and he stuck out a hand to stop him in case he understood the looks after all.

"We have food to trade," Drake said, and pulled a few meals out of his bag.

The man would be a horrible card player. The moment he saw the meals, Drake saw his Adam's apple bob up and down.

"Credits would be better, but..."

Drake waited, giving him time to convince himself.

"How many do you have?" the man asked.

"About seven," Drake lied. As they hoped, bartering was still rife in this region, and going high now would cost him dearly.

"Shame. If you had twenty, I might have considered it. A shame." The man faked getting ready to drive off.

"Okay. Wait. If we give you our rations as well, we can scrape together fifteen."

"Fifteen?" The man confirmed.

Drake bent over the bag, careful not to show his full stash, and produced fifteen powdered white box meals.

"Fifteen."

"Okay, well, jump in then," the man replied.

They grabbed their gear and squeezed themselves into the tiny, old hydro.

"Hang on," the man replied and took off at a speed barely faster than Jimmy's running.

| fifty-five |

The radar showed the incoming vehicle to be traveling in her direction, and only slighter faster than her. It was still too early to tell if it was someone she had to worry about, but she had a feeling it was. Any vehicle traveling at that speed had to have a purpose. Besides, most of the hydros she'd seen so far could not do it. This vehicle was not local.

Lt. Wells was driving well within her ability, and knew, if needed, she could most likely outrun the vehicle. But doing so would only raise suspicion and result in a roadblock down the line. She held her speed and waited it out.

Another vehicle appeared on the radar. Traveling in the same direction, but coming in at a different trajectory. The two vehicles were going at the same speed and would join up soon. She now had multiple bogeys chasing her down. She held her speed and monitored them. They were still a long distance behind her, and with their speeds only fractionally faster than hers, would take a while before catching up.

She still had time.

A third vehicle appeared, this one almost at a right angle to her. Its trajectory also set to intersect hers. She was being hunted. She could figure out why later, but for now, she had to concentrate on keeping her Ibex on the road and staying ahead of her pursuers.

The landscape, although open, had rocks everywhere. Some barely sticking out, but with enormous mass underground. If she ventured off-road, she might rip a wheel off. So she had no choice but to stick to the road. The three vehicles were all traveling at the same speed and at the same distance from her. They would all catch up at the same time.

Wells was driving at her limit. The Ibex barely hung on in the corners, the tires straining for grip on the loose dirt surface. The back drifted out of every corner, and she had to fight it into a straight line just to have another corner show up. Today there was no enjoyment in the act. She was not racing, but escaping. The Ibex lifted a back wheel through a corner, and her heart skipped a beat. She slowed down a fraction, regained control, and went full throttle again.

To her amazement, the three vehicles were catching up. She realized she might be wrong, thinking they weren't local. Clearly they knew these roads if they could drive at these speeds. Lt. Wells slowed down, admitting defeat. She had been out classed today.

The three dots on the radar were now racing toward her.

Wells gave up.

She pulled over and switched her DDU to show the incoming vehicles on the windscreen rather than on the DDU. They had her. No point in crashing and hurting herself. The first vehicle appeared on the screen, and soon the other two were visible too. Enormous clouds of dust chased them as they hurled toward her. They were now only seconds away.

All three vehicles joined on the road and fell in line, forming a long, speeding train. Wells took a deep breath and readied herself to get out of the Ibex and face her fate.

The Ibex rocked, as the first, then the second, and the third hydros blew past her. They didn't even slow down a bit, but sped past at full bore. Wells looked on as the dust cloud enveloped her, and the three hydros disappeared. She switched the screen to show the radar and watch the three aligned dots drive away.

She waited till they were out of range. By then, the dust had also settled and she could see the road again.

"What the ..." she mumbled.

Although the entire experience shook her a bit, she was back firing on all cylinders in no time. She had been part of fast-moving security hydro caravans before. And she had seen people pull over to the side, like her, to get out of the way. Less so in the inner sectors, where people were more self-entitled, but it was commonplace for people to get out of the way, avoiding getting shunted off the road. No wonder they didn't even slow down.

But they were definitely in a hurry.

Which led her to believe something big had happened up ahead. The security officer in her wanted nothing more than to chase those hydros down and follow them to see what was up. But that would put her close to the incident and increase her chances of capture. She needed to let it go and concentrate on finding Drake.

Looking at the map on the DDU, she saw only one road. Her options were less than limited. She had no choice but to travel in the direction of the speeding hydros. Lt. Wells was not an overthinker or prone to indecisiveness. If the road forward was the only way, she would take it and deal with the consequences when she crossed them.

The Ibex kicked up rocks and dust as she pulled out, back onto the road and toward the unknown.

**

It took her only a few minutes to catch up to the three hydros. They were all parked next to an outcrop, forming a semicircle around a Hydrocomet. It looked completely out of place here in the barren landscape with its rundown villages and outdated technologies. It shouldn't be here, a fact enforced by the three security hydros surrounding it.

Wells slowed down enough to have a quick glimpse and get some footage on her ARP before speeding off again. Just a nosey passerby having a look. No one seemed to pay her any attention as she drove by. The Ibex, although unmarked, was still a new model vehicle. Something of a rarity in these parts, but whatever was happening over at the Hydrocomet seemed more captivating. She monitored her screens and radar to ensure someone hadn't decided to take an interest in her after all. But the longer she drove, the clearer it became: they only had eyes for the truck.

The road was in decent enough shape that she could activate Autodrive. Her speed fell considerably, but it allowed her to access the footage she took at the scene. She transferred the files to the Ibex's DDU and displayed them on the windscreen.

A Hydrocomet, doors flung open, stood surrounded by the three security hydros. She had never seen these model hydros before, and had to assume they were from Shangcorp or some local private corporation. The way they stood and the viewing angle she had meant that there were no clear logos on them. If she sent the footage back to Penta, someone could identify them, but she saw no point in doing that. She had no interest in who the local law was.

What piqued her interest was the Hydrocomet.

She was chasing Benjamin Drake, a hauler to the bone, and just saw an abandoned Hydrocomet. What were the odds of it being unrelated or a coincidence? It had to be connected. And if it was, it meant he left it there. Why? For a better vehicle? What vehicle would tempt a hauler away from a late model Hydrocomet? Or did something chase him away from the vehicle? That would leave him on foot if it happened quickly. The doors on the Hydrocomet were open, suggesting they might have left in a hurry.

The speed the local hydros came flying past her also told her that this happened recently.

Drake was close by.

Wells scanned the radar. If they raced to the scene, they must have thought they had a chance of catching the perpetrator. They would not be hanging around the abandoned truck for too long before they set off on a pursuit again.

The race to get to Benjamin Drake was on.

***

A second later, and he would have been dead.

Or at least injured.

Either way, when the hydro came speeding up behind him, muscle memory kicked in and Sammy moved ever so slightly to the middle of the road to block it. No one overtook Sammy Sanders, thank you very much. Although he wasn't in a big Hydrocomet or any kind of truck, he couldn't help but prevent whoever came flying toward him from passing him. Only when a crash was imminent did he remember he had to be inconspicuous and fly under the radar.

Causing a hydro crash was not being that.

So, at the last minute, he swung off the road, allowing the speed freak to blast past him. As it did, he noticed it looked like a security vehicle. Nothing he'd seen before, but then every region and territory had their own designs and insignias. It also meant that something was happening nearby. Remembering he had to be cautious, Sammy slowed down.

Better safe than sorry.

A small, unmarked road veered off to his right. He hesitated for a second, then took a gamble and turned. Drake was getting away, and there was some incident ahead, which might delay him even more. Sammy decided taking the smaller road was worth the risk.

And it was.

Coming over a hill, he had the perfect vantage point to see a small hydro, maybe a kilometer away, sitting on the road. Being super cautious, he stopped, switched on his ARP, and zoomed in.

It was a shitty, little hydro, and it seemed the driver had hit a pedestrian. There was a person on the ground, and another one talking to the driver. Most likely the passenger going to check on the injured person.

This could be a problem.

Maybe the security vehicle was speeding toward them, following a different route. Sammy looked around, but couldn't see any more alternative roads. Slowly, he drove toward the accident. He kept his ARP on, and as he approached, the injured person got up and looked straight at him. His face as clear as day.

Jimmy Something.

The other person turned sideways, and Sammy would bet his life it looked like Drake. Sammy stopped his hydro to better observe them. Sitting still on the side of the road, they would only spot him if they actively looked for him.

After talking for a short time, and exchanging something, they got into the crappy hydro and took off.

Sammy Sanders' smile appeared for the first time in days.

| fifty-six |

The town of Billiwon proved to be a huge contradiction. Driving into town, cramped in the small hydro, it looked like all the towns Drake and Jimmy had seen so far in mainland Shangcorp. Devoid of color, cold, and uninviting. Same as the people.

It was not bigger than any of the other towns either, comprising a few living units and a small business district. But it had two massive differences.

One was a huge nuclear power plant outside of town that provided the power for most of the region they had seen so far. It was an enormous plant, visible from every part of town.

The second thing was that the small town of Billiwon had a connection to the Hyperloop network. Having a power plant that provided all the power for such an extensive region, it made sense to have accessibility to it. Fast transport to get engineers, or even normal laborers, to and from the plant regularly. Jumping on a pod here, one could be in a major city in a couple of hours.

The man pulled over and parked his hydro in front of a living unit in need of some repair.

"Okay. This is as far as thirty meals get you."

"Thank you so much. We are forever in your debt. But I need to ask you one more favor," Drake said tentatively.

The moment he saw the Hyperloop, he knew they had to get on it. It would get them to Cathapore in a few hours. They have wasted enough time. Having lost their own transport, it made all the sense in the world to jump on the Hyperloop. Except they couldn't pay for it. Swiping their HICs in a highly monitored zone, like a Hyperloop terminal, would bring all the security forces in the area down on them.

"If you buy us two tickets to Cathapore, I'll get you another twenty meals."

Hyperloop tickets were pretty inexpensive and had become the primary long distance transport system on the planet. The popularity drove the prices down and made it even more popular. Drake figured two tickets should be worth just under the price of twenty meals, leaving some room for negotiating.

"Mmm, thought you only had fifteen. Smart man. But not so smart. Now I know you have more. Much more, maybe. Thirty, or no deal."

Thirty would put them down to only another thirty left, with who knows what lying ahead. It was a steep price, but a price he knew he'd have to pay.

"Thirty." Drake confirmed.

The man nodded, smiled, and jumped out of the hydro.

Drake and Jimmy grabbed their gear and followed him to the terminal.

Using one of multiple DDUs, each mounted next to a gate, the man purchased the first ticket. He moved aside, and Jimmy slipped through. Drake handed over the thirty meals, and after counting it, the man bought Drake's ticket.

"Thank you, again," Drake said as he stepped through the gate.

The man just shrugged and left, the transaction completed.

***

"Please ensure that all luggage is stored, safety harnesses correctly adjusted and worn at all times. Parents traveling with children are reminded that they are responsible for their actions, and fines will be incurred in failing to keep them under control. Enjoy your journey. Next stop, is ..."

The safety briefing and trip information were still being broadcast on multiple DDU screens, but no one in the pod seemed interested.

"So, we'll get to Shangcorp City in about three hours, then we'll need to jump on another Hyperloop to get to Cathapore, which should take a bit more than an hour," Jimmy read off his HIC.

The pod was now moving, and after the initial launch, all sense of speed disappeared. Being stuck in a windowless pod, inside a tunnel, did not make for a visually interesting journey. What the Hyperloop lacked in sensory stimulus, it made up for in speed and convenience. In a few hours, they would have covered more distance than they had in the last few days. Boring, but efficient.

Jimmy reclined his seat, closed his eyes, and said, "Might as well have a nap, ya know."

Drake wished he could, but there was work to be done.

***

Sammy ran as fast as he could toward the Hyperloop terminal.

When he drove into town, he actually passed the small hydro that had Drake and Jimmy in it. They parked in front of an old, dilapidated living unit, but there was nowhere for him to stop. So Sammy casually drove by, hoping they wouldn't notice him, and parked down the street. He watched as they got out and followed the driver of the hydro to the Hyperloop. Sammy followed them cautiously, making sure they didn't spot him.

There was only one line running from this terminal, which made it easy for Sammy to follow them. It went straight to Shangcorp City, with only a handful of stops in between. Sammy was confident they wouldn't get off until Shangcorp City.

He watched them board a pod as he activated a DDU screen at the gate. Instead of using his HIC, Sammy opted for a manual entry, which was tedious, but allowed him to stay incognito. He used a code he received from the harbormaster, and the screen went green. He was in.

Ten minutes after Drake and Jimmy left, Sammy Sanders felt the pod pick up speed.

**

The moment Lt. Wells drove into town, advertisements for the Hyperloop popped up on her windscreen. It seemed technology had finally reached the far-flung reaches of Shangcorp. She also knew that Drake and Jimmy would jump aboard it in a heartbeat.

Wells followed the coordinates on the ads and parked her Ibex in the parking structure underneath the terminal. She put the Ibex in safe mode, making it impossible for anyone to access it without triggering an alarm with Penta, who could then swipe all data onboard, or even detonate it.

She grabbed her gear and made her way to the terminal entrance. As she walked, she slipped the used HIC over her arm. Feeling the dry skin scrape along her arm made her stomach turn.

Wells tried her best to ignore it.

As she reached the terminal, she stopped and ducked behind a pillar. A man standing at the nearest terminal looked very familiar. Peeking out from behind it, she used her ARP to identify the man standing at the gate. She only had a second to do so as the gate opened for him and he disappeared.

But that second was just enough.

Sammy Sanders.

Wells raced over to the terminal, swiped her new HIC, and ran after him.

Only to see the pod leaving.

"Catch you soon, Sammy," Wells said as she waited for the next pod to arrive.

| fifty-seven |

"I'm right behind them. We're heading for Shangcorp City. I'm not sure if he's there or not, but I feel we are close now."

The transmission on the Hyperloop was horrible, and the quality of the ARP conversation poor. Still, Sammy had to make an update.

"I don't pay you to feel or guess or think. If you could, you would have had him by now. So just follow and let them do all the work."

Sammy swallowed hard. Every day, every conversation, his self-esteem took a beating. He was being clever, letting those two idiots do all the work. If he really wanted to, he could find Bob Turner all by himself. But why waste all that time and energy if someone else could take you right to them?

"I'm just saying, we are on track and should have him soon."

"Very well. Do you need anything else?"

Sammy could think of hundreds of things that would make his life easier, but his ego prevented him from asking.

"No. I've got this."

"Okay then." The call ended.

Sammy stared at the DDU mounted in the seat in front of him. It showed several interesting numbers, like speed, location, and time to destination. Sammy noticed it was less than two hours.

Leaning back, he made himself as comfortable as possible and readied himself for a nap.

I could catch him by myself.

***

The pod inside the Hyperloop had a tubular shape, with two single rows of seats running down the sides. The aisle in the middle was barely wide enough to walk through and the ceiling low enough to make everyone walk hunched over. It was efficient, not luxurious. The seats were plenty comfortable, which meant most people stayed seated for the trip. Having everyone sitting down made it difficult for Drake to spot his next mark.

Once they arrived in Shangcorp City, they needed to board another Hyperloop line, one destined for Cathapore. Which meant they had to buy another ticket. Being a shorter trip meant it would be much cheaper than this journey. The problem was finding someone desperate enough to trade for powdered white box meals.

Drake lifted himself out of his chair and peeked at the faces behind him. Jimmy and Drake sat roughly in the middle of the pod, so about half the passengers' faces were now visible to him. All of them bathed in the blue light of the DDUs in front of them, no one taking notice of the man peeking at them.

The ten or so faces all looked well-groomed and washed. Not what Drake was looking for. He needed poor and desperate.

Or young and naïve.

Three rows behind him, a young man sat staring at his DDU. He looked barely old enough to be traveling by himself. The cap he wore had an unfamiliar logo on it and some foreign text underneath it. Drake used his ARP to scan the logo and translate the text. The logo was that of the University of Shangcorp City, and the text said the same. Bingo. A young, impressionable mark.

Drake unbuckled himself, dismissed the warning on the DDU, advising him to stay seated, and half crawled to the boy. The pod was at capacity, which meant Drake had to kneel on the ground next to him. The person across the aisle gave Drake a filthy look as he bumped into them, trying to squeeze into the narrow gap. He'd have to be quick before they got upset and lodged a passenger complaint, which might get him detained when they disembarked. He gave them an apologetic smile to smooth things over a bit.

Drake motioned to his ear, the universal symbol for *switch on your ARP so we can talk*. The boy swiped his HIC, as did Drake.

"Hey, buddy. Benjamin Drake. How you going?"

The young man waited for his ARP to match the language and translate it. Once the ARP knew the language, the conversation would be more fluid.

"Hi. Do I know you? Are you a friend of my parents?"

Drake had never felt so old.

"No, not that I know of. You attend university?" Drake asked, pointing to the cap.

"Yes, it's my first year."

"Must be fun, I bet?"

"Yeah. It's pretty crazy. The city I mean. It's so big and busy."

Music to Drake's ears.

"Not from the big city, hey?"

The young man looked embarrassed.

"No. Easy to tell, huh?"

"Nah, just a guess. Traveling all the way from Billiwon."

"We live there. My mom works at the power plant. She is so proud of me."

The uncomfortable feeling of guilt tried to pull him away from the kid. Best to steer the conversation back to more pressing issues.

"Say, would you like to score some extra meals?" Drake's throat tried to close up and stop him from talking.

"Um, yeah, I mean, sure, but what would I have to do?" The student looked petrified.

"No, no, nothing dodgy, or even illegal. My HIC is playing up, and I need someone to purchase me and my friend tickets to Cathapore. That's all." Drake smiled.

"Oh. Sure. How?"

"I'll give you," Drake bobbed his head around as he did some fake arithmetic, "twenty meals for two tickets. You buy the tickets with the money your mom gives you for food, and I'll give you twice the amount of meals you would have been able to buy for the same amount. Easy, see?"

The kid looked panicked.

"I don't know, it seems strange to buy food from a stranger on the Hyperloop."

"It is!" Drake laughed. "But what a crazy story to tell your friends. Besides, I can ask someone else if you're not keen. No problem."

It was a problem.

Time was running out, and Drake doubted than anyone else on the pod would be gullible or desperate enough to trade meals for a ticket from a stranger. He kept smiling, trying his best to look nonthreatening and relaxed.

"I guess—"

"Great! I'll tell my friend. We'll wait for you when we get off."

Drake crawled back to his seat as fast as possible, in case the kid changed his mind.

"Tickets, sorted!" he said triumphantly.

A loud snore from Jimmy was his only reply.

***

Drake kept an eye on the kid as they exited the pod and grabbed him before he could change his mind. He looked like he was about to run when Drake introduced him to Jimmy, but he gently steered him toward the rows of DDUs that stood waiting. The kid seemed to be eager to get it all done as quick as possible, and Drake had the meals at the ready. Five minutes after arriving in Shangcorp City, they were through the gates and safely wandering around.

The terminal was an ocean of human bodies. Only once they were through the gate did Drake allow himself to take it all in. No Hyperloop terminal in a Penta Corporation territory could match this one for sheer size and amount of people. Thousands of commuters were walking and talking, some eating as they went, others making calls, everyone just going about their lives.

Shops filled the terminal, some selling white box meals, others clothes, and some Drake could not figure out what they did. Every business seemed to be full of customers. In fact, every available space seemed to be full of people. Drake had never seen a busier place in his life, and by the shocked look on Jimmy's face, neither had he.

"If Bob was here, we would never find him," Drake joked.

"The possibilities …" Jimmy got lost in his own daydream.

A big Data Display Unit suspended from the roof showed all the terminals and departure times. Drake found the line traveling to Cathapore and noted the number and time. It was due in only a few minutes, so they headed off in the terminal's direction.

"If Turner is, in fact, in Cathapore, we might even see him today, ya know?" Jimmy said as they walked toward their terminal.

"I know," Drake replied. "Can't wait to give that bastard what he deserves."

| fifty-eight |

The doors slid open, Lt. Wells got out, and a moving mass of humans swept her away. It took her a few strides to find her feet and go in the direction she wanted. It was a struggle, but once she found some momentum, she regained control.

She switched her ARP on, set it to face match for Sammy Sanders, and crossed her fingers that out of the hundreds if not thousands of faces moving past her, one might be his. She did not know where Drake and Jimmy would go next, but she bet that Sammy Sanders did. The pods from Billiwon were ten minutes apart, which meant he had a head start on her. She had to be quick.

It was going to take a miracle to help her find him.

But Lt. Wells did not believe in miracles, luck, or destiny. They were just excuses made up by lazy people. She made her own luck; she determined her own destiny. She had to be methodical and logical and do the work, not wait for some illogical, mysterious force to help her out.

"Watch it!" a man said as he bumped her almost off her feet.

"Hey. Sorry, but I—" Wells froze, staring into the eyes of Sammy Sanders. Her ARP confirmed it.

"Idiot," he mumbled, and pushed more people out of his way.

Coincidences, however, happened all the time.

Wells immediately set off after him.

There was a natural flow to the way the human mass moved, and once Wells found the cadence, things went easier. She could keep a fair distance from Sanders, but also move quick enough to catch up when needed.

She followed him to a bank of DDUs and immediately leaned against a pillar, taking in the posture of so many others aimlessly swiping away on their HICs. Unlike them, she wasn't reading up on the pending war, or the gossip of which friend did what, but activated her ARP and recorded Sammy's transaction. Once he finished, she quickly studied the footage and discovered his destination. Wells hurried over to the same DDU, and using her disgusting HIC, purchased the same ticket. She sprinted as the gate opened, trying not to lose sight of Sanders. She reached the terminal out of breath, but in sight of Sanders.

"Got ya," Lt. Wells whispered.

***

The three dots danced around, bouncing off each other but never merging. He tried again, but with the same result. An error message appeared, stating a poor connection. Traveling in a Hyperloop almost guaranteed a poor connection, but it was worth a try.

He sent a message instead.

Only a few minutes behind them. Traveling to Cathepore. Believe it to be the last destination.

Sammy sat back and took a deep breath. He was now less than an hour away from crushing Benjamin Drake and his stupid little sidekick.

Sammy's arm vibrated, and he swiped his HIC.

Stand down. Local team will take over. Return home ASAP.

Sammy had to reread the message to make it sink in. Stand down? Return home? Local team?

He tried to call again, but got the same result.

No. I've got this. Tell local team to fuck off.

Sammy stared at his arm, waiting for the response. The Hyperloop made everything vibrate slightly, putting most people to sleep. But Sammy had adrenaline surging through his body. How could this happen now, right at the end? Drake was his. The deal was, he brought Turner in and did to Drake whatever he wanted. Whatever. He could finally have his revenge on that smug bastard, and now he was getting pulled off the job. No way.

His arm vibrated.

Local team will meet you at Cathepore terminal and assist you.

A smile spread over Sammy's face.

Assist you.

That's more like it.

***

Wells took a seat one row back and across the aisle from Sanders. It gave her the perfect position to observe him whilst going unnoticed. The position was so good, in fact, that when he got messages on his HIC, she could partly read them. From what she gathered, he had a local team waiting for him in Cathepore. It seemed Sammy Sanders were more organized than she thought.

Wells' initial idea was to ambush him in the pod and find out exactly where Drake and Jimmy were heading. Now, knowing a team was awaiting his arrival meant she had to be more careful. If he didn't disembark when the team expected him to, it might raise suspicion and cause a scene. Depending on how law-abiding this team was, they could then attract attention of security and the whole place could go into lockdown.

No, she'd have to play it cool and just keep following him. Let him meet up with his team and then revise the plan.

Lt. Wells was not a fan of making things up as you go, but knew she had no choice but to improvise.

The ride to Cathepore was short, and according to the information on the DDU in front of her, almost complete. Wells pulled her pulse gun out of its holster, and keeping out of sight as much as she could, checked it over to make sure it was ready to go. Satisfied, she put it away.

Soon, she feared, it might get a lot of use.

| fifty-nine |

"Now what?" Jimmy asked the moment they set foot in the Cathapore terminal.

Getting to Cathapore had been the goal for so long that Drake forgot that they still had to find the beach in the old photo of Mr. Turner and Lucy Hughes. Now that they arrived, they still had to figure out exactly where this beach or island was and then get there. With no credits. Only ten powdered meals, of which they'd have to eat some soon. Drake had been ignoring the aches and rumbles in his tummy for hours now, trying to avoid eating their only currency. Looking at Jimmy's face, he knew he felt the same, without complaining once.

"I'll tell you what. We eat. I don't know about you, but I'm starving. I reckon we pour some water on these powdered meals and fuel ourselves up for the next leg of this shit show."

Jimmy's face lit up.

"Yes! Yes! Let's eat."

"Okay, let's try over there," Drake said. He pointed Jimmy toward an area full of people sitting down to eat. "Mind grabbing us some water?" Drake asked.

Jimmy nodded. Walking behind Drake, they shuffled through the maze of tables, bumping into people, apologizing profusely, and walking on clumsily. Finally, they reached the other side of the area and found an open table.

They sat down, and Jimmy produced three half empty water containers.

"Good job, buddy." Drake smiled at Jimmy's handiwork.

"Couldn't have done it without you, ya know."

Drake took out two meals, gave one to Jimmy, and mixed some water into the packet he kept. Nestem, the makers of white box meals, recommend hot water, but they would have to make do with what they had. The powder struggled to mix, and the result was a clumpy, cold, half dissolved goo.

"Yummy," Drake said in disgust.

"Not bad, ya know," Jimmy replied.

"I guess not." Drake smiled, glad that Jimmy always brought perspective to things.

They ate in silence for a few minutes and washed the worst meal in history down with the leftover water.

Drake studied the surrounding people, eating, chatting, and laughing. Most of them looked like Mr. Turner and Lucy Hughes did in the photo. Happy, relaxed, and on holiday. Something Drake had only ever heard of. Most people in New Franco worked their entire lives, then died. Holidays and traveling were only for the few in the very inner sectors of New Franco. Yet here they were, surrounded by people who had nothing else to do but relax.

"Jimmy, look at these people," Drake said.

"Okay."

"I mean, they all look like Mr. Turner did in that photo. Happy and relaxed. These are the type of people who would go to a place like the one in the photo."

Jimmy studied the people, as Drake instructed.

"Okay."

"So, let's ask them. Maybe one of them knows where it is."

Jimmy slowly nodded his head as he caught up.

Most people were happy to chat to them, but most didn't know or only wagered guesses where it could be.

"Let's go over there," Drake said, and walked off to a group of people standing at the edge of the eating area.

Drake had never seen a group of young people so happy and carefree. Not one of them had the scars or amputations associated with factory work, or the out of proportion build of a miner. No one wore a uniform or armor. There was only one place in New Franco where they would not look out of place: the inner sectors. These were the kids of the elite. Rich, spoiled, and out of touch. Tomorrow's leaders.

Drake walked up to them and became acutely aware of his dirty clothes and unpleasant body odor. Things that were commonplace in a hauler bar, but not in the company of these brats.

He shrugged it off. Not much he could do about it now.

"Hey." He pointed to his ear.

The group spread out and gave him the up and down look he expected. No one said a word to him.

"Anyway, I'm trying to locate a place and hoped that maybe one of you might have seen it?"

Despite the blank stares, Drake retrieved the photo and held it up for them to see. A girl stepped forward and had a closer look.

"They your parents?"

"Sort of. It's a long, complicated story." Drake shrugged.

"Oh, okay. Well, it looks like it could be Kohsam. Maybe. I'm not sure."

"Great! Thanks, at least that gives me a name."

"I can't be sure, but it looks like where we are going, so maybe—"

"Okay, pal. Now beat it. You're ruining our vibe here. And have a shower or something," a tall, skinny, easily breakable man said. Drake took a step back.

"Thank you," he said to the girl who helped him.

Drake turned to speak to Jimmy, but couldn't see him. A slight panic took hold of Drake. Jimmy was a loose cannon from time to time, and could easily have said the wrong thing to the wrong person. Drake spun around, scanning the surrounding faces. Nothing. He turned around again and felt relief. Jimmy stood by an exit, jumping up and down, waving his arms around. Drake walked over to him.

"I think I know—"

"Yes, yes. Let's go!" Jimmy grabbed his arm and pulled him away.

Drake followed and ran with Jimmy to a medium-sized hydrovan. Jimmy ducked behind it, and Drake followed suit.

"What—" Jimmy grabbed Drake's face, mushing his mouth.

"Shh!" Jimmy whispered.

"Those are our bags. Take care if it." It was the voice of the skinny guy.

Drake heard thumping sounds next to his head as luggage was placed in the storage area under the van.

"Now!" Jimmy yanked him away again.

As they turned the corner, Drake saw the last set of feet entering the van. Jimmy stopped in front of him and turned to face him.

"Get in!" Jimmy whispered loudly.

Crouching under the flip up door of the luggage compartment, Drake hesitated. The luggage hold looked dark, cramped, and poorly ventilated.

"Get in!" Jimmy whispered louder.

Drake jumped in and rolled over some baggage and boxes to the far side. There was almost no space to maneuver.

Jimmy followed him and squeezed in as tight as possible, trying to stay away from the open door and the more visible area. The operator of the van must have had better things to do than check the integrity of the cargo, as the door shut with no inspection.

The cargo hold went pitch black.

The humming of the electric motors increased, and the van took off, shaking them gently.

"Scoot over." Drake pushed Jimmy away from him, trying to get some breathing space.

"Oh, yeah, sorry," Jimmy replied and moved over. "I wonder what Sammy Sanders is doing here?"

| sixty |

"This is a catch and clean. Once we have the package, all traces need to be eliminated. Clear?"

Sammy's feet barely touched the platform before three men in uniform whisked him away. Once they found a less crowded space, they stopped and turned to face him.

"We are your local support. We are here to assist you, however, please follow my commands, if issued. Clear?"

Sammy looked at the three uniforms standing in front of him. They were all the same height and build, although two were men, and one a woman. They weren't Moon-miner big, but still bigger than him. All of them. They also had weapons strapped to their legs, and even to their chest armor. They looked mean and purposeful.

"Sure, sounds great to me. So, you guys just going to tag along, or ..."

Sammy looked around, but there was no way of escaping these guys. The terminal was busy, but not overly crowded. If he ran, they would simply shoot him. He doubted that collateral damage was a thing they worried about.

"Whatever you need, we'll provide. We have a vehicle waiting outside."

Sammy nodded and felt his chest close up. This crew was sent to replace him, and now they seemed happy to take orders from him. Something felt off. He also faced another problem. He did not know where to go, and feared if he admitted to it, it might be the last thing he'd ever say. Drake would only have arrived minutes before him, so he wouldn't be far, but not knowing in which direction he went, or what the next destination was, put him at square one.

"You ready to move out?"

He wasn't. Not even close. Sammy knew that if he went with them, with no clue where to go, he'd be walking toward his death. He only had value as long as he had information.

"Sure, let's go," he said as confidently as possible.

He'd have to improvise. Pick a name from a sign and send them on a wild goose chase, then give them the slip. He'd done it before, he could do it again.

The man who'd been doing all the talking turned and walked toward the exit. People seemed very relaxed here, and the energy was less frantic than Shangcorp City. They walked past an eating area, and Sammy noticed how people were chatting and laughing, seemingly with no cares in the world. He scanned the area for any DDU advertising a place with a name on it, but the three support crew members had him inside a triangle and were moving at a brisk pace. Everything was going past him in a blur.

But he caught one thing.

Jimmy Something.

He was standing off to the side while Drake was talking to a group of young people. Sammy used the crew member next to him to shield himself from them and kept walking toward the exit and the waiting vehicle.

All four piled into the vehicle, the woman behind the wheel and the man giving the orders next to her. Beside him sat the third member of the group. Sammy had no way out.

The leader turned around in his seat.

"Where to, Mr. Sanders?"

This is how I die.

Beyond the man's staring gaze, a group of young people were boarding a van. Sammy took his focus away from the man's face and watched them as, one by one, they disappeared into the van. What an absurd thing to have as your last image before you die. Young people, off to enjoy their lives. A contradiction to his own situation. Maybe it was poetic.

Jimmy Something and Drake ducked out from behind the van and crawled into the storage space underneath.

Sammy Sanders almost peed himself.

The amount of relief that washed over him almost made him lose control of his body. He felt his eyes burn as tears filled his ducts.

"We need to follow that van. Do not lose sight of it," Sammy ordered, just in time to stop the tears.

***

Sammy almost ran out of the pod, and for a second, Lt. Wells feared she might have lost him. As she stepped out, she had no visual on him. She moved a few paces to the left and did a scan, then moved in the opposite direction and did the same.

Panic would not make him appear, so she methodically moved in an ever-increasing zig-zag pattern, scanning faces with her ARP, looking for a match. She was nearing the exit, and still no match. She was certain he couldn't be that far ahead of her, so she kept at it.

She was nearing the exit of the building when she felt a commotion behind her. Turning slightly, trying not to draw attention, she saw a group of three uniformed personnel push their way through the crowd. They walked in a triangular formation, and any person or object in their way got shoved to the side. Wells slowed down and waited for them to pass her.

As they did, she saw the diminutive figure of Sammy Sanders trapped in the middle of the human tank. He was shuffling along, protected by the human mass around him. She avoided eye contact, and once they moved past her, she slowly followed.

The triangle moved to a heavily armored vehicle that sat parked in a non-parking zone. She saw them enter the vehicle, but they didn't take off. She had to react fast.

Being just outside of the terminal meant there were many autonomous taxies waiting around. Wells jumped into the first one and stared at the DDU.

Destination?

There were no other options or menu items to press. She'd have to give the taxi a location in order for it to move. Wells looked to see if Sammy had moved yet, but was glad to see the armored hydro still standing there.

Wells hated indecision, so she jumped out of the taxi and did another scan of the area. Hydros were crossing the road in front of her, but stealing one would be fruitless. The moment the driver was ripped out of the vehicle, the absence of his HIC would trigger a shutdown. In a Penta territory, Wells could use her HIC to get it going again, but here it would be useless. In fact, her Penta HIC was a liability.

Sammy's vehicle slowly moved away. There was no more time to think.

Wells walked into the traffic, and a hydro screeched to a halt, it's AI preventing a collision. Wells stood in front of it, acting confused. The driver climbed out and started yelling at her in the native language. Wells ran up to them, shoved them out of the way, and climbed into the vehicle. Instead of getting behind the wheel, she shuffled over to the passenger side. She activated her ARP and scanned for the local dialect.

"What the hell are you doing, huh?" The driver poked their head into the car.

Other hydros who missed the incident where now being held up, and horns and insults flew through the air.

Wells grabbed the man's arm and pulled him inside. She kept her grip on his arm, pulled her pulse gun out with her other hand, and pressed it against his side.

"Drive, now, before I remove your arm and do it myself!" A slight delay in the ARP translator took some of the urgency away.

"No!" the man protested once the ARP systems caught up.

"Your choice," Wells said, and pushed her pulse gun into his body.

"Okay, okay, crazy woman, okay." With murder in his eyes, the man obliged.

"See that big hydro up there, the one turning now? Follow it!"

The man glanced at her and tried to pull his arm free. Wells let go of it and aimed the gun at his head. "Keep driving."

The man mumbled something under his breath, but her ARP couldn't pick it up.

"Just drive, buddy," she replied.

***

The luggage hold was a cramped, hot, and dark hole. Also, something kept poking Drake in the back. It was rough, but he only had one thing on his mind.

"What do you mean, Sammy Sanders?" Drake asked in the direction he thought Jimmy might be.

"Yeah, I saw him, ya know, just before we left the terminal."

Drake slapped the air next to him, but didn't connect.

"Why didn't you tell me?"

"Uh, I was busy tracking your mates, trying to get us a ride, ya know." Drake could hear the hurt in Jimmy's voice.

"And you did great, buddy, seriously. Thanks to you, we are now on our way to, hopefully, find Mr. Turner."

"Don't worry about it."

"But seeing Sammy Sanders is a pretty big deal, Jimmy."

"Do you think he has been following us the entire time?"

Drake had never even considered that someone might follow them.

"But why would he? If we get Turner, he gets his share. Why track us? Unless ..."

"He wants the whole bounty for himself," Jimmy finished his thought.

If Sammy had been tracking them the whole time, it meant he wanted Turner for himself. There was no reason to believe he would change his tactics now, so close to the end. If he blindly followed them, it meant he had no clue where to go. So, he most likely would stay put behind them.

At least for now.

"I wonder what Lucy would say about him being here, ya know."

It dawned on Drake that he hadn't checked in with Lucy Hughes in days. They were about to catch up to Mr. Turner, and she did not know what the progress was.

Drake thought about calling her and telling her they were still a few days out from catching Mr. Turner. He needed to buy himself some more time, as he was still unsure what he was going to do once he saw him. It had long since stopped being about the credits. Right now, they would be lucky to walk away with the powdered meals in their bags. With Delgado, Sammy, and Lucy all having their own interests, and Drake lying to all of them, he knew he should have a plan by now.

But he didn't.

| sixty-one |

A sign popped up on the windscreen, showing a turn off for Kohsam. The hydrovan took the turn, and the leader of Sammy's local crew followed them.

"Bring up Kohsam on the screen," he instructed.

The woman sitting next to him used the vehicle's Data Display Unit and projected the results on her side of the windscreen. Sammy saw a map of the area appear. They were now on a peninsula, with Kohsam the only town, right at the edge. It had to be the last destination.

Which meant he had outlived his usefulness.

The driver gave the woman a slight nod. It was on.

Sammy didn't hesitate. Bracing himself, he elbowed the man next to him in the face as hard as he could, feeling the cartilage in his nose crumple. The man grabbed his face and yelled. Sammy unsheathed the man's enormous knife and pressed it against the woman's throat. The vehicle swerved violently as the driver reacted to what was happening.

"Is your pulse gun biometrically locked?" Sammy yelled to the driver.

"Yes."

Sammy looked at the man next to him, blood spouting out of his nose. He seemed to be in a lot of pain.

"Okay, then. Shoot him in the leg." Sammy pointed with his head.

"What?"

"I said shoot him!"

The driver looked Sammy in the eyes, but did not move.

Sammy moved the knife across the women's throat, making an incision. Blood poured out of the wound.

The driver didn't budge.

"Fine," Sammy said, and moved the knife again.

The woman yelled out in pain, grabbed her pulse pistol, and fired it blindly over her shoulder, hitting the man next to Sammy in the face.

The man's broken nose disappeared together with the rest of his face.

"Leg! Leg! I said leg!" Sammy felt vomit rushing toward his mouth.

The woman spotted her chance, twisted in her seat, and pointed the weapon at Sammy's face. The vehicle swerved violently as the driver tried to keep it on course, despite the chaos. Her arm swayed with the vehicle, and as she pulled the trigger, Sammy slapped it away.

Just in time to save himself and kill the driver.

With the driver gone, the hydro did a hook turn at speed, lifting the back rear wheel, and putting all the weight on the opposite front wheel. The result was a spectacular barrel roll. It flipped over several times and landed on its side, still sliding.

Sammy opened his eyes and felt something wet and sticky underneath his head. He felt disoriented, and it took him a second to realize he was lying on his side. On top of the man next to him. He lifted his head up and touched the side that felt wet. His hand came away covered in blood. Lots of it. He looked at where his head was resting and saw the remains of the man's face.

This time, he couldn't stop the vomit.

Once his stomach was empty, his head became clear, and he knew he had to get out. The man next to him was clearly dead, and he remembered the driver getting shot. In front of him, the woman was lying on top of the driver. Sammy poked her, but received no response. He hit her harder, but still nothing. He pushed himself up and pressed his head through the gap between the seats to have a better look at her.

She looked right at him.

She startled Sammy, and he almost slipped back into the rear, but he noticed the faraway look in her gaze. She wasn't looking at him. She wasn't looking at anything. The reason, Sammy concluded, was the knife, deeply embedded in her throat.

Opening the door skyward was harder than Sammy expected, but standing on top of the dead man, he pushed with his back and got it up. With all the adrenaline from the fight and accident gone, he struggled to climb out. Finally, he managed it and slid down next to the hydro.

"Hands where I can see them!" a female voice shouted as his feet hit the ground.

***

Lt. Wells walked toward Sammy Sanders, pulse gun drawn, ready to take his stupid head off.

Shortly after they took the turnoff for Kohsam, she watched as the hydro swerved progressively more and then ultimately flipped over. Her first thought was a tire blowout, but as she walked up to the hydro, a bloodied Sammy Sanders emerged. He had a crazed look in his eyes. It was not the look of an accident survivor, or a victim, but a look she had seen many times before.

He did something bad.

"Hands where I can see them!" she ordered Sammy.

Blood covered Sammy's face, but he seemed unharmed. He stood still, staring at her. He had a calculating look in his eyes. Another look she was familiar with. The bad guy planning his big move.

The sound of tires squealing pulled her attention away as she glimpsed her ride disappearing. She focused back on Sammy, who had taken a few steps toward her.

"Stand still, dickhead. And keep your hands up," she yelled.

He didn't listen. Most people didn't.

Wells squeezed the trigger and sent a pulse cartridge flying past his head, hitting the hydro behind him.

He stopped.

"I'm Lt. Wells from Penta Security," she identified herself. "What are you doing in a Shangcorp territory?"

Sammy stared at her.

"Okay, then. I know you are here, tracking Benjamin Drake and Jimmy Something. Not an illegal thing to do. Creepy, but not against the law."

Wells listened for any traffic or commotion around her. She couldn't risk looking around, and tried to use her other senses to keep her alerted to her surroundings. She knew having her ARP on would be much better, but didn't want to risk taking her eyes off Sammy to activate it.

The standoff continued.

Without the ability to scan his vitals, she had to rely on her own senses. He must have known this, as he kept looking over her shoulder, trying to distract her and make her look that way too. But what if there was something behind her? Maybe a survivor from the crash had circled around and was now creeping up toward her. She had no choice. She let her one hand's grip on the pistol go, and used it to swipe her HIC and activate her ARP.

The moment she dropped her hand, Sammy ran toward her.

Lt. Wells saw him take off and braced herself. There was no time to shoot. She anticipated which way he was going and planned on stepping the opposite way and using his weight and momentum to get him off balance. He looked like he weighed the same as her, as she fancied her chances in a one-on-one fight.

As he reached out to grab her, she stepped sideways, grabbed him, and pulled in the same direction he was already going. As he passed her, she popped her hip out and pivoted him over it. She felt his weight go onto her, and then he was airborne. Sammy was still falling as Wells mounted him.

His head hit the road at the same time her fist met his ear. He lifted his head up to avoid another blow, and Wells head-butted it back to the ground. Wells lifted her legs and pinned his arms to the gravel.

Sammy received two more punches to the head.

"Why are you here?" Wells yelled.

Sammy laughed.

Wells didn't care to ask what was so funny, so she punched two of his teeth out.

Sammy stopped laughing.

"Bitch," he spit the words and blood out.

That cost him another punch.

"I don't think you have anything I need," Wells said.

She was wasting time here. Wells jumped to her feet and moved away from Sammy.

And fell.

Sammy had hooked a foot behind hers and kicked her in the knee. Pain shot up her leg, and she went down like a sack of rocks. Fury filled her as she fell, hating that he'd gotten the better of her.

And then he did it again.

Quicker than she thought he could move, Sammy had his turn, sitting on top of her. She raised her arms to block the impending barrage of punches that would surely follow. She saw him raise his arm and braced herself.

No punches rained down. Instead, an enormous bloodied knife swung down toward her.

A searing pain took over the side of her body and spread through all her nerves, setting them on fire.

Wells knew she was in trouble.

| sixty-two |

The hydrovan stopped, and the humming of the drivetrain died. They had arrived.

On the ride, their eyes became a bit more accustomed to the light, allowing Drake to find the internal latch that opened the door manually—a safety feature built in to help people who found themselves trapped. Also, occasionally by part-time bounty hunters.

Drake and Jimmy rolled out from under the hydrovan and put some distance between them and it.

The village of Kohsam was small enough to be taken in one view. Everything it offered was visible from where they stood.

The hydrovan sat parked outside a hotel, and judging by its size and view, had to be the best hotel around. Drake turned away from the hotel and elbowed Jimmy in the side. It made him turn around too.

Palm trees, blue water, and white sands spread out before them. Smaller islands floated in the distance. Neither one of them had ever seen anything as breathtakingly beautiful before.

"Wow," Jimmy uttered.

Drake pulled out the photo of Mr. Turner and Lucy Hughes. He held it up in front of him, replacing the scene with an older, less colorful version of it.

They had found the spot.

"I think we're here," Drake said.

"I think so too," Jimmy agreed. "There's Bob."

Drake turned around to face the same direction Jimmy was now facing.

There, at an open-air bar, sat Mr. Turner, drinking a ridiculously big and colorful cocktail. After thousands of kilometers, it was almost an anticlimax to see him just sitting there. Drake expected and half hoped for a dramatic chase and maybe a gunfight, but this was all too calm and passive. Mr. Turner took another sip of his drink, completely relaxed and oblivious to Drake's presence. He looked much older than Drake remembered him. And smaller, somehow.

Drake's feet moved toward him, and the rest of him followed. It felt like a dream. He expected a rush of adrenaline when he found him, but he felt nothing.

The bar was open, with no need for them to go through reception or have their HICs scanned. Drake simply walked straight up to him.

"Why?" Drake asked.

Drake watched the older and smaller version of Mr. Turner slowly look up and smile.

"Hey, Drake," he said. "This must be Jimmy?"

Jimmy looked at Drake with confusion.

"You are here to shoot me or take me back. Either way, I'm sure you are in no rush." Mr. Turner pointed to the vacant seat next to him.

Drake had never seen Mr. Turner so relaxed. It was such a foreign sight that it threw him off completely.

He pulled the chair out and sat down.

"Three more, please," Mr. Turner advised the young girl behind the bar.

"Why did you use me like that?" Drake asked.

He had been rehearsing this speech in his head for days, playing off different scenarios against each other, making sure what he said had impact and meaning. And right now, he couldn't remember any of it.

"Drake, we all got used."

Drake stared at this stranger, who looked and sounded like Mr. Turner, but acted nothing like him.

"No. That's not good enough! I've known you for years, looked up to you, and you just threw me under the bus—to make a few more credits?"

"Why are you here?"

Drake couldn't answer. He couldn't form the words to tell Mr. Turner how betrayed he felt. How much it affected him, being used like that.

"I know you think I'm the bad guy, Drake. And I admit, I orchestrated it, so you hauled that bismuth to McKenna, and I had a hunch what he was going to do with it."

The drinks arrived. Jimmy got stuck into his, but Drake pushed his aside.

"I could have died! Or been thrown in detention. I know you're a heartless dick, but—"

Mr. Turner, the Mr. Turner Drake knew, would have grabbed him and thrown him over the counter by now. His short temper and violent outbursts were legendary.

Instead, Turner looked at Drake with tired eyes.

"No, you wouldn't. There is no one else who I could have used for that contract, Drake. You have never done wrong by me. Most haulers are deplorable, but you have something good in you. And you are smart. Too smart sometimes, but you always pull through. I needed that."

Jimmy finished his drink with a loud lip smack.

Mr. Turner sat patiently, awaiting Drake's next accusation.

This was all too surreal.

It was not supposed to go like this.

"That's great, but you still used me. You lied to me. You abandoned me."

"Why are you here?" Turner asked.

"I don't understand—"

"Are you here for the bounty? Did someone send you?"

Drake remembered his benefactor.

"Yes. Lucy."

Mr. Turner smiled. He looked content, but also sad.

"Lucy. I figured as much. So you've met, then?"

"Yes. I think she still loves you. She wants you back in New Franco."

"I bet she does. But it's not because of love. I've cost her a fair bit of money."

Drake's confusion grew.

Mr. Turner took a sip of the ridiculous drink in front of him. "Lucy is the love of my life, and I would do anything for that woman, Drake. But she is not who you think she is."

Drake looked over at Jimmy, who looked as confused as he.

"She is one of New Franco's biggest criminal masterminds. She used my company and many, many other companies as fronts for her illegal enterprises. She controls most of what happens in the lower sectors. She financed Santo and backed him to go to Mars. She was the one who got hold of the Bismuth and used me to get it to McKenna. Like I said, we all got used."

Jimmy sat, mouth ajar, shaking his head. He reached for Drake's drink and took a sip.

"Are you trying to blame her for everything? I've met her, okay, and I can assure you, she is no criminal mastermind."

Drake could hear the emptiness in his own words. What did he know of Lucy Hughes? The sweet lady who always had fresh fruit and lived in a mansion disguised as a dump. Who made sure they had everything they needed to bring back an ex-husband she hadn't seen in years.

"I'm telling you the truth, Drake. Lucy has been pulling the strings for a very long time. I was weak and went along with it."

Drake looked into Mr. Turner's eyes. Eyes that used to be filled with anger now showed only regret.

"I've lost everything. I knew once Penta was after me, she would get rid of me. I'm her link to the whole Mars saga. She is ruthless, Drake. What I did was wrong. I should have told you. But I was weak."

Drake struggled to comprehend the words and the man. Everything he believed about Mr. Turner was in disarray.

"What now?" Drake asked. He felt helpless.

"That is up to you, Drake," Turner replied.

"How about I decide?" Sammy Sanders' voice boomed.

Drake almost fell off his chair as he spun around. Jimmy spat out his drink. Mr. Turner got to his feet.

Sammy stood at the entrance to the bar, bloodied and pointing a pulse pistol at them.

| sixty-three |

The first vehicle that came across the carnage caused by Sammy was an electric bicycle. Sammy detested them, always taking up space on the road, going slowly and holding everyone up. But he needed to go, and an e-bike did not need an authorized HIC to work.

"Please help!" Sammy yelled as the person drew closer.

"What happened here?" they asked as they dismounted the bike.

Sammy pulled his pulse pistol out and shot them in the chest. Time was running out. There was no more time for niceties.

The ride to Kohsam village felt like an eternity, but since no other vehicles came along, he had no choice but to keep using the e-bike. Within minutes, he saw the big hotel in the distance.

It was time to make his last call.

"Sammy?" Lucy Hughes answered. "It seems I have under-estimated you."

It was music to Sammy's ears.

"Your little team slowed me down a bit, but I'm about to capture Bob. I think it's time we renegotiate our terms."

Lucy Hughes nodded. "Okay."

"First, you will—"

"Never assume to tell me what I will do, understand?" Lucy cut him short. "Here is the plan. Let Drake and Something go. They are harmless, and if their bodies turn up in Shangcorp, it could come back to us. Let them go. As for Bob, well, let's get to him first."

Sammy looked up. The hotel was a few hundred meters away.

"Why would I still listen to you?" Sammy asked in total confusion.

"Because I'm going to make you a powerful man, Sammy Sanders. You've proven yourself to be very reliable in a time when I need reliable people."

Sammy liked the sound of that.

"How powerful?" he asked, as he slowed down, nearing the hotel.

"Replacing Hector Delgado, powerful," Lucy replied.

Sammy Sanders' smile cracked the dried blood on his face.

"And Turner?" he asked.

"Make sure he knows I sent you." The call ended.

***

Drake stepped in between Mr. Turner and Sammy. "What the hell are you doing here, Sammy?"

"Finishing the job we knew you wouldn't." Sammy smiled at Turner.

"We?" Drake asked.

"Lucy," Mr. Turner said behind him.

Sammy laughed. "Precisely. Now, I need you out of my way, Drake."

"Fuck off, Sammy. I'm not moving." Drake stepped closer to Sammy.

"Idiot. I knew this would happen. Here." Sammy used his free hand to swipe his HIC. Drake's arm vibrated as he received whatever Sammy sent him.

"Your choice," Sammy said, as Drake pulled up the file. "Turner or her?"

The file opened. It was a photo of Lily Wells lying on the road. A knife in her chest. A large pool of blood surrounded her.

"It's most likely too late, but who knows? Maybe you can save her," Sammy said.

"This is fake. You're lying!" Drake yelled.

"Fine, believe what you want, but you're going to regret not going after her for the rest of your life."

A hydro came to a screeching halt behind Drake.

"Come on, we need to go! Now!" Jimmy yelled from the driver's seat of a Nikolatec sports hydro.

Drake had no clue when Jimmy had slipped away or stolen a hydro, but there was no time to question him now. Lily was dying.

"I'm sorry, Mr. Turner," Drake said, handing his fate over to Sammy.

"Me too, Drake," Turner replied, with the softest smile Drake had ever seen.

Jimmy blasted the hydro's horn. Drake turned and ran to Jimmy, who sped off the second his butt hit the seat.

Drake kept his eyes on the road, not looking back once.

***

The local authorities had not arrived at the scene yet, and Drake and Jimmy came across the carnage just as Sammy left it. A hydro flipped on its side, blocked most of the road, and they had to go slowly around it.

That's when they saw her.

Lily Wells lying on the road, blood pooling around her, knife sticking out of her chest.

Sammy hadn't lied.

Drake and Jimmy both leapt from the hydro and ran over to her.

Drake grabbed the knife, but Jimmy stopped him.

"No, don't! It'll make it worse. I'm calling for help." Jimmy swiped his HIC, calling the local emergency number. Now was not the time to be cautious.

Drake took Wells' hand in his.

"Lily! Can you hear me? Lily!" he yelled, shaking her gently.

Her head bobbed around loosely.

Sirens broke the silence and grew louder in the distance.

"Lily, please!" Drake shook her harder.

Jimmy grabbed him by the shoulder. "If they catch us here, they'll lock us up forever, ya know," Jimmy said. "But if you want to stay, I'll stay."

Drake looked up at Jimmy, who had tears running down his cheeks.

"I can't leave her here."

"I get it, ya know. But what good will it do to get caught as well?"

"I'm not going," Drake said, and cradled Wells' head.

"That's okay, partner," Jimmy replied. "I got this."

The pulse cartridge hit Drake at the same spot where Jimmy shot Lt. Wells. He fell forward and ended up next to her. The sirens sounded louder than ever. Jimmy put his pulse gun away and grabbed Drake by his jacket, dragging him back to the sports hydro. He struggled, but lifted him into the hydro. The sirens were almost deafening now.

Jimmy jumped into the hydro and saw the first emergency vehicle only a few meters away. He engaged drive, floored the accelerator, and sped past the ambulance as it stopped.

"Sorry, lieutenant," he said.

Jimmy gave up trying to wipe the tears away and concentrated on the road ahead.

The Adventure Continues